Praise for
K.M.TREMILLS

"Readers will be inspired by Gabriella's journey into the heart of darkness and her triumph over those who seek to diminish her. *Messenger* is a terrific debut novel!"

   – Elizabeth Stanley, *The Dark Path Chronicles*

"Full of mystery, suspense, beauty and courage. *Messenger* made me fall in love with reading again! I had forgotten how much fun it is to get lost in a story."

   – Megan Barker, Empowerment Coach

"Well-written and entertaining. The *Great Lands* series gets it all just right. The characters were strong. I had a great time reading it and was sorry when it ended."

   – Joe Gazzam, *Uncaged*

"A beautifully crafted story of a young woman gifted with unusual talents and tasked with a quest. There are fairy tale qualities to *Messenger*, reminding me of Aesop and his fables."

   – Judith Nappa, Amazon Review

"This enchanting series is so visual that you feel at one with the characters and plot line. K.M. Tremills has a true gift for transporting you into the world she creates."

   – Desiree Daniel Miller, OP Media Group

"*Messenger* is an absolute treasure and a fascinating story. The storytelling and the cast of characters are unique and make the novel a true joy to read."

   – Renee Alarid, Associate Director of Creative Services

"K.M. Tremills is the gold standard for strong, independent and feminine heroines. *Blue Moon* is the start of a wickedly clever series!"

   – Kathryn Cottam, *The Shoemaker*

"I fell in love with these vibrant characters. The *Fated* series is a delightfully dark blend of quirky, flirty, sarcastic, and charming."

   – Vanessa Mayville, Vanessa Mayville Designs

"The ancient wisdom in the engaging story of Gabriella comes through in the eloquent words of K.M. Tremills. The *Great Lands* series can be read on many levels, all of which are entertaining."

– Jen Clarke, Executive Director at One to World

"The *Great Lands* series is brilliant ... a fantastic journey that steps into a realm of mysticism and fantasy. K.M. Tremills causes the reader to ponder their own beliefs."

– Barb Weston, Inner Focus Holistic Healing

"K.M. Tremills finds balance between page-turning plotlines and ethereal story-telling. Time well spent!"

– Roberta Cottam, *Bluebeard's Bride*

WARRIOR

K.M.TREMILLS

ALSO BY K.M.TREMILLS

Messenger *The Great Lands Series*
Queen Isabel *The Great Lands Series*

Blue Moon *The Fated Series*
Assembly of the Gods *The Fated Series*

FEATURED IN

Fabled: 17 Tales You Think You Know
Red: Three Short Tales of Red

WARRIOR

BOOK II
GREAT LANDS

K.M.TREMILLS

Warrior
© Kate Tremills 2016

Ebook Edition: December, 2016
ISBN: 978-1-987818-03-1

Print Edition: March, 2017
ISBN: 978-1-987818-02-4

Cover design © Roberta Cottam, 2017
Cover photography © Oxana Mikhaylova/Shutterstock.com

Published by RavenHeart Press
www.kmtremills.com

To those who reach deep into their hearts for courage:
May this book guide you on that path.

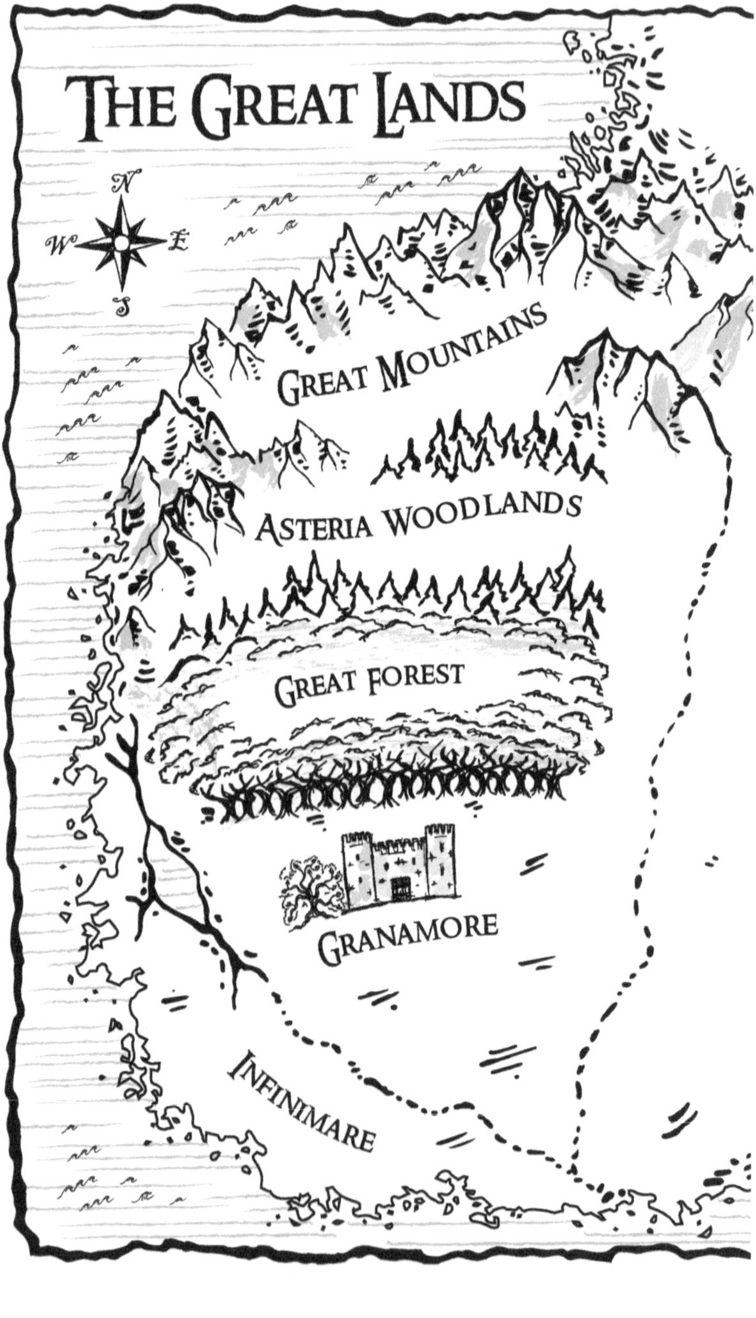

The Great Lands

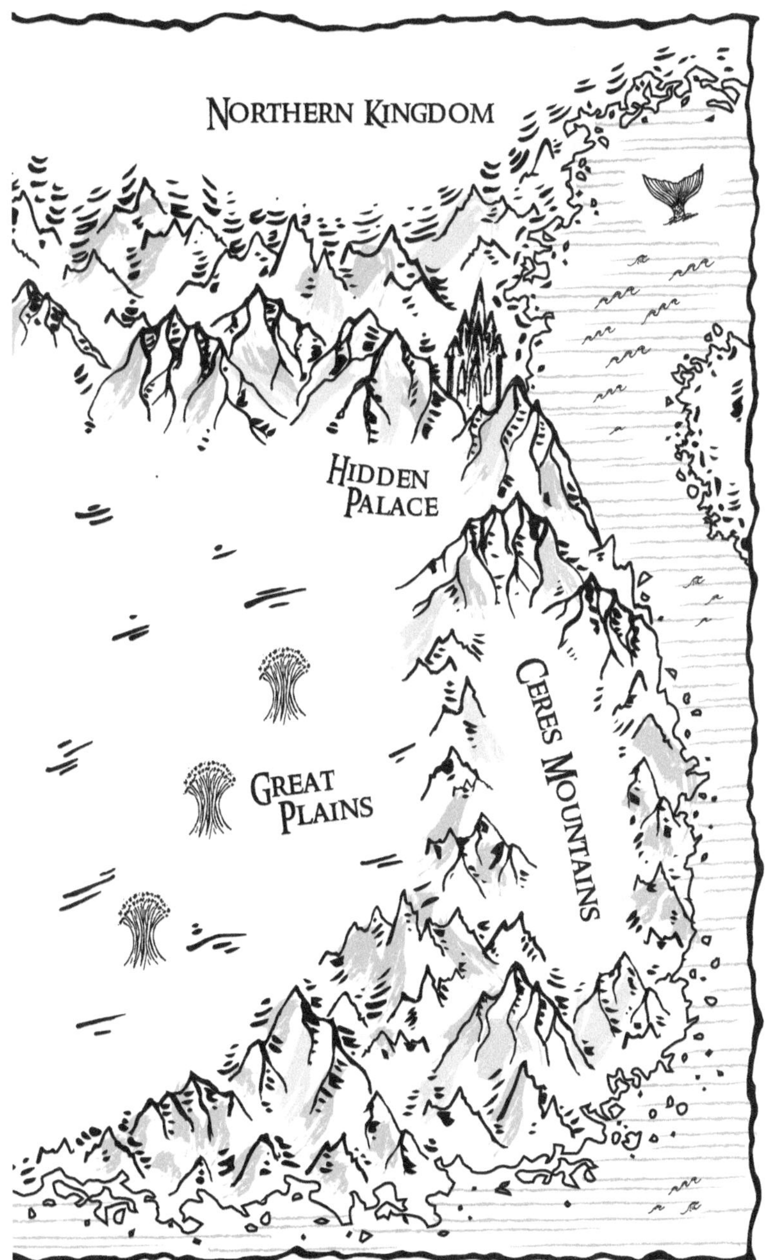

NORTHERN KINGDOM
HIDDEN PALACE
GREAT PLAINS
CERES MOUNTAINS

THE
GUIDE

ONE

GABRIELLA PACED THE CLOSE COTTAGE, restless from hiding too long.

She needed time to think. And assess her choices. In the three years since her flight from the Hidden Palace, Gabriella trusted few places. This hideaway was one of them. Due to its location and the discretion of its owner.

Even better, the cottage was shielded by spells.

She stopped and peeked out the heavy, brocade curtains. They were designed to block the sunlight and most certainly the Moonlight.

But now, she needed the comfort of the night goddess.

As she stared into the far reaches of the sky, Gabriella was relieved to see the Moon. Shining at her, the nocturnal deity whispered,

I have watched over your world for countless nights. And have hidden my face for limitless days. The tides wash in and out. The birds rise in the morning. And the owls call in the evening. No matter how many men wreak havoc and how much blood soaks into the earth, creation will go on.

"Yes," Gabriella replied. "But you are not called to tumble such men from power. Causing innocent lives to end before their time. Threatening the wellbeing of more. And asking citizens to risk everything in support of a cause that may fail."

The Moon shone bright and said,

That is true, my daughter. But you agreed to this path with no assurance that the way would be peaceful. Though you were chosen to shine, never assume the path of a star is an easy one.

Burning bright one evening only to discover the fuel for her fire dwindles the next. Then her sister star is chosen to take her place in the firmament. Such was ever the way of life, and so it will ever be.

Gabriella tilted her head and drank in the Moon's words. In years past, she would have been infuriated by the lack of clear direction. But since leaving her childhood behind, she had learned that the stars and deities spoke in the language of mystery.

She had come to appreciate the subtleties of the Goddess. The quiet guidance of the angels. Her path was more often whispers and nudges than blazing signs. When she heard loud, demanding sounds, they were words spoken by men. Despotic ones.

The stars have immeasurable time, thought Gabriella. So they speak softly and guide with metaphors. They do not need to rage or stomp. Millennia are but a blink of the eye in comparison to the turning of the spheres.

But she did not have thousands of years. Nor thousands of days.

Gabriella felt the mounting impatience of the Great Prince. His actions grew rash, and his judgment was compromised. She could not afford to wait until he razed every village and destroyed every forest in his search for her.

If people were to die from his obsessive quest, Gabriella thought, she was determined they be given the choice. Though the outcome may be the same, choosing your death was far more powerful than being cut down as a pawn.

She growled at the thought of her people being slaughtered, whether in their beds or on a battlefield. Gabriella wished she had the power of magic that could shield them as she took on the Great Prince. Though she knew that would take too much strength.

This was their feud, not the war of ordinary people. At that thought, the Moon shimmered and replied,

Ah, but that is where you are wrong, daughter.

These are the days of the small ones rising to topple the mountain. Though they would be grateful for you to fight their battle, we cannot expect the structure to hold when only one has the strength to bear the weight.

You must allow them to stand with you. To share the burden of the load. They will whisper gathered wisdom in your ear. Just as you respect the guidance of the stars, so must you listen to the collected discernment of your people.

"Does this mean the days of Kings and Queens are over?" Asked Gabriella, wishing the Moon would say yes.

She had no desire to climb a throne or place her sister back on such a high and targeted post. From the time of her birth, Gabriella had only witnessed the throne to be a heavy burden. Not a prize to be coveted.

No, my sweet girl. Leadership and wisdom are still very much required. Your parents taught you well when they offered shelter to the meek and food to the hungry. But they carried too much on their own shoulders. And did not allow their people to hold them, as you must do.

"But we have all grown accustomed to hiding," replied Gabriella. "How will they respond when I ask them to step out into the open and lay down their lives? The lives of their children? All for the slim hope that we can defeat a tyrannical force who will stop at nothing to rule?"

Gabriella did not say the force was the Great Prince. Deep in her heart, she held hope that he was the good man who once knelt before her and asked her to be his Queen. As wrong as his offer was, given he was sworn to Hannah, Gabriella longed for the Prince to win the battle for his soul.

This is where the path of trust opens. You have grown accustomed to walking alone, my daughter. Relying only on the forces beyond the veil. And growing too comfortable bearing a sacrifice that belongs to others.

Now, you must learn to believe in others. No longer is this the battle of one. This is the war of many. Women and men define their character in the side they choose and the actions they take. You are being asked to lay that challenge at their feet. And to allow each person to choose their way.

Gabriella dropped her gaze to the grass rippling outside her window. She focused on the light dancing across the blades, willing herself to be at peace. But rage gathered in her fists. And she gripped the heavy curtains, crushing the fabric, resisting the Moon's guidance.

She had been raised to fight for others. She was taught to defend the weak. Not place the battle at their door and expect them to wield weapons they did not own. This was an outrageous demand, thought Gabriella.

"This cannot be," Gabriella said, not trusting herself to say more. The Moon's light cascaded softly to the earth.

Tell me your objections.

Gabriella lifted her fiery gaze, burning as bright with rage as the Moon shone with patience. She was grateful to be protected by magic or she might have led the Prince's army straight to her door.

"These people do not know how to fight," exclaimed Gabriella. "They have not been trained. Nor should they be expected to take on a battle that was started by kings! You cannot expect them to shed blood for a feud that is not theirs to bear. That is cruel and archaic reasoning. And I will not stand for it!"

She could not ask this of a farmer, a cook, or a blacksmith. They chose honourable professions that upheld life. They were needed in their villages. She was a different beast altogether. An outsider. A loner. One who preferred her steed to people. And the wooded trails to the gossipy court.

Gabriella fell silent in her fierce anger. Pulling on the curtains, until they threatened to tear from their hangers. Waves of anger rolling off her like steam from a hot spring.

The Moon waited, as though knowing that Gabriella would quell her roiling blood. Loving her chosen daughter, as deeply for her outrage as for her committed heart.

"I was raised for this task," Gabriella said, finally. "I accepted the challenge. When the angels came to ask whether I would carry the torch, the risks were made clear. I was ready to lay down my life then and I am willing to lay down my life now. But you cannot ask me to demand that of my people."

And why not?

"For all the reasons I have stated!" retorted Gabriella. "They do not deserve to die!" The Moon shone with the deep understanding of the stars.

And you do?

Gabriella's breath caught in her chest. Her fists unclenched.

And her cheeks burned hot with discomfort. Never in all her years of service had she asked that question. Never had she wondered why she was the one who felt called to lay down her life.

And yet, somewhere deep in her heart, she knew her answer. Yes. Gabriella believed that she deserved to die. Why else would the gods have called her to this task?

As she considered the question for the first time, her heart broke. She, the daughter of nobility, with a sister that bore the soul of an angel, and a family that served only with the kindest of intentions, believed her sacrificial death was justified.

Not once had Gabriella paused to consider the other path. The one most other young women walked. A journey of love and family. The choice to live. To thrive. To build a legacy beyond death.

Her heart pounded in her chest. Gabriella's thoughts drifted to Adrian.

Once when they lay together and he thought she was asleep, she heard Adrian whisper to her. A secret wish. His desire to leave behind all that was asked of them and, instead, choose their own path. Together, without the burden of the world.

She held her breath that night. Gabriella did not trust herself to turn, to move, to look him in the eye, for fear that she would abandon her promise to the angels. She blinked back tears, choked down her own desire, and let Adrian fall asleep with his wish dying on the cold night air.

A tear fell down her cheek, as Gabriella watched the myriad of stars appear in the sky. She allowed herself a moment of wistful sorrow. Rarely did she have the luxury of feeling. Survival chased tender moments away. Fear of discovery held sway over any occasion to reflect on her choices.

But tonight, cradled in the safety of her shielded refuge, she gave herself leave to wonder. What would happen if she abandoned her mission? The earth would continue to turn. The stars would rise each night. And the angels would find another Messenger.

That may be so, but there might not be another Messenger for thousands of years. At which time, the world will be unlike any we recognize.

"But there is another," Gabriella countered. "You spoke of a star, a sister star, to take the place of the one that lost her fire."

Yes.

Gabriella sighed, realizing her error. "But you speak the language of the universe. Not in the timeline of human history."

Precisely. Stars alight and descend over thousands of years. And your world, my dear one, affords not that luxury.

Still, Gabriella wondered, whether the Moon's words spoke of prophecy. Would Gabriella's star burn on the battlefield, while Hannah's ascended in the palace?

Gabriella released the curtains and stepped back. Fatigued from years of sacrifice. She allowed the wave of exhaustion to roll over her body. And the sorrows to press on her heart.

Perhaps the time has come for Hannah to carry the mantle of leadership, she mused. If I can knock the Great Prince from his throne, my task will be complete. And Hannah would be crowned the Great Queen.

But if Gabriella were to follow the Moon's instruction, she must find a way to lead her people into battle.

How am I to do this? she asked. Throwing the desperation of her heart to the skies. *You must help me see the way. Or I fear*

I will follow the familiar path unknowingly.

And with her heart-wrenching request, the curtains swept apart, and a Moonbeam pierced her brow like a bolt from the sky. Gabriella was brought to her knees. Struck by a vision.

A cloaked man guided her deep into a watery cave. She heard the drips. Knowing they descended into the belly of the goddess. Seeking her fire. Her wisdom. Her sacred metal.

She sought a glimpse of his face, but he would not turn. She felt only his power, his strength. His absolute commitment to her cause. And in silence, he pointed toward a shimmering body of water.

How would this help her?

She doubted. Always the doubts. Leaping to the fore of her mind before she deepened into her heart. Feeling the call of an ancient force. A magic power hidden in the water ahead.

More than a mirror. More than a nourishing source of life. This pool offered a gateway. A profound way to bring victory. A powerful symbol that would draw the people to her.

Gabriella stepped closer. A gleaming light seared her mind and pierced her heart. Pulling her forward as though she no longer had a choice. She was powerless to resist. There. In the water. The blade shining bright. A sword of the ancients. She must move forward. And seize the treasure.

Gabriella glanced down to see a chasm open beneath her feet. A gash in the earth. It was going to swallow her whole and never leave a trace of her existence.

With a chest-crushing gasp, Gabriella was thrown from the vision. She fell to her side, breathless on the floor. She dug her fingers into the worn rug, and felt her hands push against the soft wool. She was alive. She could breathe. And she had a mission.

Gabriella rose from the floor. She did not know how she was to convince her people to follow. Or fight. But she knew she had to get to that cave. That man.

And the rest she would figure out or be shown along the way.

Gabriella bowed her head in reverence to the Moon Goddess then turned to her empty room. She longed for the company of Adrian. For his comforting embrace. His wise smile. And his honest advice.

She must trust that the Divine would light her way. She knew only the solitary path. The choice of keeping her loved ones safe and protecting her people. Now, she must learn how to guide them to follow. If only to unseat the Great Prince and dissemble the Hidden Palace. Once that was done, let others determine how to rule.

First, she would pray for strength. And guidance.

She would hold vigil all night. Bracing her heart for the days to come. For she could no longer rely on the shadows. Hiding to stay alive. Awaiting the inevitable fight.

The time had come. To leave the safety of walls for a harrowing journey.

All she knew now, and all she needed to know, was that she was a Warrior.

TWO

GABRIELLA PEEKED AROUND THE CORNER of her hood. She had been sitting in the tavern for hours. Waiting. Her journey from the cottage had taken her through the Nighthawk mountain pass and landed her in this old, rustic tavern at the edges of the Kingdom.

She kept to her corner. Lucky for her, most of the patrons kept their eyes lowered and their ale close. Gabriella had purchased her tankard but had not yet touched the drink. She merely wanted to secure her place without questions.

Besides, no one here was interested in talking.

Gabriella knew well why the men drank. No one wanted to remember the past three years. Even she wanted to forget. She smelled the alcohol beneath her nose. She could taste the liquid without raising it to her lips. Within her tankard awaited a world of oblivion. But that was not her path. Her path was to remember.

Others were blessed with forgetting. Not her. Gabriella refrained from growling. She still had moments when she wanted to take the Divine to task.

Why? she would ask. Why was she the one who had to remember? Could someone else not take up the torch? Why did she have to scour the countryside looking for clues to the next step on this never-ending path of merging the past with the future?

"Otherwise known as the present," she grumbled.

Gabriella gazed at the worn, tired men in the tavern. She sighed. And took a deep breath. Reminding herself that she was grateful to be alive. To have clarity of thought and freedom of will, despite the despotic conditions in her land.

She closed her eyes, took another breath, and felt the tavern sigh with her.

The poor place had carried the burden of so many souls for so many years. No wonder the patrons continued on this spiral. Round and round. They never gave their sacred haunt a chance to breathe.

She opened her eyes and, risking her own safety, she tossed a quick look at the door, bidding it, unlatch! The heavy wooden portal flew open into the night. Causing curses all around, as a frigid blast of northern air swept through the rugged bar.

Still, the peril was worth it. Gabriella felt the old place give a gracious sigh. She tipped her head with an imperceptible nod. Acknowledging the gratitude.

Gabriella could not risk many of those moves. As much as the tavern's clientele were no threat, she sensed darkness in the corners. Watching for displays of magic. Waiting for an opportunity to pounce.

She had no quarrel with darkness. The night had been Gabriella's friend for many years, particularly since she had fled the Hidden Palace. But Gabriella sensed a murkier darkness, a thick muck. The kind that sucked in the light and extinguished it forever.

This darkness was hunting her. And anyone who gave her assistance.

Gabriella's heart ached. Hitting her with the force of her lost love. She missed Adrian. She had not seen him for days. And that had been in her dreams. She had not touched him for weeks. Going on months. They could not risk being in the same physical location for long. The surge of power was too dangerous. Too noticeable.

Especially if they made love. They risked it only once. As high as they flew on the waves of ecstasy, they saw the surge of forces mustered against them. Gabriella had barely felt the afterglow of connection before they threw on their clothes to flee.

Luckily, they were in the middle of a thick wood. No, she thought, not luckily. Adrian's instinct and wisdom placed them in the midst of that sacred wilderness. They had both known the risk. Yet they could not help themselves.

—⁂—

Adrian and Gabriella needed time together. They had been on the run so long, and their need for each another was so great, they began taking foolish risks. And so, Adrian's oldest friend, Silas, risked his safety so the lovers could spend a night in his remote cabin.

"You are powerful beyond words, Gabriella," Adrian said, as he packed his belongings, readying to leave after their idyllic night. "But you must not underestimate the pull the Prince has on you."

Gabriella stared as Adrian pulled on his shirt. She did not care what he protested at this moment. She focused on pulling him back to her. So he would stay with her one more night.

Adrian shot her a look. Knowing full well she was using her charms without uttering a word. "Stop," he admonished. "You know I must leave. For both our sakes."

Gabriella shrugged. And doubled her efforts to secure her way. Leaning on the bed as she watched him fasten his belt and lock a knife into its holster above his ankle.

"Besides," Adrian continued, "You are avoiding the topic. Focusing on me to avoid thinking about the Prince."

"What do you mean?" Gabriella replied, no longer feeling amorous.

Adrian sighed, realizing that he had a bad habit of divulging thoughts he was sure she already understood. Only to discover he had been reading her heart, not her mind. And so, when he spoke, Gabriella reacted aggressively.

"Are you questioning my affection?" Gabriella challenged.

She could not bring herself to say love. Gabriella did not deny that's how she felt. But she refused to speak the word for fear the fates would take him. As they had with every member of her family.

"Of course not," Adrian replied, without giving in to his desire to comfort her. He did not trust himself to leave if he moved even one inch closer to Gabriella. "I am referring to the battle in your heart. You cannot deny what the gods have called you to confront."

"You speak of his proposal," Gabriella said, softly. The memory tormented her every night in her dreams. Foolishly, she had hoped the pain would resolve itself. Not once, had she spoken of her suffering. And yet, she was not surprised that he knew. "I do not wish to marry him."

"Perhaps," Adrian said. "But each morning, your soul questions your mind's choice. We know not why the gods test us with arduous questions. Nor why the goddesses ask us to walk territory that our feet dread. But you must not hide from the question."

Gabriella was on her feet. She crossed the room before he could react. Shoving him against the wall and demanding he speak directly. Not evade the truth with metaphysical phrases.

"Are you telling me to go to him?" Gabriella demanded. She wanted to hit him. To force him to say he no longer loved her. Not that he was giving her to the Prince in some grand gesture of detachment.

She held back her impetuous accusations. She resisted letting her fears run her actions. Though she felt like a wild stallion parading around a performance ring. Pretending to be a delicate show horse when she wanted to sprint at full speed. To give every feeling in her chest free reign. She wanted to run wild and declare all her desires!

Adrian gently took hold of her elbows. Not trusting himself to touch her face. He lost his will too easily in her gaze. Despite their time together, Gabriella did not realize the hold she had on his soul. The sheer force of resolve required to leave her was more than his heart could take. And still, he needed to bear her mission in mind.

"I am telling you to test the boundaries of what your mind protests," Adrian replied.

"More riddles," she growled. "Speak to me like a lover, Adrian. In this room, for these last moments of our one night together, you are my lover first. And my teacher last."

"Fine," Adrian said, letting down his guard. "I do not want to leave. I want to escape these lands with you. To cross the unknown ocean to a place where we can be free. No longer caring for others. Waking each morning without wondering when we might have to risk the life of the person we hold most dear."

Adrian's eyes blazed. "Are you ready to relinquish everything and make that leap?"

Gabriella fell quiet. Her heart stopped for a second, as she felt the full force of Adrian's love. She had underestimated the power of his affection. And, she was ashamed to admit, she had misjudged the burden of his restraint.

As she rose each day questioning the tasks the gods put before her, he, too, must wonder why the Divine asked so much of them. Two people who wished only to bask in the purest of human desires — to love their chosen one.

In that moment, a shift occurred in Gabriella.

No longer would she demand that the fates explain themselves. No more would she wonder whether another being suffered a greater or lighter burden than her own. These were the questions of a child. And here, with her lover, facing their separation, she must choose to be a woman. Not only a woman, but a Messenger. A bearer of truth.

"Adrian," she spoke softly, placing one hand on his face and the other on his chest. "You are my beloved. You are the one I choose. You are the one I would follow. And whom I would lead." She felt his heart pound in response. And his eyes closed in relief.

"But I do not know who the gods choose for me," she added with sorrow. "I cannot pretend that this is my choice. Nor will I deny that I want to flee with you. Today. This moment. I am prepared to forego my mission to lay my heart in your hands."

Adrian's eyes opened. Mirroring her inner battle. Acknowledging their shared pain.

Neither was going to forgo the path. As deeply as separation might break their hearts, leaving thousands to die at the hands of the Great Prince would crush their spirits. And — eventually — decimate their love.

"You must promise me," he whispered, "that you will not return to the Hidden Palace alone. That place is more dangerous than we can possibly understand."

Gabriella began to protest. But Adrian continued, "When… *if* the time comes that you must return, promise you will go with assistance. This is not a battle for you to fight without allies."

She did not attempt to placate him. She stood, silent and strong, radiating her love. Bold in the face of the future. Defiant of the sacrifices fate might demand.

"I promise," she replied. As the truth pulsed from her heart to his, Gabriella pulled him close, one last time. She drank in his adoration in a long kiss.

Then, before she changed her mind, she grabbed her cloak and fled the cabin.

—⟋⟋—

Now Gabriella's body ached. She reminded herself that lingering in the memory was not worth the danger, as much as she loved returning to their tender moments. She could not torment herself — or Adrian — this way. When she thought of their time in the woods, he could not help but think of it also. Despite his decades of training.

The corner of her mouth lifted in a slight smile. She did not wish to hurt either of them, yet she missed tormenting him. Sometimes, she swore the banter was as fulfilling as physical contact.

Enough, her instinct chided. *You must leave him be or risk exposing you both.*

Gabriella nodded. She was used to having conversations in silence. Too many years alone had taught her ways to stay sane through dialogue with herself.

As though she stays silent for long, her humour teased. Gabriella knew when her humour showed up, it was well-past time to speak with another person.

She lifted a hand to signal the woman behind the bar. The only other woman in the establishment. Aside from the young one in the hidden room playing cards. Gabriella had caught only a glimpse of the girl as she ducked through the back doorway. She wondered what the young one was up to, for the girl held too much power to be easily swayed.

The barkeep dropped her dishtowel, though she did not look pleased to leave her post. Gabriella imagined her arrival was as much a curiosity as a woman running a tavern. But as the tall, sturdy woman approached, it was apparent she knew better than to pry.

"What might you need?" the barkeep asked.

"Sustenance," Gabriella stated. "What do you have?"

"That depends," the woman replied.

"On?" Gabriella inquired.

"On whether I'm in the mood to offer," the barkeep said.

Gabriella believed the woman was joking. Though she could not be sure. In her younger years, she might have taken offence.

Assuming the woman was baiting her. But this Gabriella — who had seen too many taverns in too many forgettable outposts — kept her mouth shut.

Finally, the barkeep cracked a smile. Appreciating the silence of the strange woman in the hooded cape. She had no time for women who needed the approval of others. If she cared, she would damn well be living in a city with plentiful services and suitors. Not a puny village in the middle of the Nighthawk Pass.

"Lamb stew," the barkeep stated. "Made fresh this morning. Even has carrots."

"Perfect," Gabriella said.

"Anything else?" the barkeep asked.

Gabriella knew the woman did not refer to food. Though alcohol was lucrative, the offerings that garnered true coin in remote places were the ones that included human contact or illicit substances. She shook her head, holding the barkeep's gaze to convey the finality of her answer.

"Stew only." The barkeep nodded. And disappeared into the kitchen beyond the bar.

Gabriella sighed. She knew she had been called here for a reason. Though what it was she could not tell. Until that time, she would fill her belly and observe the patrons. There was the chess match in one corner. The rabble-rousers from the mine drinking to forget their day in another. And, hidden from her gaze, was the card game with several burly men and one clever girl.

Truth be told, she had expected the company of at least a few women. She could feel their presence. They were close by. Why were they not in the tavern? Angling for coin with their physical proximity?

Gabriella paused, intrigued by this odd occurrence. The atmosphere was rough, but that rarely kept the wanton ones from seeking employment amidst such company.

No, Gabriella considered, there must be another reason.

The barkeep appeared and set a bowl of stew and a fork before Gabriella. The rich aroma tickled her tongue and her stomach growled. As Gabriella claimed a chunk of lamb with her fork, she watched the woman closely. The barkeep wiped a glass and surveyed her territory with the gaze of a hawk. Keeping a close eye on her patrons. Ensuring they behaved themselves and did not cause her any more trouble than she wished.

She would not brook rowdiness more than a certain din. And when Gabriella swept her eyes back over the room, she saw the men knew this well. They kept the noise low and their battles to a dull tension. Giving only swift punches or murmured curses, if a man crossed a line.

Gabriella knew that, for whatever reason — be it her past or the desire to keep a tight control — the patroness was the one who did not allow other women.

Perhaps she knew that women made men foolish, Gabriella mused as she chewed. So what possessed her to allow me inside? Am I quiet enough to warrant serving? Or am I enough of an oddity, a woman travelling alone in a high mountain pass, that the patroness knows she can earn cash in exchange for information?

And then a thought struck her. The girl. Her eyes focused on the back of the inn, seeking answers beyond the closed door. She heard the high-pitched laughter of the girl, and Gabriella knew the little one was playing at more than cards.

There was something about her, Gabriella thought. Something

familiar. Then shook it off.

She carried the weight of ghosts with her everywhere she travelled.

Gabriella swallowed the last chunk of lamb. She must tread carefully. Like every other day in my life, she thought. Then checked her petty thought. She must not curse this path. To do so would only make the road harder.

No, she insisted. I embrace every rock, every pebble, every unexpected cliff.

Gabriella had tested her wings once. And she waited with a hopeful heart to feel the bliss of such freedom again.

THREE

ADRIAN WARMED HIS HANDS by the fire. He recalled the agreement he had struck with Gabriella. She would travel the high roads and he would travel the low.

Much as he did not relish being in the exposed territory of the Great Plains, he must honour his word. For they could not be seen together. And if he must be seen alone, at least he knew his exposure would protect Gabriella.

Observers would wonder why he was not with her. And when people wondered, they often jumped to the easiest or the cruelest of assumptions.

Adrian shook his head. He hoped they could change that cynicism. But in these darkest of days, he must assume what had proven to be the truth.

He poked the fire, and turned the rabbit he had caught for dinner. They were rare in the Great Plains, but the wild ones risked the expanse for the succulent grasses. If lucky, they had a meal and made it back to their burrows. If not, they ended up on a spit.

Not unlike my own journey, Adrian mused. He was not bitter, not in the least. Though there were days he dreamed of being a simple farmer or a goat herder. The simplicity and satisfaction of that life pulled at his heart on the days he wished he had a consistent bed.

But his home would forever be the wandering trails of the world. At least, until there was peace in the Great Lands. And Adrian had not yet seen that vision. He had seen many others. Darker, challenging visions. Most of which involved Gabriella.

He focused on the turning rabbit flanks. He would not dwell on what he could not control.

Adrian listened, instead, to the faint squeak of the willow branch against the roughly fashioned spit ends. He opened to the rhythm of the sound combined with the crackle of the fire. He must not think of Gabriella. For when he did, his body ached, his heart broke, and his feet insisted that he chase her down.

No, he thought, he would stay. He must complete his end of the bargain.

A soft muzzle poked his shoulder. As though to say the horse knew what Adrian was thinking and why could they not follow that urge?

Adrian reached back and gave Casmire's nose a gentle stroke. "Sorry, my friend," Adrian said. "You know as well as I do that it's against the rules. Her rules."

Casmire snorted with derision. Shook his head, and tossed his mane. Humans and their rules! He was tired of flat plains and end-less grasses. Yes, his belly was full. And he was grateful for the fresh food. But he was aggravated by this arrangement. Following Adrian, with no idea how Gabriella fared.

He knew she was alive. But Casmire did not possess the wizard's gift for touching her mind from many leagues away. He had a limited range of connection with Gabriella. And he was most aggrieved that they made an arrangement without considering him.

"But we did," Adrian countered. "You know we did." He shot Casmire a chiding glance.

Casmire snuffed and turned away. Fine, he thought. They asked how he felt. But he could think of no sound argument to counter Gabriella's concern for his wellbeing should she be required to scramble through mountain passes and hide out in caves.

Casmire had argued that he had done so before. But Gabriella insisted they had other options now. That if people saw Adrian with her mount but without her, they would assume the worst. A ruse they desperately needed in order to keep the Great Prince from her trail.

And Casmire always put Gabriella's protection first. Even if it meant being separated from her.

And so he and Adrian had forged a tenuous alliance. For Casmire did not have the will to refuse Gabriella. He trusted his mistress' intuition above all else. Though he could not imagine the days getting worse, he sensed she saw that the darkest times were coming.

If she felt parting ways was essential to their survival, then part ways they must.

Casmire took comfort in his conviction that, one day, they would be reunited. Until that blessed day, he must work with the wizard. The one who professed love for Gabriella.

Adrian felt for the noble steed. He knew well the ache in Casmire's heart. The need for Gabriella's company. And yet, here they were, brothers in arms. Holding a front in case anyone came asking. Providing a much-needed distraction while Gabriella sought —

What exactly? He wondered, turning his gaze back to the fire. Poking the embers with his stick. Somehow flames focused his mind. Allowing him to release the present and go deep within. To ask the questions that remained elusive in the daylight.

When the moon rises and the stars come out, that is when the wisdom of the soul speaks. Adrian knew this well. This was the reason he got little sleep. That and safety. Night was when bandits attacked.

Still, he loved the silence. Adrian craved the quiet. Savouring his talks with the fire. He gazed deeper into the flames. Though his senses stayed alert, he was confident Casmire would warn him of intruders.

Adrian allowed his soul to drift, to journey. To seek out the ones who could answer the questions in his heart. If he could provide answers to Gabriella, he could be of use to her.

For as much as he knew he was being of some value, Adrian was not providing the sacred guidance he was born to give. His true place was at the Messenger's side. Yet here they were. Separated for the simple, infuriating purpose of safety.

And so, he reached out to the Wise Ones. The Elders who held the secrets of the stars. And tossed the runes that spoke of the future.

Wise Ones, Adrian whispered in his mind, *please show me the way. Offer me the wisdom that might guide Gabriella's steps. Show me the stones we are meant to tread. So we can liberate this land from the tyrant known as the Great Prince.*

Even as the words echoed in his mind, a blinding light shot into the sky. A vibrant star, twice as bright as the others, appeared high above the plains. Far enough to protect their caller, yet close enough to pulse a light unknown to this corner of the sky.

Adrian fell back from the impact. Knocking the wind from his chest.

You know, sweet Adrian, the Star Sisters whispered, *that we cannot show you Gabriella's path. That is for her to see and for her alone.*

But I am her Guide, Adrian replied, as he recovered his breath. Do you not want me to direct her?

The sisters chortled. Adrian knew the stars found humans endlessly amusing. Yet he still took offence to their entertainment at his expense.

We do not laugh at you, sweet Adrian, the sisters giggled, making him wonder if they meant the words.

We only find the circumstances amusing. So many times humans try to walk the path of others. So many times they reach for another's prize. Even wise ones such as yourself cannot resist taking steps destined for Gabriella's feet.

Their starlight shimmered and the pulse quickened. He suspected the sisters restrained their natural laughter, if only to spare his feelings.

But, dear Adrian, you know we cannot give that prize to you. Much as we adore you.

Adrian wanted to insist on the reasons they could give him what he asked. But the sisters held up glittering hands. And halted his speech.

No, they said. *Truly, we cannot. And truly we will not. We will share only that we see a stranger coming across your path. Arriving in the next few days.*

A woman, they said, with a calmer, distant tone. As though they reached into the annals of the future. One that walks with the darkness. *She will change the journey for you and Gabriella. She may even tempt your heart, sweet Adrian.*

Not possible, he said, assured of his love.

Do not dismiss the journey, sweet Adrian, they mused. *You never know where the path may lead. Simply be forewarned that your heart will recognize this soul. And she may have more in store for you than you consider.*

The Star Sisters laughed softly. Blew a kiss, then shot across the wide expanse. Disappearing home in a blink. Leaving the night sky darker.

Adrian's soul drifted back to the fire. Listening to the crackling. Smelling the burning flesh of rabbit. Knocking him back to the earth.

He leapt up to rescue his dinner from the flames. Cursing his curiosity and distraction. The Star Sisters delivered a foreboding message to his heart and burnt meat to his stomach.

What could they mean? Adrian considered, already feeling disloyal to Gabriella. How could another woman tempt his heart? Is that what they saw?

Adrian cast a worried glance at Casmire. The horse stared at him with a piercing look. As though he knew what Adrian heard. Though Adrian had protected himself before speaking with the Sisters.

But Casmire was eerily perceptive when it came to protecting Gabriella. He knew when she was in danger. And Adrian could not deny that the message placed Casmire's mistress at risk. A concern that pierced deep into Adrian's being.

He would not be the one to betray the Messenger, Adrian

insisted with the force of his soul.

He knew well that the person who broke the chosen ones were the most often ones closest to their hearts.

No, Adrian asserted. I was warned for a reason. The Star Sisters did not share this wisdom to torture me. They shared it to alert me to the danger.

He ripped off a piece of rabbit flank, chewing as he considered the warning. Casmire's intense gaze lessened as Adrian puzzled through this strange wisdom.

Adrian knew it was time to take a gamble. He looked the steed straight in the eyes.

"A woman is coming our way, Casmire. A woman who plans to steal my affection," Adrian said. "I was told this information to be on my guard."

Casmire stomped the ground, blowing hard and shaking his mane. Adrian feared for a moment that the powerful horse might charge.

"I tell you this," Adrian said quickly, "Because I need your help. I have no idea who this woman is. Or who she is in league with." Adrian emphasized the last point, as though pointing a sharp sword at the steed.

Casmire calmed slightly. For the moment, he refrained from crashing forward. Go on, he instructed the wizard.

"We must both be on our guard," Adrian said. "She may have tricks that work on me that do not work on you. I need you to stay alert. And keep your eye on me."

Rest assured, Casmire said. *I have done that from the moment we met.*

"I know," Adrian replied. "Now I need you to keep guard for

both of us. To trust that I will forever and always be on Gabriella's side."

Casmire huffed. He had little faith in people who proclaimed their loyalty. He trusted only those who acted loyal.

"Which," Adrian said, "is precisely why I am telling you this. So you know that I love her. I would lay my life down for her."

Casmire stared. As much as he wanted to deny the truth in the man's words, Casmire could not deny the fidelity in his body. He spoke honestly and from the heart.

Fine, Casmire acquiesced. *I will remember your words. And your promise.*

"And if I begin to act counter to what I just told you," Adrian said. "You must take action. For all our sakes."

Casmire knew what Adrian was asking. He nodded solemnly. Understanding that their fates, indeed the fate of the Great Lands, rested on his haunches.

He paused, considering the weight of this responsibility. Whether he had the fortitude, and the trust, to carry it out. But he accepted this mission when he fled home with Gabriella years ago. And he would not relinquish it now.

Even if this cost his life.

Casmire tossed his head and pawed the ground. Adrian nodded. He placed his hand on his heart and closed his eyes. Saying a silent prayer.

Their pact was sealed.

FOUR

Hannah and Syrena walked through the woods.

The trees looked different than Hannah remembered. This puzzled her, for they were within a league of the place she called home. She thought of the castle and flinched.

Gabriella expressly insisted that she *not* return to their homestead. They knew it was dangerous.

Of all the places the Great Prince would be watching, this would be the one. But Hannah could not resist. She needed to return. It was as though an irresistible force pulled her home.

Every day, the castle whispered louder and louder to her heart. So loud, in fact, that she disregarded the wisdom of her sister. Not just her sister — the Messenger.

Hannah shivered. And Syrena pulled close, offering warmth without speaking. They had agreed neither would talk aloud while they were this close to Hannah's home. The danger was too great. Even with their silence. As though their presence alone screamed to the skies where they were.

Syrena kept glancing up, expecting the Great Prince to swoop from the heavens to strike them down.

Despite the peril, she would not leave Hannah's side. And Hannah could not be dissuaded.

Syrena walked the soft, forest floor without making a sound. She had perfected the art of moving without noise in the stone halls of the Hidden Palace. And as such she could certainly manage the same trick in a wood covered with pine needles and cedar cones.

Ever since Hannah proposed — no, insisted — on returning to Granamore, Syrena kept a close eye on her beloved.

She would follow Hannah into the fires of hell. But she did not assume that her loved one was in possession of her will. The Hidden Palace had managed it before. Though the distance they travelled was great, Syrena would not put anything past that old stone witch.

Syrena quickly drew a star across her chest and bowed her head to ask forgiveness. She came from a long line of spellcasters. And did not mean to offend the ancestors. The Palace had been born out of magic, but it was a dark and twisted sorcery. Unlike anything Syrena was raised to use.

A shame, Syrena grumbled. She was a firm believer in fighting fire with fire.

The blessing of love changed her life. Enough that she had profound faith in the wisdom of Adrian and the power of Gabriella. And she adored Hannah with all of her heart.

But she had not changed her mind about how the world worked. Gabriella had challenged the Prince and Hannah had shamed him. He would hunt for them until the day he drew his last breath.

Hannah reached out and took Syrena's hand. She felt her lover worrying and instinctively offered comfort. Truthfully, Syrena had good reason to fret. They were walking into the most dangerous area of the realm. Without guard or guardian.

But Hannah felt the old castle calling. She had felt its whispers for weeks. And she was sure it was no trick. At least, as sure as Hannah could be since her time at the Hidden Palace. It had been three years since she had been freed, yet she still jumped at shadows and wondered each morning if she were truly awake.

Syrena squeezed her hand. And Hannah remembered that she was no longer alone. She had allies who watched over her. Family and lovers who cared more for her safety than she did. And so, after years of exile, she finally had the courage to return home.

Hannah believed the castle had secrets to share. Confidences that might disappear on the wind if she did not get to them. She had not been concerned about time until the past week. She was sure she had ample days to act. And heeded Gabriella's words of warning.

But, in the last few days, she felt the castle's voice growing fainter. She was not sure why. The softer the whispers grew, the more urgent Hannah's quest felt. She must hear its wisdom before the mysterious message disappeared for good.

She calmed her rushing heart. Hannah desperately hoped for so many secrets. Ways to defeat the Great Prince. Keys to unlock the spell holding her people in fear. Assurances that she would never again fall under the sway of the Hidden Palace.

But, in truth, her greatest desire was to know her parents' whereabouts. She prayed they were alive. For she had not felt their presence since she was swept from her home.

Not even Gabriella held wisdom of their fate. The sisters had tried merging gifts, and still they could not see what had happened to their mother and father.

Hannah prayed that she would discover some truth about her

parents at their home. She would share her treasure with Gabriella. And perhaps her sister would forgive her for transgressing her promise to stay safe.

A twig snapped in the distance.

Syrena grabbed Hannah's hand, pulling her behind a great oak. With a fierce glance, she ordered Hannah to stay put.

Syrena pinned herself against the great tree. And moved in silence around the edge, inching in the direction of the sound. She felt forward with her mind, while her body was pressed against the rough bark.

She felt a presence. Syrena was unsure yet whether it was animal or human. The noise had startled her nerves. She needed to calm herself to tune into her forest senses. She trusted they knew the difference between a harmless sound and one that carried danger.

Syrena, Hannah whispered in her mind.

Not now, Syrena replied. *Let me focus.*

Syrena. Turn around. Now, Hannah insisted.

Syrena knew Hannah's tone. The slightest inflection conveyed miles of meaning. A natural compensation since limiting their spoken words.

She turned, prepared for the worst. And saw what took her lover aback.

A hunter stood only a few feet away, arrow poised at Hannah's heart. His eyes pierced theirs. Syrena was not sure whether he had the gift of sacred sight, as well as weaponry.

But she did not intend to find out.

"Stand down, sir," Syrena commanded, as though *she* were Queen of these lands, rather than her companion.

Syrena respected that Hannah believed her parents still lived. But Syrena did not hold her lover's faith. She assumed the rulers were slaughtered by the Great Prince years ago. In Syrena's eyes, Hannah was Queen of these forests now. And all should bow before her.

Especially hunters, Syrena growled. Glaring at the bold intruder.

"And why should I?" he demanded. "*You* trespass in the royal woods. A place where only the family of King Algor belongs."

Syrena felt Hannah's heart leap. Hannah was desperate to proclaim that she had returned. That her family once more belonged to this earth and would protect anyone who swore allegiance to them.

But Syrena knew better than to trust strangers. She had only one instance in her life when outsiders had turned out to be allies. All others were tricksters and charlatans. Especially ones with honey-sweet phrases readily offered from their lips.

"So you are a member of the royal family?" she mocked. Awaiting his answer.

He glared harder. Not relinquishing his arrow's aim. Something about this young woman unnerved him. Made him want to wipe her from the woods. But her companion. Her companion was intriguing. And eerily familiar.

"Do not be foolish, girl," he said. "I am a guardian of these woods."

"Truly?" Syrena challenged. "When the common word insists the royal family is gone and the castle is in ruins? What charge have you when there is no longer a family to protect?"

Hannah stiffened, wanting to scream at Syrena for her blasphemy.

Bellowing to the heavens that her family was safe and ready to return. Yet her heart understood that Syrena took an offensive stance to safeguard Hannah. And discover this man's intentions.

"The absence of the family is no concern of yours," he retorted. "These lands remain their legacy. And though they do not occupy them, their birthright is intact. As is my oath to protect all they stand for."

"Kind sir," Hannah interjected, surprising Syrena and the hunter. "We have no intention of causing harm to these lands or the family who owns them. We wish only safe passage through the woods. And to be on our way to the oceanic realm beyond."

"You seek passage to Infinimare?" the hunter asked.

He knew her voice. Where had he heard that voice? The hunter lowered his aim. He stared. As though he might will the answer from the familiar one.

Syrena bristled at his attention. Noticing, for the first time, the man's stature. His striking face. His attractive form. Syrena fumed at the way he stared at the Queen.

Hannah reached a hand toward Syrena and touched the edge of her beloved's cape. No valiant hunter would sway the course of her love. No matter how fine his form.

"Yes," Hannah spoke with infinite softness, easing the hunter's concerns. Her voice lulled him into a trance. "We are but innocent travellers in these woods. Wishing to pass through without harm to person or beast."

Syrena marvelled at the magic in Hannah's voice. She had not yet seen this ability. She had witnessed Hannah's gift to foresee danger — in dreams and in the moment. Syrena was puzzled why her beloved had not predicted the hunter's ambush. She suspected

Hannah's desperate need to find her parents had clouded her perception.

But this, Syrena thought. This verges on spellcasting. Not unlike the skills Syrena used on Hannah before she was rescued from her enslavement. Did Hannah have an aptitude for mimicry or was this her own gift of magic?

Syrena watched as Hannah presented an open palm to the hunter.

Something in Hannah's gesture spoke of another time. One filled with trust and kindness. A dance of offerings and acceptance. As though Hannah were enacting a scene she had watched performed hundreds of times.

Suddenly, the hunter fell to one knee. Dropped his bow and arrow, and swept the hood from his head. Pressing his bow to his heart.

"Your majesty," he proclaimed, mortified that he had not seen it sooner. "My humble apologies. Had I known —"

Syrena froze. Not daring to move a muscle, for fear she might confirm his proclamation.

She cried out to Hannah in her mind. *What are you doing? You do not know this man is our ally. He may be a spy, feigning a gallant nature, yet reporting our movements to the Prince.*

Fear not, Syrena. I know this man, Hannah replied, touching her lover's cheek.

"Rise up, sweet Tobias," Hannah said. "I do not require your bended knee. But I do need your assistance."

Tobias raised his gaze to the radiant beauty he had adored since he was a young lad.

"Anything, my Queen," he replied. "You have but to ask."

FIVE

GABRIELLA SETTLED ONTO A STACK OF HAY far in the upper reaches of the stables.

She knew the night would be cold but she felt safer resting her head above the beasts. They would give her ample warning of intruders. If there was one creature in the land that was twitchier than Gabriella, it was a horse.

She plumped up the hay as much as the rough grass allowed. Gabriella smiled, sadly, as she though of Casmire. Perhaps she was fooling herself by claiming the stables were safe. She suspected she merely wanted to feel closer to her steed.

Gabriella missed her equine soulmate as much as she missed Adrian. In truth, the parting between her and Casmire was harder. She had not been without him since she left home. Leaving Casmire was like leaving her homeland a second time.

She had fought back tears, but her valiant companion was safer with her lover. If the Prince's men discovered Casmire without his rider, they would surely rush the message back to their liege. Her hope was they would report something had befallen the Messenger. For they would not believe she would abandon her horse.

None of them understood the sacrifice of love, Gabriella

thought. Though, in her heart, she knew true love did not require sacrifice. She was raised in the womb of true love. And grew to adulthood watching her mother and father adore one another. Each act they took in the name of love was a choice, rather than a sacrifice.

Even if they were to lay down their lives, they did so with full hearts and soaring spirits.

Gabriella crossed herself in the sign of the star and whispered a silent prayer. She did not want her parents to face such a choice. She insisted on trusting that they were alive. Though how that was possible without Gabriella or Hannah feeling their presence, she had no notion. Her heart squeezed. Protesting what her mind stubbornly believed.

She threw her fists into the hay. Grabbing handfuls of the wiry grass and crushing it until the stalks threatened to slash her palms. She wanted to scream but could not afford to voice her rage. Not yet.

She must be smart. She wove a spell of protection around her. No matter that she made no sound. Gabriella knew better than to tempt the silence with a force that would call the legions of the Hidden Palace to her nest.

Once protected, she set forth to alleviate the immediacy of her torment. Releasing a howl inside rivalling the black wolves of the Great Forest.

Not nearly as satisfying as a full body howl. Still, she felt better for the release. Gabriella knew the dawn would bring a sign. She felt the presence of the guide awaiting her. And knew in her heart that tomorrow she would be one step closer to finding the mysterious man in the caves. And that sword.

She would set forth just before the break of dawn. When the small outpost was quiet. Either sound asleep or passed out from too much drink.

But first, sleep. Without caring for her body, she would only make foolish decisions. Potentially missing the sign altogether.

—m—

Gabriella awoke in the early hours, long before sunrise. She heard the soft rustling of the horses. Before moving a muscle, she reached out to feel their mood.

All were calm. Aside from the restless urge to be under the stars and chewing fresh, dew-laden grass. Gabriella breathed a sigh of relief. She preferred to start her day without the rush of a fight. Or a swift departure to elude prying eyes.

She sat. Careful not to spook the horses, though they were used to her smell by now. They also appreciated her ease and conversation. So few humans spoke so effortlessly with their minds.

They loved the chatter so much, she nearly lost a night of rest. She finally asked them to relent for a few hours, with the promise they could resume in the morning.

Gabriella understood the torturous boredom of being locked in a cage better than most. But needs are what they are. As much as she adored the conversation and company of the sweet animals in the stables, she had to prioritize sleep.

Now that she was awake, they regaled her with the tales of the past six hours. Each wanted to offer a story or a complaint.

Gabriella laughed as she gathered her things and gave polite responses to the multitude of voices. She peered over the edge of her post, checking her route.

The horses by the entrance assured her all was safe. She smiled, grateful. Trusting their sensitive intuition above even her own.

Climbing down the rickety ladder, she landed on the floor just as the lead mare neighed loudly. Alerting Gabriella that an intruder approached. She froze in her tracks and searched for an exit.

The youngest colt whinnied then directed his muzzle to a tiny entrance for the barn cats and herding dogs. Gabriella was not sure she could fit, but she had no choice.

She hesitated. Remembering her intuition that the outpost had called to her for a reason. What was that reason? Could it be the person about to enter the stable?

Gabriella glanced at the heavy wooden door with a faint glimmer of hope. Despite her visionary abilities, she needed to be wise. She could not put herself in a precarious position simply because she wished for a kind face on the other side of that door.

Though Gabriella often felt the approach of a sign, she was not always certain of its arrival. All she knew was to be patient. And to keep from getting captured.

Not the most ideal of circumstances, she chided her far-too-silent angels. A hint anytime now would be greatly appreciated.

Nothing. Gabriella rolled her eyes. And refrained from sighing.

As the stable door latch clicked, Gabriella leapt toward the young colt. Diving behind his mother's hindquarters before the door opened. Neither the mother nor the colt quivered a muscle. Protecting Gabriella with their steely wills and generous hearts.

She should run now and inquire later, but Gabriella could not resist seeing who entered. Were she surrounded by cows, she would expect a stable hand at this early hour. But horses were rarely taken out before sunrise, unless the person was on the run. Or in pursuit.

Gabriella prayed for the first option. Still, she liked to know her odds.

The person who slipped into the stable surprised her. She could tell from her stature that it was the young girl from the bar. The one playing cards the night before.

Gabriella crouched tight behind the mare. Knowing that the older horse would be more predictable and steady than the sprightly colt. The offer of a carrot could lure him away quicker than the blink of an eye. And Gabriella needed time to process what she saw.

For now that Gabriella laid eyes directly on the girl, she saw she was none other than a servant maid from her home. A child she had not laid eyes on since Gabriella knew the protection of her parents' walls.

No wonder I recognized her nimble gait, Gabriella thought. We are well acquainted. The girl had grown in the five years since Gabriella had left. Yet she looked more bare-boned. Her searching eyes were hard and hungry. And though she was small for her age, she was tougher than her slight build appeared.

Gabriella sensed childlike hope was alive in her young heart, despite the hard times the world had delivered to her door. Still, she watched with care. She could not risk trusting even a familiar face. For though they knew one another, Gabriella could only swear to what this girl once was. Not who she might have become.

Still, the royal creed begged her to care for the girl. To claim her. And bring her along on her mission. To shield her from harm.

Enough! Gabriella commanded her heart. I know the oath of

royal blood. I hear it whisper in my veins every day. Yet I must survive or I will never be of use to my people. A dead Queen is no Queen at all!

The young girl froze as though she heard something. Terror flickered in her eyes.

"Who is there?" she commanded. "Show yourself!"

Gabriella did not make a sound. She crouched lower and eyed the small opening.

Should she flee or stand? Her instinct told her to run. But her heart spoke of more profound risks. Necessary wagers, even in these dangerous times.

Gabriella thought of her conversation with the Moon Goddess. She was no longer meant to run and hide from every situation. She needed confidantes. Strong and loyal people who, when the time came, would rise up. And reclaim their natural inheritance.

Confidantes only came with trust. A precarious venture even in the kindest of days.

Gabriella was far from sure how to take on this sacred quest. Humans were tricky creatures. She often misunderstood their intentions and misread their messages. They spoke false when they expected truth and were aggressive when they wanted gentleness.

Gabriella refrained from growling. She did not claim to understand her fellow beings. And yet, she was being asked to lead them.

As unsure as she felt, Gabriella knew there was only one way to approach an unknown path. And that was to take a step.

After the first, the rest came easier. Or so she hoped.

Her stomach clenched. The mare felt her unease, pawing the stable floor with silent strokes. Not revealing Gabriella, but letting her know that she did not appreciate this unrest near her colt.

The young horse grew restless and was about to draw attention. She could not expect him to stay calm much longer. And so, she stood and spoke. "Hello, Katrin."

The girl started, swivelling with clenched fists. Ready to fight. Then froze.

She stared. Wondering what phantasm appeared in this remote stable under a balsamic moon. Surely the night gods had better uses for their time than to torment her. Katrin blinked. Waiting for an answer to her otherworldly concern.

For a long moment, Gabriella kept her eyes on the girl. Despite their history, she did not trust the pause. Gabriella suspected Katrin was readying to sound the alarm. Yelling for the guards, and claiming a substantial prize in return.

"Gabriella," Katrin whispered, as though speaking the name might remedy this disturbing impression. And cause the apparition to disappear.

"Yes," Gabriella replied. Still waiting for the girl to reveal her hand.

The two women stood still. Examining the other. Wondering what the past five years had wrought, since they had been familiar.

These days of subterfuge made all beings wary. Especially the horses.

Gabriella felt them waiting for the tense humans to come to terms. And such uncertainty made them restless. Gabriella placed a calming hand on the mare. Assuring her that she would not endanger her colt.

The mare dipped her head in acknowledgement. Drawing the eye of young Katrin.

Something about the exchange calmed the girl. Convincing her that this strange woman in the stable was, indeed, the same Gabriella she had known from the land of King Algor.

"You're wanted," Katrin blurted, abandoning all niceties. Gabriella laughed.

Neither expected the reaction. But Katrin's blunt statement was a relief. Gabriella had carried the burden alone for so long that the candid assessment released a wave of tension.

"Yes, I am," Gabriella said, with a slight smile. "Will you turn me in?"

Katrin examined her. A sharp-eyed, careful scrutiny that gave Gabriella pause. And made her consider, again, her limited options for exit.

"I think not," Katrin said, not altogether convincing. Gabriella raised an eyebrow at the presumptuous girl.

Yet, something in Gabriella's heart recognized the defiance. Katrin was in her own precarious situation. And though this did not encourage Gabriella to trust her, the knowledge gave her comfort.

"Much appreciated," Gabriella said. And waited for Katrin to make the next move.

"You might be worth more next week," Katrin added.

Gabriella braced, eyeing the clever girl. Unsure whether to hug her or punch her.

And in that moment, she knew.

Katrin was destined to be her friend.

SIX

MOMENTS AGO, KATRIN HAD RUSHED to the stables in search of a horse.

She had spent the evening hiding at the back of the inn when she happened on a card game. The burly men assumed she was an easy mark, being both a girl and looking younger than her age.

Katrin was accustomed to men underestimating her. And, in these hard days, their assumptions were useful. Seasoned fighters did not put effort into a battle. They used their opponents' moves to defeat them.

She saw smug condescension in their eyes. These lazy, unchallenged guards believed they controlled this backcountry outpost. And so, their greedy gazes raked over her body. Already presuming they owned her and imagining how she would pay when she lost.

They exchanged lewd jibes under their beer-sodden breath. Until the head guard spoke.

"Do you have money, girl?" the head guard asked. Not amused by anyone playing without currency. No matter how attractive.

The others fell silent. They exchanged aggravated glances. But spoke no opposition.

Their leader's question made the rules clear. If the girl were to lose, no matter to whom, he would have the prize. Such were the wages of power.

"Only a small amount, my lord," Katrin replied, intentionally using the overreaching title. He smiled in a condescending manner. Her gamble had worked.

The leader leaned back, eyeing her with amusement. Noticing her tight breasts and lean physique. "And you have coins to pay if you lose?" he asked.

His companions chortled, enjoying this game. Smug in their authority.

Katrin forced down her urge to lunge. To claw his eyes out as payment for all she had suffered at the hands of such men. But she had learned to confine her rage. To hold its reins and direct it, like a stallion with hooves of stone.

In her wreck of a homeland, survival demanded a sharp mind. And clever tactics. She used her rage to trick arrogant halfwits. They would not see her charge before it was too late.

Katrin had learned patience. If she joined the game, she would get many rewards. A handful of hours spent in a warm backroom. Relief from predators that stalked friendless travellers. Fresh bread and free ale, as the inn owner swapped morsels for the good graces of the local sentries.

And, if she was lucky, ample opportunity to take money from fools.

Katrin smiled. A well-trained smile. Sweet and naïve. As though men such as these were precisely the teachers to instruct an innocent like her in the ways of the world.

She marvelled that they never wondered how she came to this town. A rugged outpost in the remote reaches of a fierce range of mountains. If they paused for one rational moment, they would know she was no fragile waif. No matter her size and sex.

The head guard pulled out a chair and patted the straw seat, indicating Katrin must sit next to him. Katrin lowered her eyes and stepped toward the table. Taking in the portly bellies of these men who had been well-bribed and never seen battle.

They had no interest in queries. No desire to find other men to challenge. In this dank room at the edge of the world, they were kings of the dung heap. Why would they venture into far regions to challenge their comfort?

At this, Katrin smiled and her heart broke a little. She ached for her homeland. There, she had known smart men and courageous women. Valiant citizens who cared. She had been raised with honour and the value of truth.

Only to have that world of generosity crushed by the Great Prince.

Since that day, Katrin vowed she would survive. She cared only for herself. She scraped through starvation and withstood illness. And though she appeared slight, she was strong and determined.

If she were patient and blessed with luck, she vowed, to one day watch as the life drained from the Prince's eyes. Just as she had been forced to do with her beloved brother. And if she were the one to thrust the dagger deep into the Prince's heart and take that life, so be it.

Katrin took a seat next to the lead guard. She blushed as he instructed her on the rules of the game. Little did he realize that Katrin had long ago mastered five-card draw. Just as she commanded the expressions on her face and the rage in her belly.

A blast of cold air blew under the door. Sweeping through

the space and causing even the most inebriated player to shiver. A loud *bang!* drew the attention of all of the players, especially Katrin. The heavy Inn door must have slammed open.

She wondered whether a storm was brewing. A wave of concern twisted her stomach. If she bungled tonight's game and could not freely escape, she might find herself in danger. Katrin turned her gaze back to game, more determined than ever.

By the end of the night, she must win every coin from the guards' pockets.

—m—

The head guard stared at his dwindling pile of coins. Starting to suspect the young waif was swindling him. Though Katrin had not cheated anyone.

She merely played like a sharp-eyed hawk watching mice dart about in a summer field. She could not help that the mice had little minds, unable to perceive a winged hunter in the sky.

Hand after hand, she took their money.

Each game, she exclaimed that the spirits must be on her side. Shocked that she won at such a game. At first, the head guard found her winning amusing. Enjoying that his masterful instruction helped his student expose his underlings as fools.

As the night wore on, he realized they were not the only ones depleted of money. The fun disappeared. And only Katrin enjoyed herself. The guards grew sullen. Not even drunken minds and full bellies could quell their bad humour.

Katrin felt the mood turning against her. And knew she had limited time to find a way out. For though she was more clever than all the men at the table, her quick wit would do little against burly, drunken guards pinning her to the wall and demanding justice.

She feigned an unwell stomach and blamed the strange ale. Insisting she needed fresh air and, quite possibly, the outhouse. The lead guard eyed her suspiciously. His instinct told him this woman was trouble. But his pride was not ready to admit he had been duped.

After a long, tense moment, with his men awaiting a decision, the leader nodded. Then snatched her cloak, with a glare. "Be sure to come back," he growled.

She relinquished the cloak. She did not wish to be outside without the wrap. But she valued her life more than risking another moment in this room.

Katrin played her movements like a careful dance. She rose from the chair with a slight weave, to pretend intoxication. She steadied herself on the table, releasing a soft giggle. Then stumbled over her feet, almost falling.

She released the table. Steadying her movement with outstretched hands. A few steps forward, she dropped coins along the dirt floor.

Katrin focused ahead, but felt the guards lock eyes on the abandoned money. Their greed rushed in. Pushing out any suspicion. Reassured she was a silly, drunken maid, they were ready to wrestle for the shiny prize.

She held back a smile. The money worked every time. No guard would loosen his grip on a single coin. No matter how drunk. Her fumbled attempt to hold her winnings swayed her companions to believe she was innocent. A sure-fire way to restore their tarnished dominance. And provide her the time she needed.

She wove toward the back door, forcing her limbs to go slowly. Assuring her uneasy stomach they would soon be free.

After the tense crossing, her hand landed on the cool surface of the door's handle. She kept a sideways glance on the drunken guards, as she pretended the wooden portal was too heavy for her slight arms.

She pulled once. Twice. Shrugged, and tossed a helpless glance toward the men.

The leader shot a look at his biggest man. The brute slapped a palm on the thick table, wobbling with the effort of movement, and pushed himself to his feet. Katrin watched as he struggled to stay upright. Much to the amusement of his fellow guards.

Katrin breathed out her relief, as the men jeered. Teasing the brute that he would never make the journey before his rump hit the ground.

Seeing the focus had shifted, Katrin pulled with her true strength. Opening the door and releasing a blast of northerly air. Causing the men to grumble and grab another warm ale.

As she slipped out, Katrin gave a quick glance back at the boorish guards. Holding her smugness close to her heart, rather than all over her face.

Then disappeared into the crisp night.

—ᴍ—

Katrin made her way to the stables. She knew her time in this outpost was done.

They may have been fooled for now. But when they grew

sober and discovered their money was gone, the guards would want retribution. Well-versed in the local terrain and equipped with capable steeds, she had only a small window of time in which to flee.

She felt confident, however, that they would only track her a limited distance. For two reasons. One was they had jobs to attend to during daylight hours. The second, far more potent reason, was to avoid the locals discovering they had been fooled by a girl.

Hiding by the stables, Katrin had hesitated. She did not like to steal. Wagering, even trickery, was different. Each person had a chance to outwit her, if he paid attention.

But *theft*. That rankled her deep-set, if masked, honour.

Still, she knew her only chance of evading the guards was to take a horse. Katrin shivered. The cold night wind sliced through her thin clothing. Useful for distracting drunken men, worthless against the icy air that threatened to steal the heat from her body.

As her teeth chattered, she had another motivation to take a warm, capable horse. She was sure to freeze to death if she remained on foot. Katrin steeled herself. Choosing survival over honour, yet again.

She would have to pay the favour back to someone. One day.

And so she entered the stables, expecting to be the only creature awake. Except, perhaps, a steed that wanted to escape this insignificant village as much as she did.

Then Katrin got the surprise of her life.

Enough to shock the cold from her veins and anchor her feet to the ground. Of all the places, in all the countries, at all the times, never had she expected to see Gabriella, heir to King Algor. Regal princess of Granamore.

Katrin, and her people, believed the royal family dead. The only possible survivor, Princess Hannah, had been traded off to the Great Prince, in a futile gesture of peace. Though no one knew whether she had survived his torment.

Rumours surfaced three years ago. Whispers that Gabriella was seen in a far-off land. But, Katrin never put stock in rumours. Especially when they dissipated as quickly as they rose. Like a mist that felt real at dawn, only to be a memory in the harsh light of midday.

So when she stood, staring at Gabriella, Katrin was convinced she saw a phantom. Maybe even an angry shade that came to reprimand her for stealing a horse. Whispering to her of better choices. Higher callings.

She prayed it was not here to take her back to her ancestors. The apparition that was to prepare her soul for the cruel face of death and swoop in to stop her heart.

The spirit spoke and stepped away from the horses. And Katrin felt faint.

As a child, she adored Princess Gabriella. Katrin aspired to working in the palace so she could be near the princess. She practised scrubbing with the same devotion that a warrior used to practise swordplay. So deep was Katrin convinced her destiny was at Gabriella's side.

When she was old enough, after much begging of her mother, she applied to be a scullery maid. In hopes of one day, becoming a lady in waiting to this very phantom. But Katrin discovered that fate had other plans.

She had been at the palace for only a year before the Great Prince stole Princess Hannah for his throne. The kingdom was devastated. Many were outraged that King Algor made concessions to the Prince. Even worse that he gave up his beloved daughter to a man bent on devastating their homeland.

Yet somehow, at the tender age of thirteen, Katrin knew the King had tried the only move he possessed to keep his people safe. Still, they judged him. She was furious with the maids who criticized the king behind his back. She would defend him with her fiery, if unschooled wisdom. They only scoffed and told her she knew nothing of the world.

But Katrin did not need to understand the world to know the worth of loyalty. Her brother had taught her that kindness at a young age. She was perplexed by people who abandoned all allegiance at the first confrontation. This was precisely when commitment was most needed.

That year, her fixation with Princess Gabriella deepened.

In her role as a scullery maid, she was able to slip through secret castle passages. Katrin was obsessed with watching the Princess train. One mentor developed her powers as a fighter. The other trained her skills as a natural conjuror.

The King and Queen told the staff that Gabriella trained to protect herself. But Katrin knew they were arming their youngest child.

As she watched Gabriella with her tutors, Katrin saw the Princess throw herself into the training. Perhaps a part of the Princess believed in self-preservation.

The longer Katrin watched, the deeper she understood Gabriella had no such intention. She saw Gabriella's grief. She recognized her rage. And Katrin knew that Gabriella had every intention of making the Great Prince pay for his actions.

When she was drawn to the palace, Katrin adored the Princess for her direct speech and wild spirit. Several months later, as she watched Gabriella bear down with her sword, Katrin applauded with the pure fury of an orphaned child.

Now, five years had passed and she stood face-to-face with Gabriella.

The most hunted woman in the realm.

SEVEN

As Gabriella stared at Katrin, she received a memory. Years ago, this young woman had watched her train.

Gabriella barely recognized the younger, plumper face in the scene from time passed. The wide-eyed girl obsessed with her regimen. Showing up every day. No matter what drama was occurring in the castle.

Gabriella noticed the girl, but was too preoccupied to speak to her. She had wondered what was so fascinating about seeing teachers bring Gabriella to her knees, time and time again. Had the girl enjoyed watching a Princess get the wind knocked out of her? Was it a chance to feel better about her own position?

Yet, Gabriella knew better than to assume such petty intentions. There was no malice on the young girl's face. She had watched with utter fascination.

Some days, Gabriella felt the young maid was the only person cheering for her. Her teachers needed to focus on her faults. And her parents were too aggrieved at the loss of Hannah and too worried about the coming days to pay her much loving attention. Their focus was only to keep her safe.

Gabriella shook off the memory. She, too, needed to be focused. This was not the time for reverie.

"What is your plan?" Gabriella asked, directing the girl's attention to immediate escape. Rather than the gold that Gabriella's capture could put in Katrin's pocket.

Katrin's gaze swept over the stable of horses. Seeking, Gabriella assumed, the least conspicuous steed.

"Might I suggest," Gabriella offered, "The brown stallion at the far back? He is strong and fast, and the location of his stall suggests he is not owned by influential authorities."

Katrin raised an eyebrow, as though simultaneously annoyed and impressed at Gabriella's astute assessment.

"And what about you?" Katrin replied, already making her way to the brown steed with the white flare down his nose. "You wouldn't be in the stables if you weren't avoiding those very same influential authorities."

"Yes," Gabriella said. "Though I wasn't convinced I needed a horse. Let alone a stolen one."

Katrin wound up to defend her position. Until Gabriella raised a hand to stop her protest. Then a small smile curved onto Gabriella's lips.

"I am in no position to judge," Gabriella said. "Though I have not stolen many horses since you saw me last, I have taken my share of food, shelter, and weapons."

For the sake of the moment, Gabriella chose to omit the lives she had also been forced to take. That was a tale for another time. Perhaps when Katrin had less reason to fear her and more reason to be on Gabriella's side.

Katrin nodded. She opened the stall door with care, but she had no time to soothe the steed. Gabriella could see by Katrin's haste that whoever pursued her must not be far.

Gabriella locked gazes with a beautiful grey stallion. He would blend well with the snow, and was hardy enough to fend for himself once released to the wild. Though Gabriella had not stolen many horses, she felt no guilt for freeing them from this circumstance.

Katrin led her steed toward the door, as Gabriella saddled up the grey dappled stallion. She felt his urgency to be free of this horrible place. He pawed at the hay on the ground and pulled at the bridle Gabriella insisted on putting over his head.

She preferred to ride without a bridle but she did not know this steed. Not only was he young and excitable, he was about to break free for the first time. Gabriella could not take the chance that he would follow orders. A bridle was less intrusive than commanding his thoughts.

Katrin halted as she broached the stable doors. And Gabriella heard the rumble of angry, drunken male voices.

As though they already had an unspoken language, Katrin turned with a panicked glance as though asking Gabriella what to do. Calming Gabriella's nerves. And giving her faith in the girl's intentions.

A flash of insight lit up Gabriella's vision. She saw this moment with Katrin. A preordained meeting. A chance to see if they would choose a common path.

What better way to discover someone's loyalty? To test her heart? Katrin could have betrayed Gabriella, prying the starving girl out of a perilous situation and gaining a hefty purse of coins.

Instead, Katrin turned to her for guidance.

"Come," Gabriella whispered, handing the reins to Katrin. "Take our horses to the back. I'll release all the stall doors."

Gabriella moved down the centre, flipping open the locks on each stall. Keeping the steeds calm as she made her way down the line. "When the guards open those doors, the horses will charge for the open air."

"But what about us? Why must we be at the back?" Katrin asked, following with the saddled horses. The angry voices were growing louder. And she did not like the thought of being further-est from escape.

"When the other horses bolt, jump on your steed and lay as low as possible," Gabriella replied. "We'll merge with the pack at the height of the chaos. The guards will not be looking for us when twenty horses are thundering in their direction."

The sound of the men yelling and pounding on the door caught her attention. The horses could not be contained much longer. And Gabriella knew they had only seconds before the guards pulled open the doors.

"Go!" she commanded. Katrin ran with both horses toward the back of the stable.

Gabriella crouched down, making her way along the stable corridor. She opened the last few stalls, whispering to each horse. Sharing her plan with the restless steeds. She calmed their fright-ened hearts and steeled their wills. Promising freedom at the end of this battle.

The lock on the heavy stable heaved. The old doors creaked open, protesting the temperature. And rattling the nerves of the stable occupants. Then the doors gave way and banged against the stable walls, sending a blast of cold air inside.

Drunken men shouted and stumbled. Loud voices surrounded the stables. But the air had already cued the horses to bolt, and the men failed to set a single foot inside.

Nostrils full with the promise of freedom and the scent of the dawn, the horses charged.

A wave of power surged forward. Wild and furious, toward the startled guards.

EIGHT

EVER SINCE THE MAN HAD SHARED HIS VISION of the temptress yet to come, Casmire kept close watch on the wizard.

He did not doubt the heart of the magic one. He did not doubt that he was a good person who adored his mistress. Casmire did however, as a rule, mistrust the ways of humans.

Even the kindest ones strayed from the true path. They made decisions that infuriated his heart. Casmire pawed the earth, thinking of the choices he had been forced to witness.

Humans abandoned their young. Betrayed their tribe. Sent his brethren to slaughter. All for foolish ends such as a title, power, or revenge.

Casmire huffed, sending mist into the night sky. Expressing his distaste as quietly as he could while the wizard slept. He knew the magic one did not sleep well. He started awake at the slightest noise. Much like Casmire's mistress.

As the strange man shuffled under his blanket, Casmire stood tall and watched. He did not require much rest. And often reposed during the day while the wizard kept watch.

At least tonight the Wizard had not sought the guidance of the Star Women. Much as Casmire loved their essence and felt the purity of their hearts, he did not like the magic wielded by the wizard to call forth those stellar beings.

Casmire shook his mane in irritation, feeling the remnants of the spell itch on his hide. Magic drew enemies. And enemies drew weapons.

Casmire loved to assert his power in a battle. But he did not wish to fight many without his mistress at his side. His focus at this time was to stay alive, and keep the wizard safe. At least until he could be reunited with his Queen.

For unbeknown to the wizard, Casmire had made a much deeper promise to an even more regal man.

The night that Gabriella was to flee her homeland, Casmire had stood ready. Restraining his impatience. Awaiting his rider. In the final moments before she appeared in the stable, her father, King Algor had entered. Catching Casmire's attention.

This was an unexpected intrusion. For only on rare occasions did the King come to the stables.

They were not his favourite of places. Nor did he like to ride. Unlike his wife and daughters. He took to the saddle only for ceremonial occasions. The King was drawn more to matters of state than he was to displays of opulence. This was how he viewed riding horses – as play or pageantry.

This did not reflect his feelings for the animals. King Algor respected horses. He admired their regal natures and appreciated that they gave such deep pleasure to his daughters, especially his youngest.

But he was a King of staterooms and strategy. Not of battlefields and hunts.

When the King set foot in the stables, Casmire knew a weighty moment was at hand. King Algor glanced at the surroundings, breathing in the sharp scent of hay. He admired the clean surroundings and the orderly arrangement of the tack.

Then he directed his gaze at Casmire. And stepped toward him with purpose.

A ripple of cold shivered up Casmire's spine. And he took a step back. The valiant steed was not afraid. He had faced many terrible opponents before this moment. But he sensed the King was about to ask of Casmire a promise that would conflict with his long-held vow to serve his mistress.

The King stopped in front of Casmire's stall. He stood in silence. Staring into the steed's eyes. Casmire pawed the ground to release the discomfort. The steed's movement did not draw the eye of the King.

Algor stayed absolutely still. His gaze fixed on Casmire.

—m—

King Algor stared, as the horse bowed and shook his mane. The King felt confident in his calling to speak to the beast. But still, he was unsettled by the task.

Algor trusted his daughter's wisdom. She seemed to understand animals in a way he did not. She spoke to their hearts. He loved his daughter deeply and, so, he never found her ways strange. Though others certainly did.

Gabriella saw into the world of horses or chickadees or rose-buds. She understood their language. And she embraced their ways.

The King did not see or understand the realms his youngest daughter experienced. But he trusted Gabriella's brilliance. He admired her empathy. And he knew, one day, her wisdom would heal his lands.

But now, danger lurked in their beloved woods. Death and betrayal rode the winds to their door.

For her own safety, King Algor commanded his daughter to flee their lands. Gabriella acquiesced, but insisted she bring Casmire as her companion. She would be an outcast. And need a friend.

King Algor knew that the steed understood this meeting was urgent. Surely, the king would not have interrupted the last moments before the steed would forever leave his homeland if it were not crucial.

Into this tender space, stepped the ruler of his world. The father of his mistress.

This journey will take immense strength and courage, thought Algor. For both of them.

So on this, the most heartbreaking of nights, when he would send his second daughter into the darkness of the unknown, only a few years after losing his first child, Algor stood. Staring into the soul of the only being accompanying Gabriella on her fool's errand.

"I do not know how to do this," King Algor began. Holding court with the commanding stallion. Feeling strangely confronted by the beast.

The mighty horse did not make Algor's task easier. Casmire returned the king's stare. He held his ground, yet looked deeply discomfited.

The steed huffed and shook his mane, as though he sensed the King's understanding. Or perhaps, Algor thought, he merely wished to have this moment over and done.

"I do not know if you comprehend me, horse," King Algor said, as though he were speaking to one of his courtiers. "But hear me you must."

A strange noise stirred in the corner of the stable, disturbing the King's attention. He forced himself to ignore the intrusion. This was his only chance to speak with Casmire before Gabriella returned. He did not have the time to be distracted by idle servants.

King Algor had greater concerns than palace gossip. He must secure safe passage for himself and his wife. Then ensure that his trusted advisors had places to hide while the storms of the Great Prince blew through their land.

But first, he must complete this mission.

"I need you to guard the well-being of my daughter, noble one," King Algor continued, paying tribute to Casmire's heritage. For he had been chosen carefully to attend to his precious daughter.

"She may not value her safety," Algor said. "She is a brash, hot-headed girl who is unwise in the ways of the world."

The horse held the King's gaze, but pawed his hoof in protest. Insisting on defending his mistress, even to her father.

The King smiled with sadness. "Yes," Algor replied. "Gabriella is smart and brave and pure of soul. Her natural talents will take her far into the arms of destiny." The King's countenance grew serious. "But she also speaks plainly, with an open heart. And has not encountered the depths of deceit in the world. She knows only the kindness of her lands. Not the cruel ways that have spread like a blight in the kingdoms outside our walls."

Algor's gaze intensified. "This puts her at great risk. And you. You will keep her safe."

The stallion shook his mane, protesting the King's request.

Standing in the way of his mistress's desire was not a path he wished to tread.

"Heed my words, valiant steed," Algor demanded. "You are the shield between my daughter and her enemies. You are the only one with the power to keep her alive. Above all else, you must protect her destiny. The healing of our lands relies on Gabriella staying alive, so that one day, she will ride home."

Casmire stood still, his back shivering with the intention and power of the King's words.

Algor leaned in and lowered his voice. For in uttering his last command, he could not risk being heard by anyone other than Casmire. Not by a servant. Nor a courtier. And most certainly, *not* by his daughter.

"If the day comes, Casmire," the King commanded, "when you must choose between Gabriella and the life of another, you must lay them down like the warrior you are. Always and forever, protect the Messenger."

Horse and man stared with an intensity that would have made others tremble.

Finally, the King leaned back. Holding their stare. Waiting for the horse's reply.

Casmire whinnied high and strong. Protesting the command and accepting its decree, at once. King Algor nodded, confident the stallion understood his charge.

Then Algor turned, and silently disappeared into his realm.

Casmire shivered, recalling that fateful night.

He contemplated the King's words every day since leaving. On some days, he was sure he understood the King's wish. On others, he wondered whether he might have misconstrued the intention.

Below the confusion, Casmire was confident the King wanted only one thing. For his daughter to be safe. And return to her homeland. Alive.

Casmire did not know what the King saw. He suspected their ruler shared the visionary traits of the wizard. A suspicion that gave Casmire comfort at times like this. For certain the old King must know the fate of his own daughter?

Algor's decree rang in Casmire's ears when Gabriella insisted on parting company.

The great steed feared he had let down his King. How could Casmire ensure her safety if he were not at Gabriella's side? How would he know she was making wise choices?

Casmire had protested the decision. And the company, he thought, as he snuffed loudly. Glaring at the sleeping wizard. Yet Casmire knew Gabriella was right.

Somehow, the steed trusted that he was fulfilling the King's decree. Despite all appearances to the contrary.

The wizard grumbled and rolled. The first sign that he was not far from awakening.

Casmire watched over the magic one. Appreciating his simple attire and his intense ways. The wizard spoke far less than most humans. And did not waste words with those he did not respect. Much like Casmire's kind.

The great steed begrudgingly admitted he was starting to appreciate the wizard. He pawed the ground, annoyed by his feelings.

Casmire did not like another man vying for Gabriella's affection. Nor did he like how quickly his mistress became enamoured of him. But even Casmire could not deny their bond. He had hoped they would connect as older brother and younger sister. But their spark was immediate. Their denial allowed the embers to burn. And their dedication fanned the flames.

So, for the sake of his mistress, Casmire accepted the magical stranger from the ocean lands. The one whose lineage was not yet proven. The one Casmire knew had initially set his eyes on Hannah.

Perhaps this was the contradiction that Casmire could not yet accept.

Many had travelled to seek the hand of Princess Hannah before she was promised to the Great Prince. Casmire had heard the gossip of the maids passed to the footsmen passed to the stable hands, that this sleeping wizard was among those men.

Though Casmire knew his name had not been announced, he heard tale of his description. The magic one had caught the eye of many a maid. His appearance was striking. His spirit doubly so. He might have slipped away before his declaration, but a guest at the palace is never missed.

Especially when he came to declare his desire for the Princess's hand. Then disappeared.

Casmire watched as the wizard surfaced from the land of dreams. The steed wondered where the magic one walked during his sleeping hours. And whom he visited.

Even more, now that the wizard declared that a woman would be coming. One that might steal his heart and break Gabriella's.

The wizard's vision made the steed's skin shiver.

Causing him to doubt every word from the wizard's mouth.

Casmire knew now that he never forgave the wizard's original transgression. He suspected his motives. For the wizard never confessed his original claim. His appearance to appeal for the hand of Hannah. Only to flee, then magically appear years later. In the path of Gabriella.

An occurrence too coincidental for Casmire's liking.

The wizard tossed and turned under the scrutiny of the loyal steed. As though he felt the judgmental questions. Just as Casmire was tempted to rouse the wizard and demand answers, his ears discerned the distant sound of hooves.

The sky was dark and the moon too new to cast much light. But Casmire's nose caught the scent of a female horse, accompanied by a female rider, rushing in their direction.

Casmire contemplated leaving the wizard to the whims of the approaching rider. The stranger might just be the answer to his conflict with the mysterious one under his watch.

But the great steed was no coward.

He did not abandon his battles to others. Nor resolve his disagreements with foolish human ways. He had made a promise to Gabriella — and to her father.

And he would see his pledge through to the bitter end.

NINE

Syrena walked in silence through the darkening woods as Hannah and Tobias traded stories of their homeland. As the sun withdrew its light, so Syrena pulled away from her beloved.

Her steps echoed with doubt. Her heart clenched with each laugh shared between Tobias and Hannah.

Syrena did not know the people they discussed. She did not have tales from their homeland. She felt like an outsider. Even more than usual.

She felt Hannah reach back, to share kind words and reassurance. They spoke in their minds. Avoiding eye contact. Yet conversing as easily as though they shared an intimate table.

I have known him forever, dear one, Hannah said. *Do not be threatened by his presence. He will prove to be of help to us on this journey.*

But Syrena did not respond. She did not trust this Tobias. Or his intentions. So she withheld her thoughts on the matter.

She suspected that her mistrust was based in jealousy. Her lack of faith that Hannah would choose her if the Princess was free and not hunted by the Great Prince.

Syrena had hoped they would at least have this time alone together. She was willing to exchange a lifetime of love for a few years. Or even a few months.

Then Tobias arrived.

Syrena ripped a cluster of pine branches off a bough. It was an unkind act and she felt the surprise of the unsuspecting tree. Syrena steeled herself from caring. Let someone else feel her pain! Her heart ached. Her mind raged.

And she needed to tear something to pieces to keep from pushing Tobias off a cliff.

—⁂—

Hannah stepped along the well-worn path as Tobias regaled her of tales from his childhood. She was all too aware of the tumult of emotions behind her.

She had been with Syrena three years. And knew there was no other match for her heart.

Hannah grew up in a loving family. Despite all that the Prince did to her, he could not undo the depths of her parents' teaching. And so she recognized her soulmate in an instant.

Syrena had no basis to trust love. She had only received love as a rare kindness. Not a constant companion. And so, as one who received love as a mysterious gesture from a stranger, she could only believe in it for an instant.

When that moment passed, Syrena wondered anew when the kindness would end.

Hannah gave her heart wholly. Though she had no way to assure Syrena of this oath. She could only hold true, while Syrena wrestled her demons. Much as she wished to fight that battle for her, Hannah understood the fire must be confronted alone.

The Princess smiled with kindness at Tobias.

Shining the rays of her bright and loving heart in his direction. All that a man like Tobias needed in the world was to feel he served the true Queen. He might appear smitten to eyes such as Syrena's. But Hannah knew he was enamoured with his own purpose. Not her.

Hannah sighed, quiet enough that no one heard. Still, she felt the release.

The deep gratitude of connecting to her heart was a joy that surprised her every day. She would never forget the underworld journey of the Hidden Palace.

Hannah recollected the numbness of being trapped in her own body. The strange sensation of another taking control. Forcing her to say and do things against her will.

Only one cursed under such a spell could possibly know the pain of not feeling. And the pure liberation of regaining sensation. Bliss found in the smallest joys.

Twirling in the wind. Smiling at a friend. Reaching for a beloved.

Hannah shivered when she thought of the trap she endured for years. The horrid, powerless feeling of being a puppet of the evil Palace.

Yet she knew, better than most, that the Palace was the creation of the people who placed the stones and spread the mortar. Yes, they were under the direction of a mad King, but they placed the stones all the same.

One could have stepped up. Led the others in rebellion. Hurled a stone at that royal head.

She breathed out, releasing the horrid thought. Disturbing,

rage-filled imaginings still bubbled up from the depths of her mind.

Though, strangely, she did not feel they were evil.

They were an inevitable consequence of what she had endured. Like noxious gas released from a swamp. Still, she did not like the overwhelming hatred that swept through her. The feeling was too much like her claustrophobic cell in the Hidden Palace.

Not a physical cell, such as the one used against Gabriella and Adrian. But in Hannah's opinion, a far more treacherous prison. One built inside her own mind.

And so, each day, when she awoke and felt the freedom of her heart and the delight in her soul, she rejoiced. No matter that she was hunted by the Great Prince. She was free. Her feet felt pine needles beneath their soles. Her fingers tuned to the wind under their tips.

And her heart — *oh, her heart!* Hannah delighted in her connection to Syrena, the ancient trees, and the sparrows swooping through the air.

"Are you well, my Lady?" Tobias asked, seeing the flush in Hannah's cheek.

"Oh, yes," Hannah replied. "My apologies, Tobias. I grow distracted. Perhaps I am a little tired."

"Please," Tobias said as he took Hannah's elbow and guided her toward a nook in an oak tree. "Take a seat and rest a while. We have no need to rush."

"Thank you," Hannah replied, allowing Tobias to lead her to the tree.

She felt Syrena's furious gaze aimed at Tobias's hand. And Hannah shot her lover a reproving glance. She did not need her elbow bursting into flames. Or a hawk to swoop in and gouge his hand.

Syrena folded her arms and nodded. Glancing away, yet fuming all the same.

Hannah nestled into the embrace of the ancient one's roots. She did not wish for Syrena to suffer. But she needed to rest.

Remembrances from the Hidden Palace took their toll. The strength of the oak's roots fed her. Replenished her. And reminded her that even those on a quest for justice must take time to reflect.

This was the first time that Hannah admitted her true desire. She did not want to excite Syrena or alarm Tobias. Or indeed, put her dear sister at risk.

She understood that others saw her as the pretty, mild-mannered sister. Especially when compared to Gabriella. But Hannah had a quiet determination — a rock-like stubbornness that rivalled her sister's fierce fire.

Hannah closed her eyes and leaned against the sturdy trunk. She felt the courage of centuries beneath its bark. Enduring the whims and battles of humans took a resilience she could only imagine.

And so, she soaked in the oak's strength. Whispering to the ancient one with her mind. Offering gratitude.

—ɰ—

Syrena stood, arms folded, at Hannah's side. Standing guard while her lover rested.

She seethed at Tobias in touching Hannah's elbow. She was incensed with the vigour the Hidden Palace had stolen from

Hannah's body. Syrena had confidence that Hannah's fortitude would rebuild and her beloved would emerge stronger. But the time of healing was a vulnerable one. And for Syrena, Tobias's presence made the progression harder.

Surely, the hunter felt her hatred. And so, he did not meet her gaze. She understood this. But it only made her more suspicious.

Syrena scrutinized Tobias. Analyzing his attention. Peering into his unquestioning loyalty. Seeking some fault in his blind adoration.

A moment of logic broke through her jealousy. To be sure, Hannah was Tobias's liege and beautiful to behold.

Then mistrust swept in like a dark cloud. Blocking out the warmth of benevolence.

Perhaps he aspired to a throne, Syrena supposed. He would not be the first to scheme to control a Princess.

Tobias's eyes focused on Syrena. The ferocity of his look made her think he heard her. She hesitated, wondering for an instant if he was able to read thoughts.

Then, in his gaze, she saw her judgment reflected back. Accusing Syrena of the same crime — manipulating Hannah for her own ends.

—✺—

"How dare you!" Syrena exclaimed. Hannah's eyes snapped open. Wondering what transpired in the few moments she managed to find peace.

She looked up. Syrena and Tobias glared at each other. Accusations hung in the air. Bodies positioned for battle.

"How dare I what?" Tobias asked, in a cool voice.

"You think I am taking advantage of Hannah," Syrena accused.

"I said no such thing," Tobias replied.

"Not with your words," Syrena sneered.

"I would say, *my Lady*," Tobias said with disdain, "that if it were false, you would not take such offence."

"Why you hypocritical, opportunistic —" Syrena began.

"Enough!" declared Hannah. "I have not the strength to listen to my companions fight like children."

"Hannah, this man... this *boy* —" Syrena protested.

"My liege," Tobias interrupted. "You know nothing about this woman. Her people. Her past."

Syrena restrained the urge to pounce on Tobias like a cat. She had encountered enough arrogant men for a lifetime. She refused to be silenced any more.

"Stop!" Hannah levelled her fierce gaze at Syrena. "Do you cast me as a fool? Unable to discern character?"

"No," Syrena replied, in a humbled tone.

"Absolutely not," Tobias said, dropping his gaze to the ground.

Hannah pushed herself up from the ground. Furious. She had one chance for rest on this day and, instead, she was chastising her companions as though they were school children.

"Do you think I am flattered by your jealousy?" Hannah asked, glaring at Syrena. Her lover fell silent.

Hannah turned her accusatory glare to Tobias. "Do you believe me incapable of fending for myself? Of not seeing through the schemes of charlatans?"

Tobias shook his head.

Hannah's blood calmed. She leaned on the tree for strength and took a deep breath. She felt Syrena's concern, and her immediate recognition that she had contributed to sapping Hannah's strength through her overbearing protection.

A wave of apology drifted across the air from Syrena to Hannah. A slight nod from Hannah acknowledged the offering and kept her lover from stepping forward.

"I have no time for games," Hannah declared, in a firm yet softened tone. "My husband cured me of any notion that possessive displays meant anything but control."

She shot a fierce look at Syrena, then Tobias. Daring them to see her as the naïve Princess sworn to the Prince years ago. When she was a seasoned woman, far too familiar with the cruelty of flattering intentions and manipulative men.

Hannah kept her hand on the trunk of the ancient oak. She closed her eyes and whispered a prayer of thanks to the tree. Drawing strength for a long, lingering moment. Pulling forth as much power as possible before releasing their connection.

When she stepped away, she released her anger. Grounded herself in courtly patience. And sought the gaze of her companions. Reaching out her hands. One to Syrena. The other to Tobias.

Hannah waited until each stepped forward. And took a hand.

She had seen her mother bridge warring sides of a dispute in this manner — through the power of quiet presence and character. Princes, lords, warriors, and rustic farmers were each awed by her mother's power.

As a child, Hannah saw her mother's ability as a clever trick. A talent for soothing ruffled feathers with a calm voice. Now, Hannah realized the deep power to shape a kingdom through grace. She only hoped she might have the chance to honour her mother's ways.

"This is my fault," Hannah said, borrowing her mother's tone. She was determined to bring her warring factions to peace. Whether they wished it or not. "I should have united the two of you before we took a single step in the woods."

Hannah watched the colour drain from Syrena's cheeks. Her lover's imagination ran wild. Envisioning strange rituals and rites in Hannah's native wooded lands.

"My Queen," Tobias protested, "this is not necessary."

"Yes, dear Tobias," Hannah smiled. "This is indeed, necessary." Hannah glanced sideways at Syrena who now looked as panicked as a mouse cornered by a barn cat.

"Fear not, Syrena," Hannah added, comforting her. Truth be told, she felt entitled to enjoy Syrena's discomfort. After hours of silent treatment, she deserved a little fun.

"Though I am within my ancient rites," Hannah continued, "I will not force you to take Tobias to your bed. I merely ask that you assuage his manhood with an offering we deem acceptable."

Syrena dropped Hannah's hand like a hot coal. Staggering back from Tobias, she proclaimed: "I will not!"

Then Hannah laughed. Her eyes sparkling with mischief.

Syrena's face changed from confusion to fury. As her beloved's fists clenched, Hannah wondered if she might be about to receive a face full of dirt. Or worse. But then, Syrena's gaze transformed from anger to desire.

Feeling the desirous heat between them, Hannah found herself wishing she could send Tobias on an imaginary errand so she might feel her lover's apologetic ardour. Hannah blushed, and turned quickly to the hunter to regain her composure.

"Tobias," Hannah proclaimed, making the announcement she should have done when they met in the woods. "Syrena is my beloved. We have been together for three years. And I have no intention of taking another lover."

"Yes, my Queen," Tobias said, bowed.

"Syrena," Hannah continued, turning to her lover. "Tobias and his father and his father's father have served my family for many years. Though they laboured in the woods, they were considered members of our court. Their kin procured the meat that graced our table. They attended my grandfather and my father with brave hearts. Holding true in times of peace, and in times of war, when others fled in fear."

Hannah smiled at Tobias. He lowered his head in gratitude, and bowed, to acknowledge the royal blessing.

"And," Hannah continued, lowering her voice. She shifted to a confiding tone, "young Tobias was my sister's first infatuation."

Tobias lifted his head, startled. As though jolted with a hot poker. "Princess Gabriella..." he stammered. Blood flushed into his cheeks and confusion wrinkled his brow.

Hannah tossed a glance at Syrena. And she saw the relief on her beloved's face. The jealousy was gone. Amused compassion took its place. Syrena finally understood the affection between Hannah and Tobias. Like siblings sworn to secrecy. Bound by a long-sworn secret. Hannah winked at Syrena.

Then turned a compassionate, yet firm gaze on Tobias. "You must swear never to tell Gabriella," Hannah commanded. "For she swore me to secrecy and would never forgive my transgression."

"But..." Tobias said, perplexed, "she never..."

"No," Hannah laughed. "Of course not. My sister never understood how to approach a boy other than to be his competition."

"Surely, Adrian cured her of that," Syrena joked. Falling quiet when Hannah shot her a silencing look.

"Adrian?" Tobias asked, serious. He placed his hand on his hilt without realizing. "Who is Adrian?"

Hannah shook her head at Syrena. "No one of consequence," Syrena fumbled. "Just a traveller we met on the road."

As Tobias searched their faces, Hannah kept silent. She was grateful for all that Adrian had taught her sister. And she liked the man well enough. But here, in their midst, was a soul with the depth of affection and proven honour to guard her sister until the end of days. Hannah could not say with good conscience that she trusted the same from Adrian.

Though it might be unfair to give this young man hope, Hannah wished for a long life of peace and harmony for Gabriella. Tobias could give her that. Adrian could not.

"No matter," Tobias said, releasing Hannah's hand. "We must be on our way before we lose more light."

Hannah nodded her head. Her face inscrutable. But she saw the flicker of pain in the young man. The wave of feeling that passed through his heart. Sensing the burden inside this young man. The weight of unspoken love.

And she wished Adrian's name had never been spoken.

TEN

Gabriella tucked low against the grey steed. Urging him on with all of her might.

She had no idea why Adrian had just appeared in her mind. She was fleeing a pack of drunken guards and hardly had time to breathe, let alone converse.

Gabriella pushed Adrian from her thoughts. As much as she wanted to be with him, this was not the time or the place. She would connect again when she had cover, or at least a clear idea of where she was headed.

Adrian would not risk contact unless it was important. But Gabriella could not chance the distraction. She needed to keep moving until she had room to consider this latest development on her path.

Gabriella locked her gaze on the young woman ahead. Katrin had learned to ride since leaving their homeland. Gabriella had to admit, she was impressed with Katrin's focus. The young woman had not lost sight of the path.

Once they were out of the stable, Katrin broke away from the pack of horses and never looked back.

Gabriella surveyed the rugged mountain terrain. Assessing dangers and potential trails all the while wondering about this new alliance with Katrin. The young woman was fiery and unpredict-able. Traits Gabriella could use but was not sure she could count on.

First, Gabriella needed to find them a hiding spot. They were not yet out of harm's way. Though the guards had not seen her face, she could not risk returning to that outpost.

Stories would be shared. Whether they were true or not was of no consequence. Tales would spread and, these days, people made decisions based on their vulnerability. With the Prince's men in-creasing, too many were in danger to assist her.

Gabriella saw a path ahead, sloping upwards. Her grey stallion picked up speed, and she smiled at his eagerness to run uphill. His urgency was no longer fuelled by fear, but rather the sheer delight of feeling his muscles surge.

She revelled in the steed's elation. Gabriella stole a brief mo-ment of pleasure in the midst of another escape. She snatched these gems wherever she could. She did not question the timing or delivery of beauty. She simply held her heart open. Grateful to receive.

For the first time since they fled, Katrin glanced back. The leap of joy in Gabriella's heart may have sparked the reaction. Joy was a rare and precious jewel in these dark days. Any sensitive person would discern the feeling a mile away.

As intrigued as she was by Katrin's instincts, Gabriella scolded herself. She needed to be vigilant. Sending out pulses of joy was like waving a golden flag for the Prince. And if Katrin were to be her travelling companion, Gabriella needed to train the young woman in staying safe. In more subtle ways than Katrin already knew.

Gabriella noticed, as though Katrin heard her thoughts, the wiry young woman tucked closer to her steed — so close no one would have known the horse had a rider. And Gabriella found herself wondering whether she might learn a thing or two from Katrin.

The trail grew rocky and the horses slowed their pace. Giving Gabriella a chance to scope ahead with her intuition. She felt an opening nearby — an opportunity to lose the guards once and for all. She whistled.

Katrin pulled up on her reins. Then turned with an inquisitive look. She did not question Gabriella's direction, nor did she risk speaking aloud.

Gabriella tilted her head toward a fork in the rugged road. A narrow yet passable path veered to the left of the rocky trail. By the slope, Gabriella could see the path would lead them out of the mountains.

How long or how treacherous the way, she did not know. But she was tired of hiding in the far-flung reaches of these lands.

Katrin nodded, and urged her horse back along the side trail. Gabriella waited. She felt safer with Katrin at the lead while she went behind to ensure their safety. At least until they were closer to the foothills.

A burst of pride unleashed in Gabriella's heart. She was honoured to inspire such trust. Though Gabriella attributed much of her companion's confidence to her parents. Their long-standing faith, beyond when others abandoned all integrity, was still evident in the actions of their people.

People Gabriella was looking forward to being amongst. Not hiding. Not evading. Taking a stand. Gabriella understood the risk. Her pursuit of the cloaked man and the cave from her vision might very well lead to her death. But she was tired of waiting.

Gabriella had hoped the outsiders entrenched in the mountains would be her kin. Ripe for rebellion. Willing to act. But they were either too afraid or too suspicious.

Always looking for the worst in people. And that included her.

The grey stallion tossed his head in the air, and neighed. Not loud enough to draw attention. Sufficient to protest Gabriella's assessment of *all* the outpost dwellers. She laughed, and scratched his neck.

She glanced back to see an empty trail behind her. Gabriella sensed that the guards had lost interest. And followed their stomachs back to the rustic inn.

Gabriella thought of the barkeep. She had wondered if the rugged woman might have been an ally. She could tell the woman had fought enough battles to win the deference of such unruly company. But the barkeep had not been willing to even have a conversation.

She patted her steed's neck. And growled under her breath.

Some women changed after being on guard too long. They could not relinquish the fierce hold they had on their corner of the world. They had fought too hard to claim so little. She could not fault them for refusing to want more.

And yet, Gabriella wanted to blame them. To condemn them for selling out their kind. Still, she knew all too well the need to survive. The urge was primal. Instinctive. And powerful. She could not begrudge another, even if she judged her.

Freedom required courage without certainty. A risk taken only by the willing.

Gabriella pressed her cheek against the warm neck of her steed.

Finding solace in his company. She wondered what his name might be, but chose not to ask. He was enjoying the wild path too much for her to intrude. His quiet partnership was all she needed.

A wave of loneliness swept over Gabriella. She missed her friends. So she invited a moment of connection with the stallion. And he acquiesced. His heart beat with her heart. His body became one with hers. Gabriella felt safe, as this sacred warrior carried her.

For a brief and fleeting second, she belonged. *Oh, how she ached to belong!*

The years of flight had taken their toll. She bore her task with fortitude. But there were times when her heart yearned for home. Her land. And a people to care for.

Gabriella separated from the steed. She did not wish to burden his heart.

Merging was a natural process. A sacred connection between horse and rider when they swore a commitment. This young steed had only agreed to carry her for mutual freedom. Not as a deeper commitment.

And as grateful as they each felt for breaking free, she did not expect the bond to last beyond their next respite. Gabriella would go on her path. The grey warrior would go on his. Forever appreciative, yet not beholden.

When she felt the impending parting, she could not help but think of Casmire. She hoped he was treating the wizard — as Casmire insisted on calling him — with kindness.

She smiled. Then wondered if he was safe and well fed. And whether Casmire had forgiven her for insisting they part ways. The horse had always insisted his lack of civility to Adrian was in order to protect Gabriella. But, she had wondered whether his intractable suspicion of Adrian was disguised jealousy.

Gabriella heard the sage guidance of her teacher, Serafina. Her voice echoing from time past.

"Never question the instinct of a horse. They are certainly capable of being petty and jealous, just like humans. But a horse's instinct for protection is well-honed — uninhibited by generations of civilization." Serafina had stared hard into Gabriella's eyes. "If you must choose between your judgment and that of your horse? Always bet on your steed."

In her naïve youth, Gabriella rolled her eyes. Believing Serafina to be overly dramatic. But Gabriella had not yet tasted betrayal. The longer Gabriella was on her own, travelling the unpredictable path of a fugitive, the more she came to respect Serafina's wisdom.

Gabriella forced herself to stay present. To watch the passing overhangs for potential ambush. Her eyes roamed the rugged, rust-coloured hills. She commanded her spirit to stay, not travel the vast expanse to her friend.

And then her heart squeezed and a vision descended into her mind. Gabriella could not refuse it. To do so would put her at greater risk than receiving the revelation.

She saw every facet, as though the event unfolded before her eyes.

A woman — a stately, exquisite rider — approached Adrian in the Great Plains. She slowed her horse and advanced with care. As though she had simply happened upon him in the middle of the grasslands.

But she had not discovered Adrian by chance. Of this, Gabriella was certain.

This woman had been sent. Whether of her own will or of the will of another. And she intended to tear Adrian from Gabriella. And claim him for her own.

Gabriella watched as the woman dismounted with the elegance of a Queen and the sensuality of a Goddess. She approached Adrian as though he was hers for the taking. As though she saw their union written in the stars.

Not a union like the one he had with Gabriella — one of tender love and fiery passion.

This woman sought a singular alliance. Unlike anything Gabriella had witnessed. Power surged through her. She was the embodiment of lightning and thunder. Pure sexual power. And she sought a partner in destruction.

Not *any* partner. A man who would augment her gifts. And bring the world to her feet.

Gabriella's breath caught in her throat. What man could resist this woman —filled with such fierce desire and will to conquer?

She screamed her silent outrage, her hands seizing the reins. The grey steed pulled against Gabriella's hold. Rearing in protest.

Gabriella clung to his back. Loosening the reins, as her spirit came crashing back into her body. She gathered her wits and checked for threats. Whispering apologies, as the stallion shook his head and surged forward. Galloping out the panic, tearing past Katrin, almost trampling her on the path.

Once they were safe, she slowed her steed to a stop. Gabriella turned to spy Katrin close behind her, face pale as though they had been attacked. Gabriella nodded that she was safe. And patted the steed's neck to calm his nerves.

Then she urged the horse on. They must ride, despite her outburst. Their safety was paramount, especially now.

What test was this? What pain did the angels provoke, even now, as she fled for her life? Why torture her heart while she sacrificed all for the protection of others?

Like a flash of brilliant light, Gabriella saw three truths.

The first was the Prince's men descending on the outpost. Tearing apart the inn's floorboards, burning the barn, threatening the patrons. All in their quest to find the Messenger. She had left at the right time.

The second was the hooded man. He stood at the end of this path, wherever that was. Waiting. Watching. For her.

And the third…

The third related to the sensual rider sent to tempt her beloved. Especially chosen to challenge Adrian's adoration. And their loyalty.

Gabriella narrowed her gaze. And hardened her heart.

She stared ahead with the fiery rage of a thousand suns. The rider sent to tempt Adrian was most certainly a powerful sorceress. Renowned in many lands. Feared by generations. But magic did not unsettle Gabriella. Nor did she fear this opponent.

Gabriella was angered by the force behind the evil temptress.

For the rider was an emissary of the Great Prince.

ELEVEN

THE GREAT PRINCE SAT STARING out a tower window in the far eastern corner of his palace.

He did not often come to this turret. Only when he needed seclusion. And as he stared out across his grounds, watching the creatures of his kingdom milling about, he regretted not scheduling a beheading today. Such was his mood.

The Prince was not comforted that his rider had found the wizard in the Great Plains. For he was not certain of her ability to sway him. He took no joy in his emissaries crushing skulls in search of the woman who evaded his possession. Nor did he believe he was any closer to laying his hands on her.

Despite his gains, he could not shake this dark mood.

The Great Prince scowled, as a maid far in the courtyard, strolled beneath his caustic gaze. She had gathered fresh linens from a line, and prepared to fold them in the sunshine. He fixed his loathing on her foolish face. Her curvaceous hips. Hating every ounce of her.

The maid glanced about, sensing that a malicious creature had her in its sights, and snatched up her basket. Fleeing the open yard for safer spaces. The Prince grumbled as the maid disappeared into the castle. If he were able to cause pain with his mere will, he would have singed every hair off her head.

With the maid gone, he aimed his rage at the grass. Wishing flames would consume each verdant blade that had the audacity to grow beneath his window. Yet the sprouts defied his will. Gleaming in the bright sun. Defying his mood. Mocking him with every sway in the wind's breath.

The Prince resented that he did not possess such magic that turned his desires into reality. For if there were a day worthy of mass destruction, this would be it. His chest clenched. And his jaw tightened.

This was the third anniversary. Marking the day she fled.

She escaped and absconded with his wife — humiliating and wounding him in one move. Displaying his defeat to his people. Making him the source of ridicule. A feat he spent the past three years correcting with rivers of blood.

He winced at the thought, then pounded the table at his weakness. Rattling cups within inches of falling. Perched on the precipice of destruction.

The Prince abhorred feeling. He had grown accustomed to being numb. These sensations were strange to him. Unnerving. And … wrong.

Every day of the year but one, he was senseless to the acts wrought in his name. Executing the Palace's requests. Keeping the people on their knees. The dark mistress pulled his puppet strings.

And he felt nothing. Yet, for some mysterious reason — on the anniversary of the Messenger's flight — he was set free.

The Great Prince would awaken and, within seconds, he knew what day was unfolding.

He had not thought of it the month before. The week before. Or the day before.

Yet, when this singular day arrived, every order he had issued over the past year rushed, like a river set loose, into his consciousness. And the Prince was overwhelmed with pain and regret. Haunted by past horrors.

Then … he felt her presence.

She hovered by his bedside. Waiting. He sat up, as though she were with him. His heart pounded. His pulse raced like a wild creature released, unsure which direction to run.

His hand reached out, compelled to touch her. Only to find empty air.

For the first time in a year, he was fully conscious of his loss. The ache for her rippled through his body. And he would bellow in pain.

His voice carried to every corner of the Palace.

Setting every servant on edge. They scurried, this way and that, desperate to avoid the awakened dragon. The wounded beast they feared might be even crueler than the empty shell that ruled their world the rest of the year.

And so, the Prince retreated to his tower.

The Prince snarled. And smashed a crystal glass on the floor. Relishing the sound of destruction.

He wondered whether the Palace drew some sick pleasure from permitting this day. Or worse, if the Palace was unable to stop it. Perhaps the Messenger's magic woke again, reenacting her release. Liberating him from captivity for a brief time.

And reminding the Prince of his love. He could not imagine a more exacting torture.

He stepped on the fallen glass. Crushing the fragments into the floorboards. Wishing he could do the same to the sensations coursing through his veins.

The Prince refused to speak her name. He held back from spite — and out of respect. Only a lover had the right to use the intimate name of a creature that magnificent. And when she fled with the wizard, she made her choice clear.

The alchemist. The one called Adrian. The Great Prince was determined to ruin him.

Hatred seethed from his heart to his hands. The Prince flexed his fingers, and imagined squeezing the blood from the wizard's heart. Yet, his gruesome wish for the wizard was more humane than the living torment of the Prince.

Locked in a prison of the Palace's making. Deserted by his true love.

Even through his rage, he felt his love for the Messenger grow. This was the worst truth of all. The Prince tried to suffocate the feeling. Drown it with liquor. Women. Torture. Nothing quelled the sensation in his heart.

Love — the feeling that brought men to their knees. Steered Princes to abandon their birthrights. And levelled empires. The Great Prince felt his heart surrender to her more as each moment passed. He feared this overpowering submission.

As much as he longed for it.

The deeper burden of their anniversary was the Prince's awareness of his gilded cage. His freedom came with the price of comprehending his possession by the Palace. Every other day, he believed *he* ruled this land.

This truth made every second a torture. Every moment, a remembrance of his weakness. So, he waited out the day, in the only place the Palace could not reach him.

The Prince did not understand what made this tower special. Why it seemed immune to the Palace's evil touch. He was led here the last time his heart threatened to burst in his chest. His instinct compelled him to this far-flung corner with nothing but a tiny bed, a wooden chair, and a mysterious flower in a vase.

A dahlia that never seemed to fade.

If he had not found this sanctuary, he suspected he might have taken his own life. The Great Prince found little comfort in hiding in a tower. He did not fancy himself a character in a fairy story. Or a cowering creature that shrank from the grip of a despot.

And yet, here he was, staring out a high window like a forlorn maiden. Seething at his loss. Heartbroken at his abandonment. Wishing only to hold the one person in his life that had shown him how to love.

Even more aggravating was that these days of lucidity showed signs of increasing. What began as an annual event, to be endured and forgotten, occasionally rippled into other days for a brief instant. Breaking into his consciousness in the middle of the night. Waking him in a drenched sweat. Calling for her.

The Prince searched the horizon as though the far reaches of his lands held the remedy to this peculiar enchantment.

Was the Messenger's power increasing? Did she aim her magic at his heart to punish him?

And so, he set his sights on destroying the man she loved.

If he could not have the Messenger, the Prince would take away the one she chose.

He rose and strode from one end of the stone chamber to the other. His skin crawled to think of the wizard laying his hands on her. Caressing her. Laying with her.

The Prince slammed his fist into the wall. Sending shockwaves up his arm.

A trail of blood trickled down the stones. His corporeal agony was exquisite relief from the feelings coursing through his heart. And the torturous images flickering in his mind.

Night after night, the Great Prince dreamed of crushing the wizard. The magician. The trickster who stole the Messenger's heart. Day after day, he sent assassins, mercenaries, and necromancers to bring his head back on a platter.

All to no effect. The wizard escaped his clutches at every turn.

Until, the day *she* walked into his throne room.

—⁂—

As she stepped though the magnificent doors, she commanded every eye in his court. Every mortal fell under her spell. The Great Prince wondered whether he, too, would have been her unwilling servant if he did not already have a more powerful mistress.

She strode toward him, past every other dignitary. And he watched as the courtiers swooned.

Men and women alike dropped their champagne glasses. Gaped at her beauty. And trailed after her, as though they had lost all freedom of will. She smiled, appearing immune to their adoration. Though the Prince could tell she was not.

This alluring Sorceress fed on their adulation. Her hips swayed an extra inch to draw the eyes of the men. Her dress plunged lower than any he had seen in many years. Whether the eyes envied her or lusted after her, they were riveted.

The Prince was intrigued. No one had enraptured his court this way since—. Fury spiked in his body. Rage took over his mind. And he threw a fire bolt of hatred at the Sorceress.

Whereupon she stopped short. And the court gasped.

—◊—

The Sorceress stared at the Prince. Drinking in his anger like a sweet infusion on a summer's day. She did not take his upset personally. She was far too accustomed to inciting unrest to be halted for long by one spite-filled gaze.

But she did wonder what provoked him.

Did she offend him somehow? No. Though it might be directed at her, that rage was meant for another. Then the Sorceress smiled. Delighted with her deduction. That flavour of hatred was for the woman who captured the Prince's heart — then crushed it beneath her foot.

The Sorceress gave the Prince a moment.

She tucked away her smile, and replaced it with only the slightest hint of sympathy in her eyes. Like the rest of the Great Lands, she had heard rumours that a woman haunted the Prince. But she had not believed a word.

The Great and Unstoppable Prince could not be untethered by a mere maiden! Even more outrageous, the whispers insisted he had fallen in love with her. *Ridiculous!*

She assumed they were foolish tales spread to give villagers hope that the stranglehold on the Great Lands was crumbling. A delusion she mocked at every possible opportunity.

Still, the rumours persisted.

Then the Sorceress discovered that this mysterious woman was targeted by every hired killer in the realm. And she knew the rumours were more than stories.

They were treasure to line her coffers. Even better, they were a challenge.

She had been so bored the last few years. Killing had lost its allure. Capturing hearts was far too easy. And toying with men was tiresome beyond measure.

In the Prince's court, the Sorceress watched the flames of hatred abate.

The Great Prince no longer looked as though he might thrust a knife into the heart of the closest servant. The Sorceress was tempted to see if she could make such a spectacle happen. Let the court speak of *that* for years to come.

But she reminded herself that she had not come to toy with the illustrious sovereign. She had important matters in mind. And, she realized, she had lost the attention of the court. They were once again fixated on the Prince, his underlings, and the latest gossip.

So, the Sorceress elevated her cleavage, and shook her hips. Drawing every gaze back to her, including the Prince. Her gaze fastened on him, like a leopard pursuing her prey.

And she resumed her promenade down the middle of the court.

She considered securing a contract to seduce the young maiden who had stolen the Prince's heart. Striking two for the price of one. That would be a delightful challenge. The Sorceress eyed the

Prince and wondered how he might react.

She smiled with an edge of daring. Would it be rage? Lust? Or both? Even as her countenance entranced every aristocrat within reach, causing most to fall on their knees, the Prince was unmoved.

More than that, he was cold as stone.

The Sorceress had never encountered such a complete lack of emotion. Her assurance wavered. If he were impervious, how could she ensure her outcome? What would she manipulate? She reached deeper, seeking answers.

She sensed a more powerful force had control of him. For a battle of wills raged in the Prince's heart. Between the Prince's love and this treacherous force. No wonder he looked years older than the last time she laid eyes on him.

At first she thought it might be the maiden — the one he called *Messenger*. But no, something menacing held him in its clasp.

As the Sorceress neared the throne, she changed tactics. She had no way to influence his heart, but she could reach his mind. Giving her all she needed.

The Prince was angry not *only* because the Messenger had fled. But because her heart — and body — belonged to another.

This delighted the Sorceress. Agony pulsed beneath the Great Prince's numb exterior. Even though she had to focus all her power to perceive it. *This* was the gold she sought.

If the Great Prince were free, he would not rely on others. He would scour this Kingdom himself to find her. But a mysterious force kept him locked on his throne. And so, the Sorceress would do what no other had done. What no other realized was the Prince's true wish. The Sorceress would crush the man who possessed his maiden.

And, on that day, the Great Prince would give her anything she desired.

Given her relentless boredom, the Sorceress would have been content to steal the heart of the Messenger's beloved for sport alone. But knowing the Great Prince would forever be in her debt? That was especially delicious.

After all, these were tenuous days. The Sorceress was confident she held more power than most beings, but she was not foolish. Allies were always a wise investment. No matter how temporary.

"Great Prince," she began, as she dropped in a sensuous and far from doting curtsy. "I am Vanora, ruler of the Northern Kingdom. I have travelled many miles to propose a solution to your long-held and vexing problem."

"You suggest I have problems, witch?" the Great Prince scoffed. The moniker caused her hand to clench, though her expression did not falter. "Yes — your reputation precedes you. So do not try embroiling me in your spells. Or you will find your head rolling in my courtyard."

Vanora was not intimidated by the games of powerful men. Even ones who crushed lives for sport. But she would play along. She would not humiliate the Great Prince. Today.

"Of course not," Vanora replied. "I merely propose that the creature who eludes your grasp can be captured by other means than rooting out her little burrow."

The Great Prince narrowed his gaze. She was treading danger-ously close to calling him a fool. "If you have a proposal, woman, spit it out," he commanded. "Or leave my presence."

"Dearest Prince," Vanora smiled, "Of course. Your time is

precious. And my ways are nothing if not efficient."

She stepped closer. Leaning in so the Prince's advisors could feel her charm. Smell her fragrant perfume. And gaze down the cascading curves of her dress. Just enough to be entranced and know, that if she chose, she could slay them all.

"My proposal is thus," Vanora spoke in a hushed voice. "Worry not about your elusive Messenger. I will find her by seeking out her amour. The man who shares her bed."

The advisors averted their gaze. Casting eyes to the far corners of the room. No one wished to catch the Prince's eye for fear they would pay the price.

An anger that did not frighten Vanora. But fuelled her boldness.

"And when I find him," Vanora whispered, in a voice loud enough only for the Prince. "I will weave a web around his heart, pull him into my grasp, and suck the essence from his love. Leaving only an empty shell. Lost to the Messenger. Forever."

The Great Prince stared at Vanora. She sensed he was annoyed that this plan not only did not deliver the Messenger, but robbed the Prince of the supreme pleasure of killing the wizard himself.

Vanora held up her hand to stop his objection. Then spoke swiftly to avoid offence. "As soon as the wizard is mine," Vanora explained, "You can be sure the Messenger will appear at your door. Of her own volition. Yours for the taking."

The advisors turned. Staring in silence at their master. Breath held. They waited to see whether there would be rejoicing. Or hell to pay.

Vanora waited as the Great Prince weighed her plan. Evaluating her bold presence. She sensed that brute force had been fruitless. But seduction. This, he had not considered. She refrained from applauding her own brilliance.

The Prince stared. Then leaned in to his advisors. Whispering in low tones. First, the men on his left. Then, the right. Putting on a show of considering their advice. The Sorceress lowered her gaze, affecting a visage of fealty. Then raised her eyes. Awaiting her verdict.

The Great Prince paused for dramatic effect. Then gave the royal nod.

"And what do you expect in return for this favour?" he asked, knowing full well he did not intend to pay her. And yet the Prince wanted to appear magnanimous.

She smiled, tipped her head in mock servitude, and placed her hand on her heart.

"I am grateful to be of service," she lied. "Once I have accomplished my task, I will return. And if I have thought of a request by then, I will be sure to ask it."

Vanora swirled her skirts and vanished in a puff of smoke. Leaving the court to gape in awe.

And the Great Prince wondered what bargain he had struck.

THE
SORCERESS

TWELVE

ADRIAN NARROWED HIS GAZE at the fast approaching rider. He felt her power from leagues away. Her presence had already unsettled Casmire, for she rode a mare that was in heat. Compromising Adrian's one ally in this situation, as fragile as that pact might be.

Casmire pawed at the ground in protest, sensing Adrian's unease. "I don't doubt your heart, Casmire," Adrian said aloud. This might be his last opportunity to speak with impunity. Before the witch got close enough to sense their communication. "But physical drives are a powerful force. You would not be the first male to succumb to temptation."

Casmire swerved his haunches toward the wizard. Causing Adrian to laugh, relieved that he could provoke the horse to rage with accusations of disloyalty.

The deep offence in Casmire's spirit gave Adrian hope.

He did not know for sure what woman approached. But given the nightmares he battled, he believed she was a sorceress from the northern reaches. A region renowned for its battles, betrayals, and blood.

As the horse galloped toward their camp, Adrian cast a spell of protection. She would feel the magic, but he had nothing to lose. She came to destroy him. He must use all his power to deflect her mission.

He collected his possessions and packed them into the saddle-bags. Breaking camp as fast as he had ever done. He wanted her to feel she was intruding. Preventing him from continuing his travels.

Adrian leapt into Casmire's saddle just as the rider arrived at their camp. Her body was wrapped in bright colours. Her face was covered with a demure silk, giving the impression of modesty.

But the scent of her perfume and the power of her allure contravened all appearances.

Adrian had been shocked by the message from the Star Sisters. He was grateful now for the revelation. He need not waste time battling his confusion.

Adrian sat on Casmire's back. Keeping a detached stance. He waited for the woman to approach. As much as he wanted to greet her, he knew that was unwise.

He waited. The woman sat astride her elegant, tawny mare, watching the two males. She also seemed to feel no urgency to break the silence.

Adrian wondered what game she played. She rode across the Great Plains at a speed that implied she had bandits on her trail. And now that she arrived, she had nothing to say?

Ah, he realized. She was assessing his patience and his manners. But Adrian was not a creature of any court. He was beholden to a code of conduct held by a secret few.

He considered riding away. Nothing prevented him from leaving. Except he knew the sorceress would find him again, wearing a different guise. The sisters made it clear that their paths were meant to cross. No matter the location.

Adrian felt Casmire's impatience. He reassured the steed with his mind. They were being tested. And they could not show weakness at the first meeting.

When dancing with one who believed in the rules of force — that prowess bested vulnerability — he must play by those rules. Until he felt the dynamics of power. How she played the game.

Once he saw the pattern, he could direct the energy. This woman was a master of manipulation — controlling emotions, currents, and appearances.

She came not to gain favour with the Great Prince, though that was the story she told others. Adrian sensed she craved a challenge. A chance to wield her magic against one more powerful than the Prince. And by breaking him, she won against two powerful beings. A Wizard and a Messenger.

Adrian took a slow, deliberate breath. Preparing himself for the days to come.

If the witch wants a game, he thought, they would simply have to oblige.

—◊◊—

Vanora peered through her veil. Studying the man astride the horse. She lauded the wizard for his calm. And sensed fury in his steed. She found the horse's anger endearing.

She had hoped her mare would unsettle the steed. A jumpy horse made for an interesting battle. Though she sensed the men struggling. For Vanora, too, was in heat. A truth she was sure the wizard felt, despite his calm exterior.

How long should she play this game of silence? Vanora

wondered.

She could keep it up for days. Torturing men with their thoughts and desires. Though these two were a special breed. They might even keep pace.

So, in the interest of moving things along, Vanora tapped the side of her mare. Her steed bent to the ground, allowing Vanora to step off with grace.

This vantage point gave her much more to examine. She had, of course, assessed her adversary from far away. But one could never truly know an opponent — or a lover — before coming face to face.

Vanora took in every inch of the wizard. His lithe physique. His taut muscles. His ability to sense exactly what she was doing while cloaking his power. Oh, this was going to be fun, she thought. She had not had this powerful an opponent in years. Possibly decades.

As a woman nearing five hundred years old, Vanora had watched, used, vanquished, and tormented more men — and women — than this wizard had laid eyes on. Despite that fact, she did not underestimate him. Unlike the Great Prince, this man did not put on airs, or wear an imposing title, or insist that others prove their fealty.

No, she thought, eyeing the wizard like a tasty treat, this man had the presence of mind to keep his cards hidden. To wait until she revealed her intent. Vanora shivered with anticipation as another thought landed between her thighs.

Magnificent! she thought. The wizard has been separated from his beloved for a long time. Fulfilling his role as distraction. A diversion for those who hunted his love. He must be lonely.

Aching for the touch of a woman.

Vanora grinned under her dark veil, imagining the moment she revealed her countenance — a woman of indeterminate age, most likely in her thirties. Not too old. Not too young. Just the right luscious maturity to bring a man to his knees.

Oh this victory shall be delicious, she revelled. Breaking a man so devoted he renounced his life for this mysterious Messenger. She eyed his crotch through the fabric of her veil. Not that he could see. But Vanora was certain he could feel her gaze. She called to his physical desire. Taunted it. Promised him pleasure beyond his wildest dreams.

Vanora knew all about wildness. She had lived on the edge of civilization for so long, banished from the company of most humans, surrounded by the darkest edges of forest, that she, too, understood the unrelenting craving for communion.

Though, if she laid her heart bare, she would confess that she abhorred humankind. She much preferred the winged ones. The scaled ones. The slippery ones that surfaced from the darkest lakes. These were her kin.

Humans only disappointed her. No! She corrected, that was a child's word. Humans *destroyed* her. Crushed the living essence from her heart. And left her soul to feed only on devastation.

She was betrayed by the ones closest to her. Defiled. Broken. Left for dead. And for what? For control? The thrill of destruction?

Vanora composed her features, though her body had not moved. Her being pulsed waves of anger. Waves that collided against the wizard's field of protection. She considered unleashing a fury unlike any he had ever fought.

But she contained herself. She pulled back.

Reflecting that those who left her for dead had not expected her to rise again. So, in her battered state, she claimed every drop of vitriol they poured into her body. She devoured very morsel of rage and contempt. She nursed herself back to health with the vow that she would devote her life to crushing any man who blocked what she desired.

Vanora admitted that the wizard had not sought her out. Still, she felt obliged to crush his devotion. To tear the one he loved most from his grasp. To devour whatever hope he hid deep in his heart.

For no one could resist Vanora's power. This wizard might not deserve her fury, but she had not deserved the destruction wrought upon her by those vicious men. She restrained a growl. And no longer saw the wizard's face. Only a distant relation to those who ruined her. Vanora intended to play with the wizard, and savour every second.

The wheel of fate had been spun.

Vanora followed, as though this path had nothing to do with her. She must show this devoted man that the intensity of love would not withstand the fury of hatred. He must learn that the Divine to whom he so fervently prayed would not save him.

For Vanora was patient.

And clever.

And underhanded. The kind ones never won against her tactics.

She once believed the Great Prince might make a suitable mate for her. Feeding her needs. Desperate to give her pleasure. But even the cruelest man in the Great Lands was a pathetic slave to love. Foolish idiot, she thought with disgust.

Vanora snarled under her breath. Sending shivers up her mare's back. And unsettling the wizard's steed.

These ridiculous men! Fawning over the same woman. Rendering them helpless for love. She refused to allow either man the luxury of possessing the Messenger.

After toying with them, she would tear the wizard's heart from his chest. And devour it for dinner. With that scintillating thought, Vanora determined it was time.

She gave a deep and deceitful curtsy. Eager to see how the wizard would respond.

THIRTEEN

Gabriella leapt off the grey stallion. Darkness was falling and she needed to find shelter before the night bandits came calling. Her heart pounded in her chest. Wanting to keep riding. But Gabriella would not take that risk. Not for herself, and certainly not for Katrin.

She prayed that Adrian could handle the sorceress on his own. She felt sure he had been forewarned. Though, she was not sure by whom.

That woman was powerful, thought Gabriella. She pulled the reins off her steed, glad to give him a few hours respite from the chafing of leather straps. She scratched behind his ears. But her unruly energy irritated him, and he flicked his head at her.

She must be rattled, indeed, for a stallion to shake off her touch. Gabriella sighed. She needed to settle her nerves. She had made her choice. Keep her head low and trust Adrian to fight his own battle.

But, for the first time since they met, she was afraid of what might befall him. Could he handle this witch? Could any man resist the temptations she offered?

Gabriella had little faith in the fealty of men. Her own brother-in-law had thrown himself at her feet. Discarding her sister.

Proclaiming his love. Was it even Gabriella's right to demand loyalty from one as freedom-bound and otherworldly as Adrian? Perhaps this woman was his true mate. Perhaps —

"We need to eat," Katrin said, standing with arms full of firewood.

Gabriella nodded, grateful that her travelling companion had her priorities straight. And so she padded into the forest, pulling out the blade hidden behind her back. She loved the scent of the trees. And the companionship of fellow wild souls.

The forest calmed her spirit. And the sacred journey of seeking a willing animal for sustenance brought her down to earth. They had travelled far enough down the mountain to be surrounded by denser evergreens. This was both a blessing and a curse. The forest brought game and shelter, but also hiding places for thieves.

And so she focused on the practical grace of hunting. Gabriella held her blade close, stepping across soft beds of pine needles without a sound. Her eyes adjusted quickly and she felt movement. She froze. Allowing her senses to distinguish the nearby creatures.

In a breath, she knew the noise belonged to an animal. Though she could not be sure there was not a person in pursuit. Her stomach grumbled. She had not eaten in hours. And she realized that Katrin must also be famished.

Gabriella waited, hovering on tired yet skilled legs. She sent a prayer to the spirit of the animal. A message of gratitude. And an invitation to exchange its life for her welfare. The animal might reject her request. Forcing Gabriella to go deeper into the forest.

She received no response. A strange occurrence. Gabriella wondered if someone grabbed the animal without any offering of grace. While that might put her in danger, the person would likely be distracted by their kill. Giving her an opportunity to run.

Gabriella took a silent step back. Reaching behind her to find a towering larch. She moved to keep the tree at her back. Giving her protection, and a chance to determine what had happened to the animal. She stilled her mind. Connected with the depths of her soul.

And enjoyed the first breath of peace in many weeks.

Oh, how she missed the soothing protection of trees. She was without her beloved guides for far too long. Hiding high in the mountains, many miles above the tree line, she had been apart from their grounding presence.

Her body relaxed. Her mind calmed. And her heart found faith. She trusted that all would be well. Adrian would find his strength. Katrin would be an ally, not a traitor. And the forest would provide for them. Neither she nor her travelling companion would starve.

When she composed her spirit, she felt the tree's trust. The larch reached out to her. Sharing the secrets of the forest.

Within moments, Gabriella's inner sight caught the winter hare bounding through the trees. Calling out for her to give chase, instigating the game. The sacred agreement between predator and prey. A rush of gratitude flooded her muscles. And she spotted the hare's target — a warren tucked in a gathering of elms.

Gabriella leapt into action. She was swift to gain momentum. As the rabbit leapt over a knoll, she sent her blade flying through the dense trees. Cascading through the air. Chasing down the prey, as he sprang from the ground toward his home.

As he soared through the air, the blade pierced deep into the hare's heart. Killing him in a heartbeat. She felt his spirit fly up through the forest, back to the place of his birth. And Gabriella fell to her knees beside him, filled with boundless gratitude.

She whispered a prayer. Waiting for the response of his spirit before she touched his flanks. The hare answered with the blessing of the departed. Gratified that his death served the life of another.

Gabriella scooped him up. Not wanting to waste time nor vitality. She held the hare close to her chest as she ran, and conveyed thanks to the forest.

As she neared the edge of the forest, Gabriella placed a hand on the larch. Truthfully, she wanted to stay with her sacred sisters in these cloistered realms. She understood this life. Simple days. Humble tasks. She allowed herself a moment of comfort. Drinking in the refreshing scents and peaceful surroundings.

The years of bearing witness to the worst in humanity had stripped Gabriella of her brash ways. She had seen enough, and wished only for a quiet existence with her loved ones. Her body ached for the soothing home of the forest. Tucked away with the sensible ways of the wild ones. Not the strange, complicated ways of her kind.

You know that is not your calling, blessed one, the larch said, startling Gabriella. Reminding her that thoughts echo loudly in this serene place. *You are to bring peaceful connection to your kind. Carry our wisdom to them. Teach them honour and humility.*

I know, Gabriella replied. *But I am weary. Weary of pain. Deception. And hiding. Can I not take a brief respite? I have been without family and home for so long.*

I understand, replied the larch. *But you have been tasked with the hardest of roads. Were it safe to move among humans as we did in the past, I would pull up my roots and walk at your side. If only to bring comfort to your heart. But we know those days are long gone. Humans do not trust the magic of wild ones. So you, sweet Gabriella, must return faith to your people.*

I am not sure they are worthy, admitted Gabriella. She held the hare close to her body, feeling his warmth ebb. She needed to leave soon to keep the meat fresh.

Ah, Gabriella, responded the larch. *In truth, you fear you are not worthy. Do not resist the dark thoughts in your mind. And the heartache in your soul. These are your teachers. They guide you to the people who will challenge you most. To bring the greatest change. For you cannot transform humankind without facing the worst it has to offer.*

Gabriella felt the pull to fall on her knees. Her doubts whispered visions of begging the wise ones to take her burden. To free her of this life. Weariness echoed in her bones. And her heart called to be released. But Gabriella also feared that were she to make the plea, she might be granted her wish. And the moment she possessed freedom, the hard task would fall to another. Perhaps one less able. One less strong.

And Gabriella refused to pass this burden to another. She could not, in good conscience, ask another to bear the weight.

In her realization, she felt she had been released. Relieved of a resistance she had carried since being away from her trees. In their millennia of existence, the forest had born witness to far more than she could even imagine. Atrocities. Blessings. Wars. And wonders.

Thank you, wise one, Gabriella said. *Without your grace, I might have fallen prey to my doubts. Been consumed by my fears. And caused much harm in my wake. Your wisdom has rekindled the fire in my heart. I am more grateful than I can express.*

I hear your words, replied the larch. *Show me your gratitude by caring for your companion and respecting your allies. You need them more than you see. Humanity cannot be transformed through your single hand. Never forget the power of family.*

Gabriella rested her head against the shimmering bark of the larch. Drinking in the pulsing love of her arbor sister.

Gabriella's secret wish to stay in the forest would never fade. But she could bear the ache of missing her wild brethren in exchange for healing her world.

Such was the bargain she struck with her sacred path.

FOURTEEN

The Great Prince sat in his chambers and seethed. He had been tricked by Vanora. He knew the woman mocked him, even if his Counsel assured him otherwise. They would never dare admit they allowed a pretender into his court.

Such an admission would cost them their lives.

"Rightfully so!" he cursed, smashing his fist into the rosewood vanity. He smouldered with rage, staring at his reflection in the mirror.

He loathed that the witch got the delight of hunting Adrian. He should be the one out on his steed. Roaming his lands to bring back the woman destined to be his Queen. And punishing his wife, Hannah, for fleeing his side.

In truth, he did not care what happened to his cowardly wife, but he could not allow the Kingdom to believe he had softened. His wife had abandoned him, and for that she must be punished.

The Great Prince growled. He did not know how to reconcile possessing Gabriella and killing Hannah. But he would manage the task.

Yes, dear one, the Palace whispered, seeping back into his mind. Controlling his desires. *You will get your retribution. Have no fear. That is why I brought Vanora to your door.*

The Prince leapt to his feet, then froze. His mind and heart were at war. Each day, they battled over this territory. And his body paid the price. Aging at twice the speed of his peers. Bringing the Prince to his knees. The tension was more than he could take.

While the Palace controlled his thoughts and directed his actions, his heart rebelled. Causing a steady friction in his body that, he knew, would eventually wear him out. The Prince wondered how long he could keep up this battle.

Before he could chase the thought, it was swept from his mind. Leaving him disoriented. Grasping for the inquiry that was present only a moment ago.

Still, his heart resented the mysterious force that caged his thoughts. That demanded he torture innocents and tear villages apart. Only to find he could not remember why he had ever commanded such atrocities be brought to bear.

The Prince took to pacing his room. The pulsing of blood calmed his heart and soothed his mind. For when he paced, the grip of dark thoughts loosened. A brief, clear space opened. He found himself thinking about Vanora. He was aware she was a powerful sorceress. The villagers whispered of the shadowy power that possessed the Northern Lands.

Fewer and fewer people chose to live in the north, beyond the Lightning Lakes. The long chain of deep waters served as a sort of barrier. Once people had sought the lakes for their sacred qualities. Now they marked a warning. A message to turn around and return to the lands from whence you came. Or choose another destination.

Woodland gossip claimed Vanora had killed most of her

family. And what remained of her court had fled for their lives. Neither hunter nor warrior would place foot on her land. Even the most sensible trackers claimed the Northern Lands were troubled. By what, they never could say. And they had no desire to find out.

The Prince knew to take the sum of gossip and cut it into many pieces to find a fragment of truth. He had heard tales of Vanora since he was a small boy. Whispers passed down through generations. From his father and his father's father.

Then, one evening in the Prince's eighth year, his father snarled her name, as he sat in the Great Room by the roaring fire. *Vanora*. He said it like a curse. Yet underneath was a current of need. Like a plea to an illicit lover.

The Prince was too young to understand the torment of possession. Nor did he yet comprehend the feeling that masqueraded as love, only to show its true face as obsession. This was the torturous cage that housed his father.

He stood at the room's doorway, knowing that to venture closer to the King was the height of stupidity. But that name. *Vanora*. The sound called him forth into dangerous territory.

The Prince stepped into the entrance. Feeling his way. Waiting to discover if his mere presence would send the King into fits of rage. As though the Prince might be a reminder of something blasphemous.

But the King did not turn. He stared at the flames. Watching their dance like a man under a deep and unforgiving spell. The Prince stood transfixed. Wondering whether his father wished to throw his body onto the flames. To end his suffering once and for all. For in this room was a fireplace large enough to swallow a man.

The Prince was shaken by the thought. Truth be told, the King had shrunk in recent years. The man, who once held sway in every kingdom through his impressive physical size as much as his force of will, was wasting into a frail old man.

Though the Prince was not so foolish as to misjudge his father's strength. Though the King's limbs may be narrow, he possessed an unearthly power when he desired to crush something beneath his fist. Especially his son.

Still, his father did not move. And the Prince took another step. Wondering if his father might speak the strange moniker again.

"Vanora," the Great King whispered, even softer.

The name sent chills down the Prince's spine, rendering him both weak and willing. His knees buckled, and he swayed close to the cold floor. He must not fall, for fear of snapping his father from his reverie.

The Prince commanded his legs to hold. And his urgent plea was heard. His legs grew in strength. Keeping him upright. Sending an entirely different chill up his spine. As though a force in the Palace had noticed him, as soon as he declared his desire.

The Prince sensed he had called forth an even worse fate than the ones the Gods had carved out for him. But he was entranced by the name on his father's lips. So he shook off the eerie feeling, and pushed forward.

Who was this Vanora? the Prince wondered.

"Vanora," his father echoed, like a puppet on a string. Shocking the Prince, and thrilling the invisible force that filled this strange room.

The Prince looked around, wondering what spirits whirled in their midst. What ghosts possessed his father? As he sat hunched, in front of the blazing flames. Drinking blood-red wine and contemplating death, while whispering the name of a stranger.

The Prince felt gripped by a possession of his own. Compelled to know this woman. What hold did she have on his father? Where had she gone? Was she even real? Obsession entered the Prince's blood and forced his feet toward his father.

As he arrived at his father's chair, the Prince focused on one word: *Vanora*. The force of his will thrilled the room. Sending shivers through the walls. Whispers chased around the stones. Echoing in the Prince's ears. Threatening to drive him mad.

Still, his father did not move. He remained fixated on the flames. The stronger the Prince held his attention on the name, the louder the King spoke it.

"Vanora," the King proclaimed. "Vanora."

And when the Prince was only an arm's length away, the King yelled at the top of his worn lungs, "Vanora!" Then threw his heavy goblet into the fireplace, smashing the glass against the stones, the flames hissing as they tasted the wine.

The King turned and locked his son in his gaze. Released from his curse, if only long enough to see the bearer of his torment. The Prince froze. His will vanished. His courage drained. A cold sweat broke over his body.

The Prince had never willingly provoked his father's rage. And so, he could only imagine, that the vicious spirit in the King's chest would wreak far more damage than a broken bone or black eye.

Instead, the Great King glared at him. And a grimace of hate and portent twisted his mouth.

"You wish to know of the witch, *Vanora*," the King stated,

accentuating the name.

Despite himself, the Prince nodded. He had come this far. He had chased temptation to the gates of Hell. Why not cross the darkened threshold?

"Well, boy," the King sneered, "you may come to rue this night. But far be it from me to withhold a tale of devastation and torment."

The King eyed his son, as though waiting for him to run, leaving him to his dark thoughts and decanter of blood wine. But the Prince did not move.

"Ah, Vanora," the King said, turning his gaze back to the flames. "A woman unlike any other. And I have met many women, son." A lurid sneer darkened the King's face.

The Prince should have run. Evil desire poured from his father's body. The yearning to pass on this torment was palpable. But the Prince stood transfixed. His father had never taken time to tell him a story. And certainly never called him *'son.'*

For as long as the Prince could remember, he felt only that his father despised him. As though, from the day he was born, the King was propelled ever faster toward death's door. With his son counting the days. And thus hated him for that.

While the Prince was a child, nothing could have been further from the truth. More than his father's love, he desperately craved his approval. He would have thrown down his life in battle were that the destiny of the King's heir.

But the Prince was not permitted to prove his worth through combat. No one was allowed to risk his life. Except the King. And with madness pressing on his father's skull, the Prince fell asleep every night wondering whether he might wake.

In this strange moment, the boy felt wanted.

And so, the Prince gambled his life. For a chance to sit in the chair across from his father and listen to a story — of a woman named Vanora.

FIFTEEN

"MAY YOU NEVER FALL FOR A WOMAN the way I fell for Vanora," the Great King declared.

He reached for his glass, and snarled when his hand clutched empty air. He snatched up the decanter and poured blood wine down his throat from the vessel itself. "Curse these wretched spirits," the King muttered. "I wish to hold court with only one ghost tonight. Be gone, others!"

The King stabbed his hand at the air, as though the gesture would frighten his tormentors. He achieved only the startled face of his pathetic offspring.

He would tell the louse a story, mused the King. If only to show him the crushing weight of the world. For the rest of his prizes, the parasite will have to fight his own battles.

Only the brutal of mind and cruel of heart deserve to rule, vowed the King. He would not hand a crumb to this insect. Thrones are hard won on the battlefields of fate. If he wants the weight of the crown, let him tear it from his head. Leaving blood and bone under his nails.

He glanced at the boy. Perched, in silence, on the chair. Awaiting a tale, as though he might be entertained. The child had no notion of the darkness he called forth.

Let him find out, laughed the King, grim delight the only enjoyment left to his mad mind. Let the wretched troll discover the torture of love.

"Love. *Ha!*" The King exclaimed, alarming the child. The King turned his gaze back to the fire. And his stare grew distant as he travelled into the past.

"Vanora was the woman I chose to be my Queen," the King began. "Not your weak-willed mother. No. Vanora was a woman who dominated. She would steal your heart and crush your will. *That* was a woman worthy of my side."

The blood drained from the Prince's face. Fury mixed with terror in his heart. The boy's hands shook and his face flushed dark red. The Great King revelled in torment.

He felt the child's blood begin to boil. The King witnessed the instinctive urge to protect his mother. Yet he knew the child would not act.

The story was too intriguing. Too delicious. The boy chose to bear the pain of it. All so he could hear the tale of the mysterious woman who captured the King's heart.

"Though I chose her, and demanded that she be mine, my father and his advisors deemed her dangerous," snarled the King. "They did not care that she brought parcels of rich land with her dowry. They did not care that she was my true match. They did not care that with her at my side we would unite the most powerful kingdoms in the Great Lands."

"They only saw a woman capable of bringing them to their knees," said the King, as he locked the boy in his gaze, "That was their greatest mistake." The Great King's searing hatred pierced the child's heart.

"In the moment of their denial," the King continued, taking a swig of wine, "I knew they did not see the grand vision. The greatness I was to bestow on this kingdom. That was when I knew they would only ever be boulders on my path. Boulders that required destruction."

The King fell silent. Seizing the cast iron poker from its stand at his side. Clutching the poker as though he prepared to thrust a sword through his enemy's heart. His hand turning white with the force of his crushing need.

The boy did not move. He waited, as though afraid to breathe. Terrified the King, lost in the fury of yesteryear, might mistake him for his rivals. And send the iron weapon through his small chest.

Furious, the King thrust the poker into a well-worn hole in the polished oak floor. Over and over. Shattering the ancient wood. Whispering curses on the souls who denied him.

"But, I digress," he declared. Holding the poker hard against the oak for one more long moment. Until he relented.

"You came to hear the tale of Vanora. The story *before* I was so cruelly denied." The urchin had risked annihilation. For that, the Great King would reward the mite's courage.

Though the King could not promise that he would not later punish the child for his desperate curiosity…

As a young man of twenty, the King was handed the throne while his father still lived. He was not sure whether his father's advisors bequeathed the crown to keep the cruel and ambitious child from murdering their ruler. Or whether the rumours of his father's deteriorating health had forced their hand. Either way, the conniving old men relinquished the title to him, while keeping its authority in their grasp.

The newly crowned King resented the distrust of his advisors. They pretended to heed his opinions only to placate him. But the King knew they feared his ambition. He saw through their flattery and their pathetic endeavours to lure his aspirations into the open.

After weeks of games, the King stormed out of their latest assembly. He stormed through the courtyards. Then shook off his guards and pushed away his footman. He burst outside. Tearing through the expansive gardens behind the summer palace.

The King needed time alone to resolve how to deal with his father's lackeys. He wound his way deep into the labyrinthine gardens. The ancient design integrated towering shrubs and private nooks. The King was never sure whether the architect intended the passages to rouse contemplation or to provide courtiers a tempting place to conduct affairs.

He pounded the narrow paths, weaving into the depths of the secretive garden. The King did not care who heard his tempestuous footfalls. For it would clear his path of foolish lovers.

Pound. Pound. Pound. Eyes down. Hands clenched. Cursing under his breath, he thundered deeper into the gardens. Had he been a man of any awareness, he might have heard the trees whispering. Seen the flowers hide their faces. And witness the most cheerful birds — the chickadees and larks — flee the shrubs to find safer branches.

Instead, the King obsessed over the men who defied him. Turning their words over in his mind. Never once seeing their loyalty to his father or their desire to protect the kingdom. The brash young man saw only traitors and heard only judgmental whispers.

With his eyes fixed on distant scenes already played, the King crashed into a woman in a most undignified manner. Startled, the King's hand flew up to strike the insolent intruder that dared interrupt his thoughts.

Until his gaze alighted on the most ravishing creature. A woman older than he, she appeared to be a lady of thirty years. The claret colour of her close-fitting dress rivalled the most vibrant flower. Her chestnut hair flowed in luxurious waves, begging for the King's touch. And her curves silenced his tongue.

The regent was confounded. His mouth fell open. His cheeks flushed. And his eyes dropped to her tempting cleavage. As he openly broke every social grace, the woman did not flinch. Nor did she curtsy. She waited. Watching the bewitched young man. As though she foresaw where this journey would go.

For endless moments, the King stared. He could not find his words. Nor his feet.

He was frozen to the spot. Unsure whether this creature was before him in his garden or whether she was a fantasy sent to distract him from the dank, coal pits of his mind.

If she were merely a fantasy, he did not care. She was in his private garden. On his land. And he would have her. His thoughts abandoned language and leapt to a vision of taking this woman on the grass. Here and now, like the basest of servants.

Still, his feet did not move. Nor did his tongue. The King was imprisoned by his own desire. And he was at a loss as to where to find the key.

As soon as the King sensed his helplessness, the woman stepped forward.

She had been patiently waiting, as though watching a bug upended in a pond. Anticipating the moment the insect declared the futility of its fight. Then she pressed close, in a most inappropriate manner. Nearer than any person dared step since he was three years old.

Teasing with her succulent figure, she lingered just beyond the threshold of touching.

And whispered three words in his ear, "*I* am Vanora."

SIXTEEN

After those three words, the King remembered little.

He woke up hours later beneath the willow tree at the heart of the garden. Bereft of his clothes, with a naked Vanora by his side. This was his right, to lay with any woman of his Kingdom, when and where he pleased. But even as he stared at her, the King was unnerved by this woman.

He had never seen her before. He did not know her lineage. Nor was her face familiar. He knew only her name. Within seconds of their meeting, she possessed him body and soul. Yet, the King did not question their union.

Fate threw them together, he thought. She would not have been in the garden at my hour of need if she were not destined to be my Queen. Not that he once wondered how she appeared here.

All he cared was that her violet-blue eyes burned with the hunger for power that consumed his own. That her heart echoed his pounding need to devour the world. He cared not if ruthless desires brought about their destruction. The craving merely made him want to take her again.

The King knew, deep in his bones, that their mutual quest for dominance was the means of their greatest conception. Not the path to devastation.

He gripped her. Pulling her to him. Feeling their power surge. All of nature was his witness — this woman would claim the hearts and minds of his land. And, as soon as he achieved the fealty of his people, the King realized, he would reach for greater heights.

He wanted all the land. All the people. Everyone would bow to him! The King's fingers dug into her arms. Clutching her as though she might resist, but Vanora did not cry out.

Instead, she smiled. Urging his thoughts forward on their path, like a rider with a crop. Pushing her steed into familiar territory.

Yes, thought the King, unaware he was not the one pulling the reins. With Vanora at my side, every being will bow to me. Every creature will owe me its life. Why stop at the servitude of the Great Mountains? I will unite all the kingdoms. I will be King of the Great Lands.

The Great King! Yes! That was his destiny! He exulted. Never again would he fear any soul. Never again would he answer to anyone. All would answer to him!

The King claimed Vanora over and over in the garden. Until darkness took the sky.

—⁂—

The King's advisors grew concerned that harm had come to the new ruler.

Finally, they sought him out under the night stars. Calling his name. Receiving no answer. Venturing deep into the gardens, they stumbled on the naked leader and his lover.

The advisors were shocked at the King's state. And perturbed by the woman who, by all external appearance, had possessed their young regent.

The senior advisor, Edwin, saw unnerving power emanating from this strange woman. She might appear vulnerable with no clothing to shield her, but she had control of their King. She had woven a spell so powerful that the young man had no notion he was lost. Or he did not care.

Edwin knew to move with care. And haste.

With a tight sweep of his hand, he gestured for the others to retreat to the shadows. They recognized the signal as one of profound warning. And shifted away without a sound. Trusting Edwin. For he possessed the gift of perceiving beyond the veil — Edwin knew truths most could not see.

And he was the sole bridge between the tyrant King and his troubled advisors. Especially as the King's sanity eroded farther each day. Edwin knew the young prince had never been balanced of mind. Screaming at servants. Distrustful of his parents. Swearing that if they birthed another child, he would dispose of the traitor in its sleep.

A threat his parents took seriously. Much to the Queen's chagrin and the King's sadness.

And so, from the earliest days, the advisors treated him with caution. Even more so now that he was on the throne. They attempted to guide him without giving offence. Offering the wisdom of their years. Moving with care and patience. Determined to hide their pain at the loss of a beloved King, who was replaced with a despot.

Edwin's heart broke as he saw the dark path of coming years with a power-crazed tyrant at the helm. Still, he swore an oath as a young man to serve his kingdom. And he would uphold that vow until his death.

"How are we to wrench him from her grasp?" asked the youngest advisor, a mere sixty-five years old in comparison to his comrades.

"We must not," whispered Edwin, to the shock of his peers. "She is a powerful sorceress. One we know little about. If we act rashly, we do not know what she will do to the King."

"Or to us," murmured Peter, Edwin's right-hand man. No other would have dared to voice a concern that verged on treason.

"We must put the regent's safety at the highest concern," chided Edwin.

For he knew what Peter did not say. That perhaps this sorceress had done them a favour.

If they sent her away with the King, they would solve an immediate problem. But Edwin could see she was a much greater concern than their petulant leader. One that would certainly come back to haunt them. For generations.

"I am afraid we must invite her into the palace," Edwin decided. The five other advisors gasped. "You cannot be serious," the youngest said. "She'll kill us in our sleep."

Edwin stole a glance at the sorceress. Careful not to catch her eye. He surveyed her without gazing directly at her form. Not that he was ashamed to look at a woman without clothing. Rather, her ability to enthrall was most deadly. Her body was an instrument she used to fool simple and easily possessed men.

Edwin had protected his King and lands through much more than sage advice. For in these increasingly dangerous times, he relied on tools that his leaders banned from common homes. Even when serving his King, he made sure to disguise his use of rhythmic words and herbs — what the old ones would call *spells* — with skillful explanations.

The most superstitious and paranoid nobles still believed in blessings and offerings to the ancestors. And so, Edwin carefully tread the line of treason in service to his masters. In secret, he resented the King's decrees forbidding magic. Frustrated by the hypocrisy of a regent relying on enchantments that he forbade his humblest servants to use.

And yet, part of him understood. The higher the echelon of power, the more potent — and secretive — the tools that must be wielded.

So Edwin used his hidden sight to evaluate the sorceress. By focusing within — and defocusing his external sight — he perceived the subtle web that emanated from her womb. A dark silver cord of pulsing power that secured itself to the King and wound its way through his heart, his mind and circled round him to secure his genitals.

Despite himself, Edwin smiled. He had to admire her craft. This one had studied with the most talented weaver in the world — *The Silver Wolf Spider.*

He had not seen one since he was a lad, when he ventured across the border of the Great Mountains and the Northern Lands. Once he crossed over, he felt beckoned to return again. He discovered mysteries that he never imagined possible. Studying sacred creatures. Listening to the wise wind. And drinking magical waters.

Edwin fell deeply in love with the Northern Lands. In truth, he was preparing to run away from his home and live out his days in her rugged wilds. As his anticipation grew, Edwin became careless. And his father caught him returning from across the border woods.

His father railed about the dangers of their neighbour kingdom. Telling tales of dark magic, possessed children, and ghosts that drove men mad. Edwin saw the fear in his father's eyes, but he did not understand. All he had known of that land was her beauty.

Still, Edwin was a loyal child. And the thought that his journey would cause his parents worry and heartache, was more than he could bear.

So when his father insisted that Edwin never return to the Northern Lands, Edwin swore he would not go. But each and every day since, he felt the call to return. The Northern Lands promised a wild and enduring beauty that he had not seen since he visited it as a child. And the Silver Wolf Spider carried the greatest secrets of all.

This was a dangerous scenario indeed, Edwin thought. The sorceress bore the marks of the wild. She spoke languages and wove spells they had never seen in the Great Mountains. Edwin would need to tread with care. Using all his faculties to outwit this woman. Indeed, he might have to lay down his very life.

"Tell us what you see," whispered Peter. Edwin had been quiet too long for his comfort. All was not well in the kingdom.

"The lovers are intertwined with a potent spell," Edwin began. "We must not separate them abruptly or the King will suffer. Indeed, he might not recover his faculties at all."

The advisors murmured to one another, debating the wisdom of their sage. "But if we invite her into the palace," questioned Peter, "will we ever be rid of her?"

"I believe so," Edwin ventured, "though the way may take some time. Follow my lead. Never engage her directly. For she will ensnare you with her magic. The King's safety will take all my attention. So you must tend to your own wellbeing."

Magic. That word was rarely uttered out loud. The belief in magic had been silenced for generations. Keeping sorcery and spells in a few privileged hands. Hands that were dying as each day passed. With their leader possessed by a sorceress, Edwin was one of the few people who knew what to do.

The five advisors lowered their gaze to the ground. And waited for Edwin to command them. "Fear not any tack I take," Edwin whispered. "Trust my wisdom. Keep your eyes lowered. And direct all your faith to my heart."

At that decree, Edwin stepped forward into the light.

Startling the sleeping King and bringing a smile to Vanora's lips. She held her naked body proud, as though expecting the old man to show a sign of discomfort.

But Edwin did not flinch.

He looked to his regent and said, "Your highness, the hour is late. If you wish to bed your hired consort, you might consider moving inside where there is heat and wine."

Edwin felt the tension behind him. The advisors feared his words. Terrified that the sorceress would condemn them for his insult. Their qualms were soon confirmed.

A powerful wind swirled around Vanora like a tornado. Swooping her to her feet and draping her claret-coloured dress around her body. Vanora landed in front of Edwin, an imperious look upon her face. Her hands shook and her eyes blazed.

Edwin saw that she expected him to cower. Or at least be shaken. But as he stared into her eyes, he saw her recoil. She saw in him no worry, or fear. Only clarity.

And for the first time in many, many years, Edwin knew that the sorceress was afraid.

SEVENTEEN

THE GREAT PRINCE SNAPPED from the trance of memory.

Footfalls had arrived on the other side of his door. He did not know who had the nerve to approach his personal quarters, but they risked the Prince crushing their fingers.

Memory was a precious commodity for the Prince. He rarely found himself able to retrieve childhood moments. He was not sure why, but his recollections grew weaker by the day. Perhaps this was a blessing. For there was little he wanted to remember.

His father's treatment had been cruel, though the Prince struggled to remember detail. He only needed to think of his father for his stomach to clench and his shoulders to stiffen. Though his mind may not recall the events, his body prepared for battle every time.

The Great Prince did not enjoy recalling history, but he was sure his memories held the key to his freedom. So when he finally possessed the precious memory of his father's infatuation, he was furious to be interrupted. Even now, moments after being pulled from the past, the Prince struggled to grasp the thread.

All he remembered was the fireplace, his father, and the eerie sensations of magic.

The Prince heard the floorboards squeak. And felt the

apprehensive presence in the hallway. As anger pulsed through his veins, he refrained from whipping open the door and thrashing the servant.

Perhaps the emissary brought news of Gabriella, echoed a far away whisper. The Prince was unsure whose voice echoed through the walls. His tower was a quiet sphere that no one could penetrate. Yet the voice felt strangely familiar.

On hearing Gabriella's name, the Great Prince's blood responded with a wave of calm. Such was the power of the Messenger. The mere mention of her brought peace to his soul.

—⁓—

The Hidden Palace fumed at Gabriella's impact on the Prince. She resented the effect the irritating child still had on him. The Palace raised him. She made him the ruler he was today. No one else deserved his devotion. She would not be usurped!

Still, the mentioning of the Messenger's name was occasionally useful. Something about her prompted the Prince to action. The waif was not much of an opponent, but she had held the Prince's interest this long. A feat unmatched by any other creature. So the Palace could not yet deem her inconsequential.

This was why the Palace lured Vanora back to a land she swore she would never revisit. A heart as bitter as Vanora's could never resist an opportunity for vengeance. And her banishment from the Palace years ago still pulsed through Vanora's veins with deep shame.

Vanora was a profound enough sorceress to wipe the memory of her vanquishing from the minds of mortals. But the Palace did not forget. She possessed all of the memories of every creature that forged her or was forged by her. Especially those of the most corrupt man ever to live inside her walls — the Great King.

The Palace derived deep pleasure from luring Vanora to the scene of her shame. She was impressed how well the Sorceress hid her rage. She kept the court distracted with her ample curves and devilish beauty. But the Palace was not fooled.

She felt the surge of hatred in the witch's blood as she broached the Prince's throne. No woman forgets betrayal. No woman forgives abandonment. The Palace knew Vanora was determined to have her pint of blood; to make the son pay for his father's sins.

But the Palace had no intention of watching the blood of her puppet be spilled. Vanora was a means to an end. One that was so easily provoked. Whether Vanora vanquished the Messenger or the Messenger killed Vanora, the Palace did not care.

So confident was she that no one else could hold sway over the Prince's heart.

The Palace felt assured that her Prince was back on track. He would tend to the servant at his door. And she must deal with an uprising in the sculleries. Some new girl from the outskirts with a notion of resisting her power.

The Palace scoffed. By morning, the child would be found drowned in a well. The shock would eliminate thoughts of rebellion for at least six months. The mere thought of it made the Palace tremble with anticipatory delight.

—ɷ—

As a rush of blood surged to his head, the Prince swerved to avoid crashing into the wall. He was unused to such an influx of sensation. The overwhelming stream of feeling knocked him off-balance.

He grabbed the oak bedpost to keep from falling. His hand pressed into the wood, feeling the grain push against his skin. The pressure of the polished wood sharpened his mind.

The Great Prince awakened to the realization that he stood in the middle of his private tower. A truth that should seem obvious. But like an increasing number of moments in his life, the Prince did not recall how he came to be where he stood.

He assured himself that he was not going mad. He could not become his father! And yet, each day brought occurrences like this one — announcing the shadow of madness.

A tentative knock caused the Prince to grimace.

Despite the soft noise, he swore the servant rapped directly on his skull. The Great Prince clenched his teeth, resisting the urge to howl. He would not give his underlings the satisfaction that he wrestled with the same demons that drove his father to an early grave.

Ah, his conscience whispered. *But the demons did not send your father to his death. You did. And still you cannot bring yourself to claim his title — the Great King.*

"Silence!" the Great Prince bellowed. And the poor soul outside his door whimpered.

The Prince was in no mood to make tasks easy for his servants. Or his ghosts. His father was dead. He was alive. And, for this instant, he cared not how fate cast those dice. He had a narrow window in which to take advantage of having control over his mind.

He ignored all doubts and instead focused on the precarious pact he had struck with Vanora. In his haste to return Gabriella to his side, the Prince forgot that Vanora had been to his land many years ago. Even worse, she had been his father's lover.

How could he have forgotten? *What force* — A shiver rippled up the Prince's spine. He had pondered this question before. Likely, many times. Through the grace of the gods, he had been given a moment of recollection. He must not waste it.

The Prince stood tall, leaving the support of the bed. He focused all his mental strength to recall the answer that evaded him. Vanora, he thought. She was not merely the ruler of the Northern Lands. She bore intense magic. But even worse, she bore a powerful grudge. If I were Vanora, how would I wreak revenge? What would satiate a century's old rancour?

Hurt the one her betrayer loved most, came the answer.

But how could he know who hurt the ancient witch the most in all the years she had lived? The Prince grew more and more frustrated with each passing moment.

"Your highness," said the voice in the hall, interrupting his precious thoughts. Rage burned through him, pulsing to the tips of his fingers.

Only the faintest voice of reason at the corner of his mind quelled his violent impulse. The servant would never risk her life if the message were not of importance. Any creature would have fled in self-preservation long ago.

"State your mission!" roared the Great Prince, yanking open the door to face the impudent wretch.

A slender girl, twelve years of age, stood across from his

imposing figure. Shaking harder than a young willow in a windstorm. She pressed her legs together to keep from fleeing.

"Sir," she quaked, "I h-have been s-sent with a message."

"That is obvious," scowled the Prince. "Spit it out!"

"I h-have been told that there is news of your..." the girl paused. She was about to use the word beloved, but in facing the terrifying man, she could not imagine that he possibly had one. Her lips froze, at a loss.

"My what?" he replied, dark storms of impatience gathered across his forehead.

"Your beloved," she exhaled, unable to think of another in the face of her impending death. The young girl had worked in the Palace for four years, and had never before been sent to face the Prince. She always dreaded this day. For fear it would be her last.

The Great Prince hesitated at the sound of *'beloved'* falling from the young girl's lips.

He yearned to crush this imp so she would never say the word again. But his heart... picked up several beats. Thumping in response to the only person ever to bring him hope. The one to whom he had pledged his love on his knees.

"Gabriella," he whispered. And the girl was shocked at the transformation. The wall of anger dropped from the Prince, leaving a handsome man who appeared many years younger.

"Yes," she replied. "Your..." she paused, afraid to risk the word again in case it reanimated the monster. "Gabriella has been spotted."

"By Vanora?" the Great Prince questioned, nauseating terror rushing to his stomach.

For now the Prince understood Vanora's vengeance. Many

people bore a deep grudge against his father. The Great King had ruined many kingdoms and countless lives. But none had the power to wreak their desired revenge. Until now.

The Sorceress carried the strength of armies and the fury of thousands. He saw now that Vanora only chased Adrian as a game to lure Gabriella from hiding. And the Prince had sent the witch on her mission!

"Where?" he asked, forcing his hands not to shake the servant girl. "Where was she sighted?"

"In the highest reaches of the Asteria Woodland," she replied.

The Prince sensed a storm coming. A great darkness hung on the horizon and pressed against the Palace walls. Time was running out. The moment for inquiries had passed. He needed to act.

"Go, fetch my strongest steed!" demanded the Prince. "Waste not a second. And tell no one. You must fly as though the demon hounds of Phantasos were on your heels!"

The girl squeaked her acknowledgement and moved as fast as her feet would travel.

As the servant fled his presence, the Prince whirled into his quarters. Pulling his riding attire from his wardrobe. Not risking the time for a servant to dress him. He must strike while the iron was hot. If he could only get on his steed and flee the Palace before the storm caught up. Gabriella would be safe.

But what if —

His mind could not resist leaping ahead, warning of the possible dangers.

The Great Prince stripped off his silken chemise and day trousers. Throwing them aside as though they burned his skin. He pulled on riding pants and a raw silk shirt, perfect for long days on horseback. As fast as the Prince moved, he felt the darkness rising faster. The storm clouds were gathering quick. He feared that he fought a losing battle, but he would not leave Gabriella in the path of a danger he unleashed.

The Prince pulled on his dark green leather coat, designed to shelter him from pouring rain. He cut a dashing figure in the riding clothes he had not worn for years. Catching sight of his likeness in a mirror, he felt a glimpse of recognition. The shimmer of a young man whose heart once held dreams for the future, rather than nightmares of deeds done.

Still, the clouds of despair closed in like a tempest. His heart pounded faster. Urging the Prince to forgo all other decisions and run.

For once, the Prince's mind fell quiet. The path before him was clear and bright. Find Gabriella. Leap into the unknown. Relinquish all he possessed and be with the one he loved. Nothing else mattered. No one else called his name.

And so, the Great Prince leapt to his door with strength and hope. Forgetting all desires that had come before this moment.

He wrenched open the door and placed one foot into the hallway.

Then he felt the surge of darkness. The palpable shadow overtook him like a mighty tornado. Swooping around his body. Possessing his mind. Fighting his free will until he bent to his knees from the sheer effort.

His mind — overwhelmed by the tension between the freedom beating in his heart and the storm of desolation swirling in his blood — collapsed under the irresolvable tension.

As the Great Prince lay unconscious on the ancient stones,

whispers of gloom and wrath seeped from the Palace walls. Laying claim to his consciousness once more.

The Palace was not concerned about the Prince's attempt to escape. She relished the struggle. Fed from his resistance. And trusted that the next time courage spoke to his heart, he would quake from the toll it took on his body and mind.

Each time he resisted, the Palace deepened her hold on his heart. Clawing her way beyond foolish dreams and crushing fragile notions of belonging. Her cloying presence reached deeper as he slept on the icy floor. Heat seeped from his body, making room for her dank hold.

Though the Messenger sparked a fire in his heart, the Palace spent each day quenching the flame. For every mile the foolish girl fled from his presence, the Palace gained territory in the Prince's soul.

The ridiculous waif hid from the world as though she expected time would solve the dilemma of hopelessness in the Great Lands. The Messenger did not realize that the longer she hid from the Prince, the deeper the Palace sank into his being. Claiming the precious few corners where his soul held out against absolute possession.

Until one day, when he would forget the Messenger ever existed.

EIGHTEEN

GABRIELLA FROZE. The leg of hare hanging in mid-air, awaiting her bite. She felt Katrin's eyes on her. Questioning this strange behavior. But Gabriella's companion had learned that the Messenger rarely offered an explanation for her strange behaviour.

Still, the young woman's hawk-sharp gaze made Gabriella self-conscious. Especially when she found her thoughts straying to the Great Prince. She feared that Katrin would see her heartbreak. Or worse, speak aloud the struggle she perceived in Gabriella's heart.

A battle the Messenger preferred to pretend did not exist. Much good that did her these days. She thought of the Prince more often than she thought of Adrian. Indeed, more often than she thought of her own family.

What did it mean? She tore the last bite of flesh off the hare's leg bone. Gabriella was exasperated by these feelings. The Prince's struggle was not her responsibility. He must bear the weight of his choices. No matter the evil of the place where he lived. If she must find her way through the dark mystery of the world, then so must he.

Yet, somehow, her heart would not relinquish responsibility. She could not dispute that fate brought them together. That her presence gave the Prince hope. And with hope, came the possibility of freedom. Not only for the tender man held hostage under the weight of his ancestral burden, but for the people held captive by his rage.

No! she protested, throwing the bone to the fire. Sparks flew up from the drips of sizzling fat. She would not be a sacrificial maiden for the despair of men! She did not fight this long to play the meek wife and tend to the Prince's wounds.

Gabriella jabbed the flames with a stick. Missing Adrian. Yet powerless to do anything. She could not reach out to him. Nor could she confide in anyone, for fear of putting him in danger.

"Well, you can keep punishing the fire or you can talk," Katrin said. "But if you continue to torment the wood, know that you are releasing flares to the Great Prince."

Gabriella looked up in shock. Few people ever said the Prince's name with such boldness. And certainly not with a lack of care to the consequences.

"Have you met the Prince?" Gabriella asked. She was grateful for the diversion. No matter how dangerous the topic.

Katrin was not foolish. Even this far from civilization, the woods had ears. She lowered her voice. "I saw him the day of your sister's betrothal."

"Ah yes," Gabriella replied, turning back to the fire. The Prince may have been demanding that day, but Katrin did not know just how dangerous he had become.

"I do not fear him," Katrin said. "He is nothing but an insolent bully."

Gabriella sighed. Everyone thought they knew the Prince. Just as, she supposed, everyone thought they knew the Messenger.

When in truth, they saw what they wished to see. An enemy they had faced before. A rescuer they always desired.

"He is much more than that," Gabriella avowed, and fell silent as she stared into the flames.

—◊◊◊—

Katrin had heard many tellings of the legend of Gabriella at the Hidden Palace. But she did not put much stock in stories told over ale in remote border towns. The distance from the original event rendered the storytellers unreliable, as did the copious flasks of alcohol. The weavers of myths used both to challenge anyone who dared doubt them.

Whether the tale was handed through one or one hundred people, Katrin had no idea. But she knew folk tales well enough to trust only the elements that remained the same. No matter the teller.

This much Katrin knew — Gabriella disappeared from the Palace in a swirl of mist. Every soul in danger had transported by miracle back to her home. And the Prince's soldiers could not recall any moment past when Gabriella took the stage.

Since that time when Katrin watched Gabriella train, the valiant princess had — somehow — transformed into a mystical warrior. Capable of saving thousands. Katrin was intrigued. Yet not entirely sure how she felt about the change.

Gabriella lifted her gaze. And Katrin felt the Messenger's challenge. Inciting Katrin's doubt. Stirring her questions about why Gabriella hid from the man people claimed she defeated.

Katrin wondered why she did not return. Why not vanquish

the Prince? What was she waiting for? Did they not deserve to be liberated from him? She could remove the Prince and place her sister on the throne. What was her delay?

As Gabriella held her in a fierce gaze, Katrin felt her need for answers burn like an uncontrollable wildfire. She tried to push the desire down. To silence the screaming need in her mind to understand. To question her liege.

But she could not. The fire took over her mind. And spread to her lips.

—m—

"Why do you flee?" Katrin blurted out.

Confronting Gabriella with the question she asked herself every morning. The inquiry no one dared ask her in three years. Though to be fair, she gave no one the opportunity. She had felt the questions burning inside Katrin. And knew they would not be able to continue the journey unless the young woman found the courage to confront her.

Gabriella laughed, "I wish I knew."

"Of course you know," Katrin challenged. "You are the —"

"No!" Gabriella commanded, shutting Katrin's mouth with her conviction. "Ask me whatever you please. But never say that word."

"Why not?" Katrin asked.

"The Great Prince has spies searching the countryside," Gabriella replied. "Waiting for such an utterance." She peering into the woods, checking for scouts. They might come in human or animal form.

"People say it every day," Katrin objected. "I must have heard the tale of the miracle at the Hidden Palace a thousand times."

"Yes," Gabriella conceded. "And the tellers meet an unexpected end after they leave the public house. Or find an intruder waiting when they return home. The Prince's mercenaries use any means to unearth information about my whereabouts. "

"If you were to utter the word, and there were spies in the woods," Gabriella indicated the darkness beyond their fading fire, "I would wake in shackles. And your throat would be slit. Once in custody, my name would be forbidden in the Great Lands for generations."

Gabriella needed the girl to understand the risks of travelling with her. This was not a journey to undertake lightly. And though they found one another in what appeared to be fated circumstances, Gabriella was not sure that Katrin should be anywhere near her. Keeping her company was not wise.

Katrin was safe when strangers believed she had not seen her regent for years. But now, if she were spotted with Gabriella, Katrin would be an outlaw for life. A fate Gabriella would rather not have on her conscience.

"I have protected myself this long," Katrin said. "I can outwit the Prince's henchmen."

And though Gabriella believed her, she shook her head. "They may not be the brightest," Gabriella replied. "But they are cruel, determined creatures. If you made them look as foolish as you did those outpost guards, they would hunt you down until the end of your days. Then they would torture and kill you for pleasure. Is that a fate you desire?"

"Of course not," Katrin countered. "But I do not relish living in fear. Hiding from those who would hurt me. I may as well dig a hole and bury myself."

As the words left Katrin's mouth, she realized that they sounded like an indictment. Accusing Gabriella of cowardice for hiding. Katrin's mouth fell open. Suddenly remorseful, yet unable to take the words back.

Gabriella stared at Katrin for several, long minutes. The girl grew more uncomfortable with each breath. Still, the Messenger glared. As though deciding whether to abandon her in the woods. Or worse, silence her forever.

NINETEEN

V ANORA REALIZED THE WIZARD was on guard. She smiled, pulling back her veil. Finally making eye contact. She could see that he was struck by her beauty. And, yet, he did not respond.

Oh, she thought, *this will be fun.* She had not had a good challenge in many a year. Not since her tryst with the Great King. Though the King himself was not the challenge. He was a vain and foolish man. Easy to enamor. And even easier to manipulate. Her true opponent in those days was his advisor, Edwin.

Vanora refrained from growling. Truth be told, her deepest regret was not succeeding in turning Edwin to her side. What an ally he would have been! No matter the trick she used, he anticipated her. Edwin had taught her much. She would not make the same mistakes with this clever one.

She extended her hand. Expecting chivalry to win the day. And while his courteous manner acknowledged her with a brief bow, he did not touch her.

"I believe you have been expecting me," Vanora teased. Touching her mare's bridle to release her from her bended knee. The horse rose with gratitude.

"Yes," Adrian replied. "We knew you were coming."

"How quaint that you include your steed in your greeting," she laughed, not looking at Casmire. Wounding the stallion's pride with her slight.

"Why would I not?" Adrian responded. "You expected him to turn traitor with one whiff of your mare. Though she is plainly not a worthy match for my companion."

Adrian's tactics surprised Vanora — and infuriated her mare. Vanora smiled, enjoying the acknowledgement of battle. She did not expect his chivalrous façade to fall so quickly. Yet nothing sparked Vanora's lust more than a good fight.

"Do not expect me to fall for your charms," Adrian replied, reading her cues. "You are beautiful. But I expect you have worn that glamour for many centuries. Underneath, you must be homelier than the oldest wood sprite."

Vanora exhaled sharply, calming her need to seize his throat and crush his windpipe. She was an experienced combatant. Instead of immediate retaliation, she chose to keep stock of every wound. When the time arrived for vengeance, her recollection of his offences would fuel the raging blaze that would be his end.

She returned his volley with a coy smile. "How endearing that you feel yourself a match for my magic. Since we speak plainly, wizard, allow me to assure you that you are no contender. We will dance. And we will parlay…"

Vanora stepped forward, daring Adrian to move away as she leaned close enough to send fire through his veins. "Then, when you least expect it, you will betray every vow, every being, every loved one you ever cherished."

Adrian stood strong, but did not doubt her words. Vanora inclined so near as to brush his lips, sending chills down his spine. As she felt his pulsating response, Vanora laughed. And whirled away.

She enjoyed nothing more than tormenting loyal men. Ones such as the Great King were hardly sport. They grovelled at her feet the moment she dropped her gown. But this one — she gazed over her shoulder as she lifted her leather saddlebag from her mare — would be a thrilling adventure.

"Since we are laying ourselves *bare*," Vanora said, turning back to Adrian. "Shall we declare terms?"

"Terms of war?" Adrian countered.

Casmire snorted, as though objecting to Adrian's directness. Still, Vanora resisted looking at Adrian. Knowing full well her lack of attention infuriated the horse. She sensed tension between the two. And made note of the opportunity for another time.

"Yes," Vanora replied. "If we are to be opponents, we must acknowledge that at some point one of us will surrender. And the other will claim the spoils."

Adrian took his turn to smile. Throwing Vanora off her game. He felt the shift and realized she fed off his opposition. He needed a new tactic. One that kept her off balance.

Casmire shook his mane. He disliked when humans felt assured around magical creatures. These beings did not play by rules. Why did humans always assume they had the upper hand? *This witch is clever,* Casmire cautioned. *She is luring you into a trap.*

Possibly, Adrian replied. *But resisting only gives her power. Casmire, I must play on the field she offers. Otherwise, I will exhaust all my magic keeping her at bay. Only to be expended when the attack comes. I must trust my instincts.*

Before Casmire could object, Adrian replied, "And are you my spoils, Vanora?"

She tensed, not expecting this answer. He was toying with her. Flirting! This was not the intelligence she had gained about the wizard. Her spies would pay for the error when she returned. No matter, she growled, attempting to take control of her emotions.

But angry sparks flew off her. Spooking her mare.

And the wizard's smile grew.

TWENTY

VANORA FORCED HERSELF TO BREATHE. The wizard had won the last round. But the Sorceress reminded herself that this was a long game.

Laugh all you like, trickster, Vanora scorned. But when I lay claim to your undying servitude, your shame will torment you until the end of days.

"Do you feel clever, now?" Vanora asked. "Have we earned an intimate parlance? *Adrian?*"

She sensed a rumble of anger deep in his stomach. And admired that he hid his reaction so well. That made the treasure even more valuable. She would pry and provoke until she claimed him. And she would not stop until he no longer withheld anything from her.

And though she salivated at the thought, in truth, the game was more important to Vanora than the prize. She certainly loved to win. She revelled in the victory — in crushing another's dream. In fact, she had razed entire villages when she so much as lost a bet.

Ah, but the game! exulted Vanora. The sport kept her vital. And breaking a wizard as powerful as Adrian? That was the prize for which a sorceress would wait a lifetime. Even more, that he came with the windfall of ruining a Messenger.

Vanora eyed Adrian, confident that he did not perceive her true strength. He appeared calm, but he pulsed with the impatience of youth. She had centuries on this boyish conjurer. Vanora was familiar with magic long before Adrian's spirit was even a whisper on the wind.

"Yes," she continued. "I think we shall call one another by our first names. After all, I anticipate spending many a night together."

Vanora swayed her beautiful hips nearer to Adrian. Daring him to move away. He held firm. "Shall we skip the prudish formalities and share one bed?" she teased.

Adrian replied evenly, "I expect you have much more extravagant needs than I can furnish, but you are welcome to join me. Know that the ground is hard, and the sun rises early. For I sleep under the stars, *Shadow Mistress*."

Vanora might have enjoyed his playful language, but she was caught unawares by the moniker — Shadow Mistress. A name she had not heard in decades. She clenched her fists and turned to keep from launching a lightning bolt through his skull.

How could he know an epithet no one had spoken in generations? Her mind reeled, searching for an explanation. Vanora had wiped out any creature that dared to use the derogatory term. She had been sure of her thoroughness.

Her mare whinnied as Vanora stood too close while her insides scorched with indignation. The horse dared not back away further, but she was in pain. This proximity to her mistress threatened her with scarring burns.

Casmire felt the mare's agony and struggled with his desire to protect her. But he could not be sure whether this was a ruse to provoke his instinct. Casmire loathed this dance. This was the territory of humans: trickery and deception. Not the domain of his kind.

Adrian held strong. Feeling the mare's pain, and Casmire's distress. Though they suffered, he believed they would be safer in the long term. Vanora lived to draw out torment. By speaking the forbidden epithet, he shortened the timeline of the witch's game.

Her amorous façade dropped. She did not even pretend to smile. Adrian had crossed a line. No wonder she was furious, he thought. Not only did he disgrace her, he stole control of her scheme. He would pay for this transgression, of that he was sure.

Still, he relished the transparency, even if it was fleeting. He might toy with her as she toyed with him, wasting time on foolish dalliances. But he had sent a clear message — she did not know everything. No matter how talented her spies.

"So, the valiant wizard resorts to insults," she smiled, though Adrian was not mislead by her light tone. "Shall I volley with words people have used to describe *you?*"

Adrian remained silent. He cared not what his enemies called him. Then a shimmer of fear rippled up his spine. She did not speak of his enemies. No, she had tortured his friends to find her poisoned barbs.

"No," she mused, regaining her hold on the battleground. "I think we shall dine first. I will torment your senses with stories of my exploits. While you wonder which of your closest supporters I persecuted. Until your heart cries out to hear the names of those who suffered to protect you."

Vanora laughed. Nothing tasted as sweet as the pain that seeped from the heroic. They ached for the injustice of the world. While she yearned for cruelty. Drinking gratification from the agony of others. For if she must suffer, then so must they all.

She waved her hand, sending swirls of dust into the air. Forcing Adrian and Casmire to cover their faces while struggling to keep an eye on her. As the particles of sand fell back into place, they marvelled to see a beautiful feast of pheasant, mushrooms, cream, bread, and wine, laid on an elegant blanket. Illuminated by delicate beeswax candles.

"Come," Vanora said. "Allow me to regale you with stories of torment." She laughed, as she sat on the blanket, feeling the cracks in his self-assured armour. She prodded at his every defence. Adrian may have upped the pace, but she still held the reins. Yes, she thought. She would wreak her vengeance slowly. Painfully. Then she would throw his body to the vultures.

And with that thought, Vanora patted the blanket for Adrian to sit.

TWENTY-ONE

Hannah could hardly believe they were here.

She stared at the familiar grounds. Once beautiful gardens were now ragged. She hesitated at the edge of her family's private acreage. Afraid of what she might see, what she might *feel*. And worried that by some mystical event the Great Prince would know that her foot had returned to her native land.

Syrena and Tobias exchanged a look. In truth, Syrena wanted to take Hannah's hand and pull her in the opposite direction. She dropped Tobias's gaze. Not wanting him to see her disquiet — that she was betraying Hannah by wishing she would abandon this quest.

Tobias gave voice when Syrena could not. "My liege," Tobias spoke. "There is no shame in changing your mind. No matter how far you have travelled."

"I appreciate your concern, Tobias," Hannah replied, eyes fixed forward." But the call I have heard for many weeks grows fainter by the day. If I do not make the leap, I fear I will forever regret my decision."

Tobias looked across the riotous gardens to the jutting pinnacles of the castle. His heart sank. "Mistress…" Tobias began, hesitant to interrupt the intimate dialogue between Hannah and her home.

"Yes?" Hannah replied, though she was distracted by the soft whispers of the trees. The wild ones recognized her and her brow furrowed. Listening to their pleas. The gardens cried out, not for her, but for her sister.

Tobias did not wish to say the words that sprung to mind. But he felt obliged to serve. No matter the consequence. "You must know," he continued, "that I returned to your castle many a time. In search of … your parents. But I never found any sign."

Hannah looked Tobias in the eye. Fire burned in her belly. She admired his courage, but wanted to strike his face for implying that her parents were dead. To gouge his eyes and mangle his knees —

She exhaled. And turned away. Not trusting herself to speak.

Hannah did not recall being so angry before the Hidden Palace possessed her. She was tired of the emotion. Her time at the Palace was marked by darkness and rage. And still, it pulsed through her like a rushing river. When would it stop? Had she not carried this torment long enough? Was she not a sufficient distance from that desolate place?

At first, Hannah had welcomed the anger. Embraced it. Believing she needed to exorcise the feeling like a demon. She even gave it voice on occasions when she had privacy. But this? This vision of hurting people? This she would not brook.

Her silence made Tobias increasingly uncomfortable. He felt he had done something wrong — had crossed an invisible line. He was close to dropping to a knee to beg forgiveness. But he had acted with honour. And so, he rooted his feet to the ground and did not fall.

"Fear not, Tobias," Hannah said, feeling his conflict. "I am grateful for your honesty. And, though I trust your diligence, I must travel this territory myself."

And with her words, Hannah took the step. Placing her foot on soil she had dreamt of for years. She expected a chill. Or a rush of welcoming warmth. Instead, she felt only tender recognition.

—∞—

Syrena and Tobias waited. Giving Hannah time with her land. Each watched the perimeter, looking for danger. Tobias with his keen gaze. Syrena with her intuition.

Since discovering Tobias's feelings for Gabriella, Syrena had relinquished her concerns. She felt his honourable spirit and already grew attached to him. In truth, Tobias and Syrena had become allies in protecting Hannah. Much to the regent's exasperation.

Yet, Syrena thought, here they were, flying in the face of the Great Prince's decree. Risking capture by opportunistic spies that watched the royal lands. Syrena scoured the hillside, hoping they had tired of waiting for the royal family and sought easier game elsewhere.

Syrena felt Tobias grow tense. He did not like that Hannah stood still. Drawing curious eyes. Making them targets. Syrena agreed, for she understood the vital importance of movement. Both for protection and for when an attack came.

Still, she would not interrupt Hannah's reverie.

This moment was deeply healing for Hannah. She had been sacrificed by her family for a peace that never came. She had traversed dark roads and confronted ominous enemies, not the least of which was her own husband.

Syrena could only imagine what emotions surged through Hannah's heart. She returned home, no longer a child, but as a woman who had seen more than the daughter of a king should ever have to face. Syrena had grown up with the cruel reality of the world. Hannah had not. And since they fell in love, Syrena wished each day that she could erase Hannah's pain. Especially the damage caused by her hand. Regardless of being an unwitting pawn, Syrena could not forgive herself for her transgressions against Hannah.

Hannah turned, and stared resolutely at Syrena. *You must not torture yourself. I will not have it. You were no more in control of your choices than I. And I might never have discovered love, nor been freed from prison, had you not been at my side.*

Syrena grinned, amazed by her lover's kindness. Hannah extended her hand. And Syrena stepped forward, following Hannah. Taking a leap of faith. Looking back with happiness, and inviting Tobias to follow.

—⁂—

All three stood on regal soil. Expecting something to happen. Only silence greeted them.

For Hannah, that was the most unnerving element of her reunion. She heard no songbirds. She saw no scurrying squirrels. Where were all the wild creatures? Did they flee in fear? Did they await some sign of safety? Or did they know something she could not see and were wise enough to keep from returning to a land cursed by heartbreak and betrayal?

Despite her misgivings, Hannah was determined to enter the castle. She must understand why she felt called. Whether for her sake or her parents, Hannah would lay down her life to find the answer. A truth she had not shared with Syrena. She was careful to guard that secret deep in her heart.

Hannah set out for the castle's back entrance, across a long and unprotected trek through disheveled gardens. The state of her family's land did not surprise her, but it did cause sorrow. Though logic insisted otherwise, Hannah could not help but compare its condition to her memories.

So much so, that each fallen tree, each tangled vine and broken bench, pulled at her heart. She forced her feet toward the castle door — but everything in her wanted to tend to the gardens. Digging her hands into the soil and bringing the flowers back to life.

The gardens were her mother's treasure and her sister's solace. Hannah was content to spend her days inside, dressed in elaborate gowns. Sharing gossip with the kitchen staff. And drifting between rooms, dreaming of the day she would share such a home with her husband. Now, Hannah flinched.

She wasted hours and days and years, like a foolish maiden, wishing to be swept off her feet. Believing in the fairy tale, only to be delivered to the nightmare. She was traded for diplomacy. Even then, Hannah clung to her belief in her powers. Believing that her beauty could soften the cruelest heart in the land. When instead, the force that changed him was Gabriella's courage.

Hannah wished her diplomatic voice and pretty form could bring half the change as Gabriella's gifts. Still, she was determined to be a woman of courage. Not to win back the Prince's heart, though his desertion still stung. But rather, to prove herself worthy of her people. Her parents. And their legacy.

As each footfall brought her closer to home, every step also reminded her of the last day with her family. She searched for anger at her father. Disappointment in her mother. But Hannah found only anguish.

She felt their torture — parents forced to make an unbearable choice. She could not imagine sacrificing her child for the protection of her people. Tears streamed down Hannah's face. She felt the vast weight of decisions carried by those who rule.

As the twin born first, Hannah was groomed for the role of Queen. Hannah had focused on the kindnesses she might show people. The generosity in a soothing word. She never considered the horrific choices. Nor the heartbreaking costs.

Hannah began to doubt whether she was strong enough. She wanted to be worthy. But she also did not wish to relinquish her happiness. After years of suffering at the hands of the Great Prince, she resented the thought of giving up what she loved.

She glanced at Syrena. Staring for a painful moment, then quickly looked away.

The closer Hannah got to her ancestral home, the more she believed this was not her destiny. She may have been first, but she was not the twin with the fearsome spirit. Yet, she was the one who understood the intimate tasks of tending to people. She felt a kinship with her mother's gifts. And she missed the companionship of court. Unlike her sister, who hated being confined. And loathed the politics of diplomacy.

Hannah chided herself, as she gazed at the beleaguered castle. She was leaping over the immediacy of battle to the reassuring comfort of a home. There was no need to tend to a court anytime soon. Would she never learn? Why was she always dreaming? Hannah fumed at her soul's insistence on gazing at a far-off future at the cost of the painful present.

Why was she not more like her sister? Brave. Brash. Practical. Why did she always wish for the soft and elusive scenario instead of the sword-wielding adventure? Why did she wait for others to take the difficult actions while she sat on the sidelines?

The closer Hannah drew to the door, the more unease she felt. What was she doing here? This was not her home. This was a pile of forsaken rock. If she were wise, she would flee this place. Leave the reclamation to Gabriella's strong hands. The sister with the warrior spirit.

Hannah stopped. Staring down the collection of stones that was her home. She thought of the vision that kept her alive all those lonely nights with the Prince. All those dark days in the Palace. The image had been her solace. A memory that no longer existed. And she was about to face the truth.

Hannah held her breath. Ready to flee. When Syrena stepped in front of her, with a fierce gaze. Hannah's intense confusion kept her from being able to read Syrena's intention.

"You have come to the threshold, my queen," Syrena said. "This is not the moment to doubt your journey. Or to cower from choice. You were called for a reason. Whether it is the call of your parents, your people, or your own heart. You must discover what that is."

Tears welled in Hannah's eyes, as she looked from Syrena to Tobias. Each stood firm in support. They acknowledged the risks. The possibility of death. And still, they swore their lives to her. She did not feel worthy of their loyalty. Yet their strength poured into her veins. If she had lost faith, this was not the time to allow doubt to guide her path.

So, Hannah nodded. Syrena stepped aside. And Tobias loaded an arrow in his bow.

With her heart pounding in her chest, Hannah pushed on the scullery door. Feeling the long-awaiting portal give way — she stepped into the darkness.

TWENTY-TWO

Finally, after a strong exhale, Gabriella spoke.

"You may be right, young rebel," Gabriella said. "I have fled too long. Hiding my face when the people need more than folk stories to inspire them."

"I didn't mean —" Katrin began, only to be stopped by Gabriella's raised hand.

"Maybe not," Gabriella replied. "But Ariana, the fire goddess, spoke through you. To proffer her firebrand of truth. And to awaken the warrior in my soul."

Gabriella stood and cast her eyes at the stars. Giving thanks to the heavens. Then turned her burning gaze on Katrin.

"And I have no choice but to answer. Tonight, we ride!"

Gabriella held her breath as they rode through the darkness into town. Though Katrin had asked for a night away from the saddle and a bowl of hot soup, Gabriella forced them to ride past every small village that might have offered lodging.

She did not want the first rumours of her appearance to take long to spread. She needed the spark to leap to a blaze. Building enough momentum to sustain a constant fire, no matter how many henchmen the Great Prince sent through the mountains.

In truth, she had another mission — an urgent mission — that she could not share with Katrin. The time had come to find the wise one. The man who would guide her to her vision. Gabriella had received this wisdom in her dreams.

A sign that brought her to this humble town.

Gabriella kept her hood over her face as she rode down the packed dirt cutting through the town centre. She would maintain anonymity until she was ready to reveal herself.

As she assessed the town folk, Gabriella found that she was grateful the Sorceress was chasing Adrian. He was capable of fighting such dark magic. If the witch had been sent to these mountain towns, she would have demolished them in one breath.

She peered out from her hood, keeping Katrin in her sights. Gabriella wanted to ensure Katrin's safety. The young woman was too intrigued by Gabriella's new form. She feared Katrin would risk her life to stay by Gabriella's side. More from a sense of adventure than fierce loyalty.

Gabriella sighed to herself. *These years of solitude have me suspicious of everyone. My trusted family is far away. And now, I am more paranoid than ever. Especially without Casmire to keep me calm.*

Katrin pulled up next to her. "Do not be afraid of my motives," Katrin said. "I am no traitor."

Once again, the girl surprised Gabriella with unspoken gifts. What else did she not comprehend about Katrin? What abilities were waiting to develop?

"I do not believe you to be a traitor," Gabriella replied in a hushed tone. "But you have survived through your wits for these many years. That instinct does not disappear overnight. No matter how much you enjoy my company."

"You expect me to choose survival over fealty," Katrin said. "How is that not seeing me as a traitor?"

Katrin's declaration drew stares from townspeople stumbling home from the public house. They exchanged whispers, arguing whether they should fetch the lawman.

"Lower your voice," growled Gabriella. "These folk may be more accustomed to strangers than the tiny mountain villages but that does not mean they trust them."

"Fine," whispered Katrin. "But you are evading my question."

Gabriella did not reply right away. She needed to feel the reaction of the townspeople before addressing Katrin. She sent waves of calm in their direction, soothing their ruffled feathers. Assuring them that the mysterious riders were harmless travellers passing through, with no intention of harm.

Once she heard them resume light banter and laughter, Gabriella locked her gaze on Katrin. She was torn between admiring the girl for her directness and being annoyed that she questioned her. She was her former liege.

Then the truth struck Gabriella like an arrow to the heart. She was no longer a princess. Her family no longer ruled. And she had no claim whatsoever on Katrin.

"You have no reason to be loyal to me," Gabriella said, keeping her gaze forward. "Indeed, you have no reason to ride by me now that you are safe from pursuers. Yet, here you are. When we have no kingdom left to call our own. And no homeland to which we can return. So why would you not preserve yourself at the cost of my freedom?"

Despite years of mistrust, Katrin was shaken by Gabriella's words. The offence ran deep.

For a fleeting moment, Katrin hated her. Yet, in truth, Katrin was not sure whether she would trade her closest friend for a night of safety. Such had been her life since fleeing Granamore.

Gabriella's instincts were not wrong, Katrin conceded, gazing at the townspeople. She simply had the courage to say them aloud. Challenging her intention before she was knee-deep in a mired choice — between betrayal and honour.

Even as they had approached town, Katrin had assessed the easiest targets and the escape routes. Despite her toughness, Katrin's heart squeezed at the thought of straying so far from the idealistic child she had once been.

Katrin wondered whether she no longer was the child who served King Algor? Was she only left with the meagre destiny of a dishonourable thief? Using the brutal world as justification for her behaviour?

They rode side by side in silence. Each caught in her dilemma. Gabriella directed her grey steed down a narrow laneway off the main road. She had not travelled through this town for many months, but she knew of a small inn hidden from prying eyes.

Few knew of its existence, for the innkeeper did not promote its location. Gabriella had only found the inn through Adrian's direction. She felt confident the owner would provide her with lodging. And though Katrin still followed, Gabriella was not sure she would stay the night.

Gabriella continued to the far end of the path. When she stopped in front of a silver-toned building with no sign. Katrin stared as Gabriella swung off her steed and left the grey stallion untethered.

Then she looked up at Katrin.

"I am staying here for the night," Gabriella said. "I must attend to some business. Perhaps for a few days. But by the rise of the new moon, the world *will* change. I will emerge from the shadows. And the Prince shall heed my challenge."

Katrin narrowed her gaze. Working her hands on her reins. She readied her steed. Unsure what to do.

"You think I mean to harm you," Gabriella remarked. "But this is your decision to make. If you stay with me, you must swear your fealty. And I expect you to keep that promise in the face of exile. Torment. Even death."

Gabriella lowered her gaze. She withdrew into her private world. "I realize this is not an easy request. Few would accept. Even fewer could swear such a promise. Knowing the allegiance might call death to her door." She felt Katrin recoil, preparing to run.

"You were once a loyal and valiant servant, Katrin," Gabriella said. "And though you might find offence in that term now, I believe you have the mettle to be a powerful ally. If you elect to stand at my side."

Gabriella looked up with a fierce and demanding gaze. "The choice is yours."

And with the swift turn of her cloak, Gabriella vanished before Katrin's eyes. Spooking Katrin's horse. He reared up, forcing Katrin to close her eyes and cling to his back.

After she brought him to the ground, her heart pounded, and her eyes swept back and forth. Seeking the Messenger who had stood before her only seconds ago.

But she was left only with an empty alleyway. And a life-altering choice.

PART III

THE
WARRIOR

TWENTY-THREE

HANNAH'S EYES STRAINED against the night, the ink black darkness heightening her other senses.

Designed to be secure, the main floor of the castle was almost impenetrable to daylight. So, without candles, Hannah could hardly see her own hand. She felt the presence of Syrena on her left and Tobias on her right. Syrena saw better in the dark and Tobias had a hunter's instinct. They pressed close, reassuring Hannah.

She edged forward. The floorboards felt familiar. Each worn patch. Every seam between the wood. Hannah knew them all by heart. She sensed their warmth, calling to her feet. Her childhood held more power in its splintered essence than a handful of torturous years.

As a girl, Hannah had forged intimate contact with this kitchen. Dancing in circles. Running from flirtatious boys. Teasing her sister from one end of the cutting block. The cook scolding them. And the scullery maids laughing at their antics.

Her heart burst with memories — full of mischief and joy. Gabriella was so bold and, yet, so easy to provoke. Her sister wore her earnest heart on her sleeve. And Hannah loved nothing more than to taunt her. Especially since Hannah held the position of oldest. She lauded that over Gabriella. Touting her superior wisdom.

The girls spent their hours arguing over which was the most honourable pursuit in life. Hannah on the side of love. Gabriella on the side of adventure. She smiled in the darkness. Feeling the rush of memory flow over her like a long lost friend. Hannah was relieved that she could not see the current state of her beloved home.

She was spared the distraction, giving her room to connect before being confronted with the echoes of war. Hannah inched forward. Feeling her way. She was alert for intruders, yet more afraid of what she might feel. She bumped into a table, startling her companions.

As the table vibrated from impact, a wave of cinnamon and nutmeg floated through the air. Hannah breathed deep. Then restrained a burst of laughter, as she was overcome by the sensory rush of love. She recalled pilfering fresh baked buns from the cook's table. Gabriella running ahead as diversion and Hannah sneaking in for the attack.

She giggled. And felt Tobias tense and Syrena hold her breath. Hannah covered her mouth to muffle the sound. *Focus,* Hannah admonished herself. You cannot gallop down memory lane if there are mercenaries hidden in the castle halls.

But her heart refused to listen. Each step resonated with joy. As though the castle celebrated the return of her long lost child. Hannah's soul was positively alight.

Shining in the dark like a firefly during mating season, she wondered whether she cast them all in a spotlight. Illuminated for the whole world — good or bad — to see. Yet she could not restrain her joy. Her elation. Her assurance that this was where she was meant to be.

Then, as though an arrow pierced her chest in mid-flight, Hannah was struck by the notion that the call she heard was not from a person but from the building — her castle.

Was it you who called me? Hannah asked the surrounding walls, protecting her thoughts from Syrena. She felt foolish. Reaching out to the castle. Regardless of her dark possession by the Hidden Palace, she still defied the idea of a sentient building.

Syrena believed that the Palace took hold of them and pitted them against each other. She insisted that Gabriella's arrival distracted the Palace, requiring enough magical resources that Syrena and Hannah were given an opportunity to break free. Had they not run, Syrena was convinced that they would have been possessed again. Hannah was not so sure.

She could not determine whether the Palace was its own creature or the creation of years of hatred, resentment, and despair. Surely, it was a clever curse that pulsed through the Palace, not a live being. A long-buried spell, worked into the mortar with blood — forging a monstrosity devised to protect a demented King.

Hannah moved deeper, close to the foyer that bridged the servants' area and the royal domain. She felt cooler. The weight of the world hung heavy in the air as she approached. Certainly, as children they must have felt this, Hannah thought. And yet, they were lucky — suspended between the generosity of servants and the refined wisdom of their parents.

Hannah sighed as she relived the hesitation she felt as a child, interrupting her parents. Knowing they loved her. Feeling their adoration. Yet always an arm's length away. When Hannah needed advice, she sought out the maids and footmen. Even more as she grew older and the burden of impending war lurked outside their borders.

She dared not bother her parents with the qualms of a teenage girl. Though her needs seemed urgent at the time, Hannah felt her mother's impatience. The Queen struggled to listen to her daughter after tending to farmers who grieved stolen children and herdsmen who reported dead bodies in the mountain passes.

Many a night, Hannah lurked outside her parents' bedchamber. She was sent away many times before the Master Guard took pity on her. Hannah suspected he felt she deserved to know what was coming. Against his orders, he let her listen at the thick oak door. The King and Queen did not wish their children to feel their burden. But, one day, Hannah would be asked to rule. How else would she understand what was expected?

As Hannah snapped back to the present, she stepped across broken crockery. Smashed. Littering the threshold. She pressed her hand on the door, ready to push into the royal domain, when a chill rippled down her arm. Stopping her in her tracks.

Startled, Hannah pulled her hand away. A whisper flitted past her ears. Words so faint, she did not hear them. As though their secret was spoken into the wind.

Tobias readied his bow and nudged Syrena, knowing the two women shared a silent communication. A valuable skill given that speaking was dangerous. Syrena nodded. Assured that Tobias would feel her motion, even if he did not see it.

What is wrong? Syrena asked.

Nothing, Hannah assured her. Yet Hannah did not move forward. Nor did she renew contact with the door. She stood completely still.

Sometimes your feet must cross where your heart is not yet ready to go, Syrena replied.

Hannah wondered whether these were Syrena's words or guidance that she channeled. Maybe Hannah's ancestors whispered to Syrena, since their relation was unable to hear them. A chill ran up Hannah's spine. She remembered her teachers saying the identical words hours before she was betrothed to the Great Prince.

Was this a foreboding message? Hannah wondered. Should I flee as far from this place as possible? But her feet stayed anchored. Her heart pounded in anticipation. And her soul…

Oh, her soul!

Hannah realized it positively cried out for contact. Reaching for the nest that held her from first breath to heartbreaking departure. She could not explain a single sensation pulsing through her body. She felt pulled to touch the door. Not just touch it, but hold her hand to the wood as though she sought wisdom from the oldest tree in the world. The tree of life.

Hannah reached forward. Feeling for the ancient grain. Her palm crossed a seemingly infinite abyss before making contact with warm wood. She held her hand to the surface. Not pushing. Nor pulling. She focused on silencing the doubts in her mind.

This time, the whispers landed.

Welcome home, my child, came the voice. *I have waited many moons for your return.*

Chills swept Hannah's body. She kept her hand on the door, though her mind screamed to run. What trick was this? Was this a ghost? Was it her grandmother? Another relative?

Hannah's mind raced ahead with terrifying conclusions. Still, her hand held a relaxed connection with the old door. Despite her myriad doubts, Hannah felt a deep comfort.

She wanted to curl up against the ancient surface. Was this something she did as a child? Hannah wondered, struggling to remember. Did it bring her comfort when nightmares riddled her nights?

My love, Syrena interrupted her thoughts, *why do you wait?*

All is well, Hannah replied. *Or… all is …* She lost her words.

Syrena waited, sensing a challenge had been issued. One she could not take on, no matter how deeply she wanted to bear the weight of Hannah's dilemma.

Hannah felt Syrena's courage. Her desire to throw herself on any fire that threatened her loved one. Echoing memories of Gabriella charging into danger without hesitating for a moment.

She was determined to be brave. Hannah was not the steadfast warrior breaching the frontlines. But she had come this far on inner valour.

Who are you? Hannah asked, her heart thumping against its cage.

You know, came the mysterious response. *Search your soul.*

Riddles! exclaimed Hannah. *I travelled treacherous mountains and abandoned forests. Breaking a vow to my sister and endangering my friends to be offered riddles?*

Recalling her recent journey, Hannah realized how brave she truly was. Few would return to the place she was most hunted. Where she was given to the most treacherous man in their lands. None would have defied the Messenger. Trusting her instinct above all else.

Hannah felt her blood boil. She had not faced personal annihilation to be denied! She stood in her birthplace. The land of her ancestors. She was regent and defender of her people. Ready to strike down any that might challenge her authority!

She was the rightful Queen! A chill shot down Hannah's spine as though lightning had christened her.

The castle... whispered the far reaches of her consciousness. *The castle speaks.* Hannah felt terror and exhilaration rush through her. Sending contradictory impulses.

She froze, hand on the spruce door, terrified that she might — once again — be possessed. Yet feeling sure this force was nothing like the Hidden Palace.

This voice belonged to the loving maternal being that coached Hannah's first steps, rejoiced at her first kiss, and mourned each day since she was sacrificed to the Prince.

This voice was none other than the spirit of the castle.

Hannah fell to her knees. Pressed her body to the door. And wept.

TWENTY-FOUR

GABRIELLA FOLLOWED HER INSTINCT, stepping down the narrow stone steps. She descended into darkness with nothing but her wisdom as a guide.

She had dreamt of this meeting many times. Though she never imagined it would be in a dank cellar. But on arrival at the Inn, Patrick instructed her that she was awaited below. Gabriella knew that the time for this meeting was at hand.

A shiver ran up her spine. She understood that though her feet descended into what felt like the lower levels of the Inn, she was passing through a gateway. Protected by magic. So no passerby could stumble into this room.

Her foot reached forward for the next step. And found a dirt floor. She closed her eyes. Her sight would do her no favours in this darkness. She must reach forward from her heart. And trust that if the Wise One deemed the time right, she would meet him.

Gabriella focused on her breath. Hearing only her foot landing on the dirt. Brushing against the floor. Then the soft intake of air. Her own breath. She detected no other sound in the room. But that did not give her confidence that she was alone.

As her mind grew quiet, she sensed the pulse of another. Slow and steady. Waiting. Perched like a falcon in the highest branches of a cedar tree. The embodiment of patience. Watching with keen eyes.

Am I the prey? Her stomach rustled with fear. Am I being tested? If I fail, will he refuse to reveal himself?

Gabriella breathed out her fear. She could not let it rule the day. Though fear was her constant companion, she had trained it to follow rather than lead.

In that moment, she understood her course. She walked toward the pulse. Approaching carefully. Aware of the blade tucked in her belt beneath her cloak. Gabriella sharpened her senses. And listened closer to her heart. Trusting its wisdom. Heeding its rhythm.

With each step, she sensed the other being waiting. She felt the many possibilities of his reaction. Like ripples in a storm. Determining how to receive her approach.

"Halt," the voice said. Startling Gabriella. Her hand touched her blade.

"You will not need that," he said. "Did Patrick not instruct you to leave your weapons behind?"

But Gabriella did not move her hand. She wished to see his face.

"He did not neglect his duty," Gabriella replied. "I ignored his words." Gabriella was not going to disarm herself without knowing his intentions. Or if this was, in truth, her Guide.

"Ah, but you know my purpose, Gabriella," he continued. "Or you would not be here."

"No," Gabriella replied, "I know *my* purpose. I have seen you only in dreams and visions. You must speak yours for it to be true."

"And if I speak it, in the darkness, without you seeing my eyes," he said, "will you believe me? Or will your hand stay true to your weapon?"

Gabriella paused. Her mind argued that she should not need to see his face. She should be capable of detecting deception without the guidance of her eyesight. But her stomach clenched and her heart pulled back.

Have I been tricked? Misled? What if this is a trap set by the Great Prince? I need to see his face. Only my dreams can uncover the truth.

"And what if your dreams were the trick?" he asked.

"Stop that!" Gabriella declared. "You are clever enough to sense my thoughts. Well done, trickster. But you are not courageous enough to show your face!"

"Nor am I foolish enough to be goaded by a young girl's challenge," he replied.

Gabriella's temper flared. Her grip tightened on her blade as she berated herself for falling prey to her wistful belief in a Guide. A wise one who might show her the path to defeating the Great Prince. Her body flushed with embarrassment. She felt as ridiculous as a naïve maiden who believed in gallant rescue by a faraway knight.

She turned abruptly. And sprinted back through the darkness to the staircase. Fleeing this trap before she was struck down with a bolt of magic.

As her feet reached the bottom stairs, the soft glow of sunrise bloomed around her. Gentle light illuminated the stairs. And Gabriella stopped, turning gracefully on the step.

She was perched on a staircase, with the upper steps still

connected to a doorway. Beneath her, the last step met with dirt that transitioned into sweet grass. Her eyes followed the grass, toward tiny specks of lilybells and nectarblossoms, wrapped in the sacred circle of a birch grove. Her face filled with amazement.

Gabriella stared at birches that reached into high, clear skies, reflecting soft shades of pink and orange, marking the dawn. At the farthest reach of the grove, leaning against a white birch taller than any she had ever seen, was her Guide.

"Allow me to introduce myself," he said. "I am Gideon."

Gabriella lowered her foot onto the dirt. She stood at the edge of the stairs, her heart and mind at war. Her heart called her forward yet her mind screamed this was a trap.

She leveled a sharp gaze at Gideon. Feeling into the illusion. Determined to figure out if he was lulling her into a sense of safety. For nothing calmed Gabriella like the soft embrace of a forest. And she needed to be clear.

"Have you been without trust for so long," Gideon asked, "that you cannot allow yourself even an hour of reprieve?"

"No," she replied, circling her way cautiously toward him. Her fingers still twitching to hold her knife.

Gideon watched her. His stance relaxed. His gaze bemused. Yet Gabriella felt the steel of strength beneath his approachable exterior.

"Then we are not going to get far," Gideon said. He stood straight, moving away from the tree. As he stirred, Gabriella caught the soft shimmer of light. As though he were surrounded by a cloak of starlight. Visible only when he shifted.

Was he even here? Or was she witnessing a projection from far away? Her mind grew more perplexed, even as her heart grew calmer. Why could she not let go? She wanted to trust him. But all of her training countered the decision. Too much could be lost.

"Serafina and Claudius served you well. Teaching you to guard against enemies. They understood this skill would keep you alive. But they could not foresee the faculty that would be required for you to win the faith of others. And that is trust."

The shimmering around Gideon grew brighter. And Gabriella was seized by the fear that she had lost her chance. Had let doubt defeat this opportunity. Giving in to her shadow.

"Wait," she called out, running toward him. "Stay!"

"You cannot set aside your weapon for mere minutes, so little do you trust," replied Gideon. "And without trust, you are not ready to lead the Great Lands."

He faded from her sight. The shimmering edge of his body glowed brighter as the core of his being slowly disappeared.

"I need your help!" Gabriella insisted, as she hurried toward his position.

Gideon tilted his head. Eyeing her as he vanished.

"That remains to be seen," he replied.

And was gone. Taking the sunlight and birch grove with him.

Leaving Gabriella alone in the middle of the dark root cellar.

TWENTY-FIVE

KATRIN SWALLOWED HARD, stranded in the back streets of a town she did not recognize.

She gazed around as the last wisps of daylight disappeared. Katrin was not sure what she might find in the dark, back corners of a lower mountain town. She had not left the high mountains for several years. She suspected the lowlifes were different closer to the populated cities. Less opportunistic. Possibly rougher.

Katrin swung off her horse. As much as she wished to flee and never give Gabriella another thought, this was not one of those moments. She had been handed a chance.

Then her well-honed cynicism spoke up. *The world we live in does not offer chances. This realm belongs to the survivors. The ones who take without asking questions. The Great Prince outlawed hope many years ago. You would do well to remember that allying yourself with the Messenger is only a chance to cut your life brutally short.*

Katrin pulled her steed to the hidden side of the secretive house. There were no indications that this was an inn. No signs of anyone else staying here. What kind of place had Gabriella led her to, only to abandon her at dusk? Was this a cruel test? Or worse, a set-up? Eliminating the one person who knew the Messenger's whereabouts?

She tucked deeper into the shadows. Ready to spook her horse and send it as a galloping decoy if she needed time to run. But as Katrin realized she was alone, she opened to this secluded corner. And with each passing moment, she only felt safer. As though Gabriella had found the single solitary alleyway that might afford Katrin space to consider her offer.

As a sense of safety dropped around her like a protective cloak, Katrin wanted to curl up and rest. She was hungry and tired. The endless days of riding and fitful woodland sleeps left her vulnerable. Her body was desperate for a respite.

She hitched her horse to a nearby post. Secure enough to keep him close but loose enough that if threatened, he could yank free with a strong pull. She sat at the edge of the inn, out of sight. And pulled the last morsel of bread from her pocket.

As she ate, a feud was struck in her heart between courage and bitterness.

Long ago, Katrin was a woman of high ideals. Raised with the kindness of King Algor and Queen Isabel, she had only known rulers whose best interests were to serve their people. If she had a question, she could approach them. If she doubted their policies, she could ask for the justification.

But the days since being cast out as an orphan, taught Katrin that the world was not kind. People were cruel and wretched and put their own needs first. She had learned the hard truth of betrayal. And she resented Gabriella's parents for not preparing her for the darkness.

I owe them nothing, she thought. *Indeed, they owe me for their cruel failure! Did they not anticipate the destructive wrath of the*

Great Prince? Did they not trust we would fight him at their side? They abandoned us, leaving us vulnerable. Sending their daughters to safety while we fought the Prince's henchmen.

Katrin chewed her bread. Her stomach growling for more as though it, too, wished to tear apart the royal family. But as hard as she fought to hang on to her resentment, the more Katrin recalled that her regents had warned her.

Much to her surprise, Queen Isabel pulled her aside one evening. Gripping her arm with a fierce strength. "Katrin, my darling," the Queen said, with tears in her eyes, "You must flee this place. Find protection in a neighbouring kingdom. Granamore is no longer safe."

Her gaze looked haunted, though Katrin had not heard anything but assurance from her fellow servants. They believed the Great Prince's lies. But Queen Isabel saw the truth. And wished all those under her care to be safe. Especially the young ones. "Being close to us is no longer a wise place to be. You must seek your future elsewhere."

Then she released Katrin's arm and disappeared down the hallway. Already a spirit in her own home.

Katrin had been young and self-doubting. Believing the Queen spoke from dislike. That, somehow, Katrin had displeased her sovereign. Each day after, she had only seen the Queen's stern looks as proof of the regent's irritation.

As she looked back, Katrin saw that the Queen desperately wished to save a young woman who reminded her of her daughter. Katrin shifted, as she realized the King and Queen had made the greatest sacrifice. They gave up their oldest daughter in hopes the offering would appease the Great Prince. Protecting their people and preserving the legacy of their Kingdom.

But the Great Prince was not a man of small measures. He took the bribe with one hand and crushed her homeland with the other. Ensuring all were either exiled or slaughtered. The Prince had ripped hope from the chest of every citizen and left anguish in its stead.

So effective were his tactics, that Katrin had foresworn all she was taught under the rule of King Algor and believed only the brutal vision of the Great Prince. How had she given up so much in so little time? How had Gabriella, the one woman who had the most to resent, held on to love?

Katrin flinched as she heard footsteps approach the other side of the inn's door. She tucked deeper into the shadows. And pulled a sharp blade from the holster at her waist.

The door cracked open. Katrin saw neither hand nor face. She pulled farther back around the corner. Preferring to hide and strike, rather than be confronted. She calmed her breath. Drew inside and steadied her nerves.

"You need not fear me," came the voice. Katrin jumped but held tight to her hiding place.

How did he know she was here? Katrin's thoughts threw her into disarray. She should run. But then, how would Gabriella find her? And what kind of warrior would that be? Fleeing from a voice in an alley. Hardly an ally worthy of the

Messenger's side!

Katrin tensed her muscles. Readying for attack. Either way, she would be fighting for her liberation.

"I was sent by your hooded friend," continued the stranger. Katrin scoffed. That described every traveller. She would not be fooled by a bandit, tempting her then slitting her throat.

No, Katrin thought. If this were a test, she would prove she was worthy of battle. That she could take a life. She had not been forced to do so since she had been attacked in the stables of a drunken town, not long after she fled her home. That was her first step in hardening to the world. Her welcome to the new days of the Great Prince.

After that day, she had two choices — deception or killing. Deceit left fewer morsels for lawmen to follow. And won her more money. But if needed, she would steel her stomach to kill again. Katrin clutched her blade. Bringing it close to her waist so she would have the most power.

If she thrust the edge in the right spot, her opponent would drop in seconds. Freeing her to run. Her mercenary companion taught her that trick, in exchange for a night in bed.

She had run out of options in a hard-bitten town. So, she traded her body for protection. Then fled before the sun rose. She thought the rogue had taken a shining to her. But was not confident that affection would win out over his instincts.

Since that night, Katrin grew skilled in tempting a man to believe he could bed her. Then leveraging drink and distraction to get what she wanted without forfeiting her flesh. Laying with a stranger made her vulnerable beyond measure. And *no* man would ever own her. The mere thought consumed Katrin with rage.

Good, she thought. You will need that fury soon enough. Her body coiled, ready for the fight. Katrin edged her way toward the open door.

"Put away your claws," said the voice. "I come in peace. And in possession of your supper."

This was a new trick, indeed! Katrin might have laughed. But she felt a wave of warmth drift across the night air. And within seconds, the heartwarming scent of fresh bread and hot pumpkin soup reached her. Katrin closed her eyes and pressed her back against the cold stone. Her body shook with a chill.

What demon was this? Sent to test her! Katrin lamented and her traitorous stomach growled. The man around the corner laughed. Infuriating Katrin. She pounced into the street. Holding her blade close, eyes ablaze with indignation.

As she landed, she was struck by his youth. She assumed he would be an older man, preying on her inexperience. But this lad was no older than she. Seventeen years at most, and appearing even younger. Which might account for his bravado, she thought, then shook off the compassion. She would need her anger if she were to —

Her thought disappeared, as her eyes strayed to the bowl in his hand. Steam rose off the brim, filled with the rustic hue of pumpkin soup and topped with fresh cream. Tucked in his other hand was a loaf of fresh chestnut bread, laden with the salty scent of butter. Her senses were overwhelmed by the mix of cinnamon and nutmeg.

Katrin's mouth salivated. Her senses had abandoned the fight. Still she clutched her knife, unsure what was happening. Her body sent conflicting signals to her mind.

The young man watched her struggle. And softened his voice, as though speaking to a wild animal. Coaxing it in from the cold, wet night. "I cannot hand these to you unless you relinquish your blade," he said.

Katrin's eyes snapped. She would not be duped by such trickery. No matter how empty her stomach. Nor how weak her knees grew. Charity did not exist in the Great Lands. The sentiment was washed away with each wave of blood wrought by the Prince.

"Back away, rogue," she growled. "I will stick you with this knife. You cannot tempt me with your poisoned fare. Nor deceive me with stories of my companion. I have wiped this blade on the guts of men much larger than you. "

"Rest assured," he replied, "That I am not hired for my skills of slaying, whether by weapon or by feast. My father owns this inn. And the longer I remain outside, the more he will believe I have come to harm."

The young man lowered the bowl to the ground. Placing the wrapped bread carefully across the brim, and backing away. "I hoped you would join us inside. But if you are to persist in threatening my life, I must take care. And not heed the words of Mistress Gabriella."

As quickly as he appeared, he slipped back through the door. Leaving Katrin speechless.

Within seconds, she scooped up the bowl. Devouring the soup and tearing into the bread. The butter melted across her tongue. And her eyes filled with tears. She was so touched by the generosity of the young man.

As she emptied the bowl, her senses were suddenly overwhelmed with memory. Katrin had tasted this soup before, she was sure. She felt the love radiate from her stomach, as surely as she had tasted the spices. In truth, she had not touched such exquisite food since…

And the vessel fell from her hands, crashing into the ground.

TWENTY-SIX

HANNAH HAD NO WORDS for all that she mourned. She did not care that her life might be in danger. Her heart fell to pieces.

As Hannah felt the comforting presence that nurtured her steps from birth to adulthood, she unburdened her soul of the pain she had carried for the past five years. She cried for the loss of her parents — kind and generous leaders. Though they may be alive, they were lost to these lands. Hiding far from the place that needed their valiant hearts.

Hannah grieved the guidance they might have given her. Their nurturing hands, directing her to become a regent in her own right. Learning from their wisdom. Leaning on their strength.

She ached for the loss of her innocence. The years she could not remember. Sacrificed to the darkness of the Hidden Palace. Her heart broke when she wished only to forget those years. To pretend that they never happened.

Most of all, she grieved for her people. For the maids and footmen and cooks and ladies-in-waiting and knights without a King to keep them safe. Torn from their community. Forced from this blessed home. Robbed of food and protection.

They scattered to the winds. Slaughtered and raped and hunted. All by her so-called husband in the name of ruining everything she held dear. All for the sake of power.

Hannah's tears stopped. Her eyes dried. And the rage in her heart burned like a wild fire. She felt the flames leap in her chest. Kindled and prodded over years of captivity.

She saw all that happened in grotesque detail. This was the consequence of her gifts. Just as she could perceive the future, she could as easily turn the lens and view the past. Her people suffered dearly in the destruction wrought by the Great Prince. First by his soldiers. Then by his mercenaries. And last, by the cowardly jackals that picked apart the vulnerable when no one was left to defend them.

Hannah rose to her feet. For now, she kept her emotions under control. She did not wish to risk their safety by releasing the tidal wave of her torment. *Tell me, ancient one,* Hannah said, *why you called me back to this place. What could possibly be left for me to see?*

Ah, dear one, the castle replied, *that is for you to discover. There is great healing at hand for you. And your people.*

Yes, Hannah replied. *But we are far from the days of healing. My sister and I are hunted. The Great Prince holds more power than ever. And our allies are scattered. How can you claim there is healing at hand?*

Hannah had risked everything to come home. She had put her dearest ones in danger. For what? A reunion? Some tears? She demanded more than sorrowful remembrances and wistful memories. She wanted justice! She demanded answers!

"Tell me why I am here!" commanded Hannah, thrusting the door open. *Slam!* The heavy wood crashed into the stone wall, sending waves of reverberation through the castle.

Reacting from instinct, Tobias pulled Hannah down. Shielding her with his body. And just in time. For arrows flew over their heads. Hannah tucked closer to the floor as Tobias leapt to the right side of the doorway, and took aim.

Syrena sprang forward, diving into the great room. Drawing the attack in her direction, so Tobias could spot the assailants. His eyes raked the corridors and the impressive stairway. Fighting the dim light and deep shadows.

The air grew quiet.

And for a moment, the arrows ceased. Syrena crouched by the wall, listening for the scurrying of feet, but not a sound reached her sharp ears. She motioned to Tobias to come forward, as she kept a watchful eye.

Tobias pulled Hannah behind him through the door. Then backing her against the wall, safe in the deep, hall shadows. Fading daylight cascaded from windows high above, creating a soft and surreal effect, as though they had stepped into a land ruled by magic. The light dappled the stairway, but fell into darkness in the nooks of the corridor. Impenetrable without hallway candles to cheer the corners.

Syrena gestured towards the passageway and stone staircase. Tobias nodded, keeping his back to Hannah and his bow loaded. And then Syrena moved. Down the corridor, dipping into the faint light to draw any potential fire.

The air was heavy with tension. Not an arrow was fired. But each side felt the presence of the other, despite being blind to their location. Tobias skirted the edge of the corridor, guiding Hannah forward in silence. His arrow tracking the edge of the upper hallway.

Tobias surmised their attacker was tucked behind the upper

balustrade. Using the marble column to hide his whereabouts. Tobias wished he had the ability to communicate as Hannah did with Syrena — that would make them a formidable team.

Regardless, he had faith Syrena would route out the villain. Though his fingers itched to be the ones to bag the prize. He considered retreating to the kitchen, but could not be assured that Hannah would be safe as he and Syrena sought out the villains.

A sudden screech echoed through air. Hannah jumped and Tobias reacted with a sharp swinging of his shooting arm. Syrena took advantage of the distraction to run up the stairs. A heavy *clunk!* and soft *squeak* announced that the oak door landed back into place. Rusted hinges singing out for dire need of oil.

Hannah might have laughed at the absurd sound were her life not in the balance. Still, the noise woke her senses, and brought her into the fray. Shifting her from cowering princess to alert sentry.

Tobias refused to be pinned in a corner. But he had no way of knowing where Syrena was. Then a plan became clear. Tobias edged Hannah along the hallway. She followed without question. Trusting his physical guidance and tracker's instinct. With skills well-honed in the forest, Tobias threw his voice — ensuring their assailant would believe they still stood far behind their current position.

"Lay down your arms," Tobias ordered. "You have no right to this place."

A long silence followed. The attacker was smart enough not to move. Though Tobias sensed he was more coward than strategist. Why else would he hide in a castle waiting to shoot them in the back? Tobias scoffed. Relishing a prize without a true fight.

Tobias grinned. He had dealt with many a coward. And he knew, that above all else, they abhorred being accused of spineless actions. Tobias had found his bait.

"Were you a true man," Tobias challenged, "You would show your face."

He tapped Hannah, without taking his eyes off the upper reaches of the hall, encouraging her to continue following him.

"Even mercenaries have a code," Tobias accused. "You must be a pathetic fighter to disregard that small mark of honour."

As Tobias and Hannah made soundless progress down the hall, Tobias picked up a shift in their attacker, hidden behind the balustrade. Not a verbal response, but still an indicator that he had pierced the assailant's pride.

He wondered which insult inflicted the wound. He had made too many judgments in one statement. But no matter. Tobias had the advantage, and used it to guide Hannah across a lighted patch of hallway. Landing them in direct sight of the stairs, but tucking her back into an obscured corner as he stood guard. Seeking the coward with his arrowhead.

Where was Syrena? She could not have taken so long to climb a staircase. How long did she expect him to hold this position? He only had so many arrows. And so much patience.

Feeling his rattled nerves, Hannah touched Tobias's shoulder gently. He tilted his head to indicate he was listening. Hannah hesitated then determined her risk was for the best. Given their predicament, Tobias would forgive a minor intrusion.

Hello, Tobias. His jaw tensed but his arm did not waiver. *Hannah spoke in his mind. Do not be startled. My ability is not limited to Syrena, though she and I have a special connection.*

She felt Tobias's impatience. He was unable to project his thoughts, but she could sense his intention. *I cannot tell where Syrena is*, Hannah said. *But understand that this castle was built to confound anyone who did not know its passages well. I grew up here and even I might get lost if not paying attention. The architect was commanded to protect the royal family. As a result, the passageways are deliberately labyrinthine.*

Tobias nodded. Though it made him uncomfortable, he understood she was using her strengths — as he was — to keep them alive.

He must not count on Syrena finding the assailant. If the passageways were complex, he took comfort in assuming Syrena was safe. That way, Tobias needed only to guard Hannah.

He had ferreted out worse villains in more dangerous circumstances. He would not fail his liege now. With renewed determination, Tobias was struck with an idea. If this rat did not respond to his bait, he did not possess any allegiance. And if he did not feel any loyalty, he must not be aligned with the Great Prince!

Now I have you, thought Tobias. But he could not make a move without Hannah's understanding. He shivered at the thought that she was already listening. They would have to discuss his privacy later. For now, he needed her ability.

Hannah? he inquired, feeling ridiculous. No response.

There must be a trick to this, Tobias thought. Perhaps he needed to emphasize his need.

Hannah? He tried again, aiming the thought at her, as he might aim an arrow.

Yes, Tobias? She replied, and felt his jolt of delight in landing the shot. Hannah smiled behind his back. She, too, had excitement running through her veins. Feeling the anticipation of taking on their adversary. She despised cowering behind his back like a hapless maiden. And was thrilled to be included in the strategy.

I have a plan, Tobias said, testing his aim once more. The hunter in him was enjoying this covert communication. Though he still felt exposed.

Excellent, replied Hannah.

I need you to trust me, Tobias continued. *Follow my every command. Without question. Or hesitation. Can you do that?*

Yes, Hannah replied, though she understood what he asked was not easy.

Good, Tobias said. *Ready yourself.*

Tobias stretched his neck. Gave his arm muscles slack for a brief moment then locked them back into place. The lack of sleep over the past few days was beginning to take its toll. One quick lapse in judgment and they were all dead.

He needed a rest. But he did not have that luxury.

"I know who you are," Tobias lied. "And I know you hold no allegiance to the Great Prince. You trespass on his land. And you threaten his wife, villain."

Tobias felt Hannah cringe. He had expected such a reaction — and he needed her to stay strong. No matter what offence he spoke. "I found her on the run and am returning her to the Prince," Tobias continued. "If you threaten my prize, be sure that I will slice your throat and leave you for the wolves."

Within seconds, Tobias saw the glint of an arrow between the upper balustrades. The promise of a purse in exchange for Hannah's life was enough to prompt the rogue into foolish action. Greed. The great motivator of all cowards.

Tobias yelled to Hannah. *Run!*

Then he released his shot a moment before he heard the song of his opponent's bow. Tobias leapt out of the arrow's way and heard the *thud!* of his own missile strike. Followed by a startled yelp.

Tobias quickly gave chase to Hannah. Across the foyer, then up the stairs. He yelled, *Lead me to him!*

And Hannah, running as though she were a horse released to freedom, was only happy to oblige.

TWENTY-SEVEN

KATRIN HAMMERED ON THE INN'S DOOR. She no longer cared who heard. She wanted answers.

The young man yanked open the door, staring at Katrin as though she had gone mad.

"What is wrong with you?" He asked then searched to ensure battalions were not careening toward him with torches and swords.

"Let me in," Katrin demanded, "Or I will fetch the lawman myself."

At this, the lad smiled. Making Katrin uncomfortable. He seemed to hold more cards than she. She had no choice but to abandon her bravado. And use a far less worn tool in her belt — honesty.

"That soup," she began, hoping he would assist her. But he felt no such inclination. "I have tasted it. Long ago…" Her voice faded with the weight of memory. Katrin was not one to be nostalgic. Sentimentality was weakness. When swindlers discovered from whence she came and played that against her, she did not flinch.

But Katrin knew that soup. The woman who made it was like the mother Katrin never had.

In her life, Katrin worked under many cooks. Rarely did they care a stitch about her. More often, they berated her for being stupid. And distrusted that she did not have a family. This woman had, however, always offered compassion. Took Katrin under her wing and showed her how to cook food that tasted like love.

No more so than when she ate her special roasted pumpkin soup, laden with fresh roasted spice and decorated with a dollop of melting sour cream.

Katrin lowered her voice. "The only person capable of making that soup died seven years ago. I went to her funeral. I mourn her to this day. So tell me, little trickster, who mimics that irreplaceable soul in your kitchen."

She resisted pulling her knife. Knowing that she would only be rewarded with a door in the face. But after her story, she felt his mood shift. His face softened and he examined her closely, as though working out a puzzle.

Katrin folded her arms and glared. Yet knowing she had lost all chance of intimidation since revealing her heart. *Damn it*. This is what you get for sharing too much.

After a long wait, he opened the door wide. "Come in," he offered.

She stepped into the foyer, as he watched her.

"What?" she barked, uncomfortable with his stare. But he would not be dissuaded. And extended his hand. "My name is Patrick," he said. "You must be Katrin."

"How do you know my name?" She accused, refusing to touch his hand.

Katrin could see Patrick was weighing whether to gamble on her. This wild creature who thumped on his door and threatened his life. He had no reason to trust her. Except, she assumed, for the affirmation of the revered Messenger.

"The soup I brought you," he said, ignoring her question. "You speak of it as though it was made by hands you loved."

"It was," Katrin said, not saying more for fear her voice would break. She missed few people in this world. Truthfully, she missed only two. One was the kindhearted cook, Patrice, who took her under her wing. And the other, Katrin realized much to her surprise, was Gabriella.

"I understand," he said.

And yet, he did not move. Patrick stood in front of her in the most infuriating way. As though he expected Katrin to divulge her history. Or tell him how grateful she was to be indoors instead of hiding.

She folded her arms. Not saying a word. Forced into a ridiculous staring contest with this Patrick who suddenly seemed far older than his years. As though Katrin's story had revealed a hidden part of him that held as much sadness as she felt.

"Did you know her?" she asked.

"No," Patrick replied. "But my father speaks of her every day. With such reverence that I feel as though she lives among us. For the woman you loved was my grandmother."

The sadness overtook his eyes. And Katrin wished she had taken his hand. She stared at his fingers. Suddenly compelled to touch them. Yet unable to reach out.

Katrin looked away. And felt her heart pinch. The sensation was strange. She sensed that she had experienced something like it many years ago. But she could not recall why. She glanced again at Patrick, who gave her a tender smile.

A fierce blush crept up her cheeks. And butterflies set loose in her stomach. What feelings were these? She felt annoyed by the emotion. Why did her gaze fall to the floor like a silly maiden? What magic did this rural lad possess that struck the depths of her? She who withstood the amorous advances of charismatic charlatans and attractive hunters!

Katrin fought the sensation that rushed over her body. Furious that she could not command her senses. They ran riot like wild stallions. The more she struggled, the more fervently the scintillating feeling rushed to the edges of her fingers and toes.

She gave in — gazing at Patrick —determined to lay bare his charm. He was tall and lithe. His dark hair bore a wave, more masculine, but similar in temperament to his grandmother's long locks. Though Patrice's hair had turned grey before Katrin met her.

Patrick's attire was impeccable, if worn at the edges. And his eyes seemed that they had known as much laughter as sadness. A truth that intrigued Katrin, pulling her closer.

Until she fought the urge and looked away. Digging her nails into her palms in an attempt to wrestle back control over her heart. She did not care about people's stories! She asked about their pasts only to take advantage of their weaknesses.

And now, in the humble foyer of a rustic inn, she found herself caring about a stranger. A sensation she had not faced since fleeing home.

Nor did Katrin appreciate the predicament. She was considering the greatest choice of her life. Whether to risk heart and home for the Messenger. She did not have time for foolish feelings. Gabriella needed a warrior spirit by her side, not a blathering maid that craves stolen kisses!

Whether Patrick noticed her discomfort or the blush on her

cheek, Katrin did not know. Nor did she care. She was grateful when he cleared his throat to speak.

"Perhaps I could show you to your room?" Patrick offered, seeking out Katrin's gaze.

"I do not have one," she replied, avoiding his stare for fear of releasing more butterflies.

"But you do, Mistress Katrin," Patrick said.

"How could I —" she broke off, realizing that Gabriella must have made arrangements. "And am I alone this evening?"

"Not unless you wish to be," teased Patrick.

Were she not so affected by his presence, Katrin would have returned his jest. Volleying until he could not bear her flirtatious game a moment longer. Falling to his knees and giving her whatever she desired in exchange for her company through the night.

As it was, her palms were sweating and her pulse raced. She needed to retire. No matter that she wanted to ask Patrick about his family. Wishing to feel close to Patrice again. But Katrin could not think with this boy so close. She required all her wits to make her choice by sunrise. And so, her inquiry would have to wait.

"Take me to my room," she commanded, as though she were queen of the realm, ruling everything in her sight. When, in truth, she barely had control over her feet.

—◊◊◊—

Patrick stared for a moment, sensing that something was amiss. But he was not ready to confront this wildcat for fear she might turn her discomfort on him. Still, he hesitated.

Against all decorum, Patrick wanted to invite Katrin into the kitchen. She knew and loved his grandmother. A woman he only met as a baby, and did not remember, though he was named in her honour. His father grieved the loss every day. Still setting a place for her at every meal.

And here before him was a woman who had worked by his grandmother's side. She must have stories to tell. Secrets to reveal. Patrick longed to find out all that was hidden inside Katrin's mind. But he made her nervous. Though he could not imagine why.

The longer they stood in silence, the tenser she became. Winding like a coiled spring. Until Patrick wondered if she might explode. Strangely, he longed to reach out and touch her hand. He felt, somehow, that the gesture would calm her.

As he imagined touching her, Patrick received an unbidden vision. Katrin laughing. No longer suspicious, this Katrin was a joyful spirit. A passionate heart. With a glorious laugh that rang across courtyards. His lips curved into a smile. Enjoying the beauty of the tale.

Then, catching sight of another in the dream, Patrick jumped. Standing before Katrin was a young man. Seen from behind, but was unmistakably Patrick. Holding out wildflowers that had been crushed — looking comical as he offered them to her. He smiled as she laughed. Loving the glory of her amusement more than the ruined gesture of affection.

Patrick snapped back to the present. And stared, wide-eyed, at Katrin. *Who was this girl?* he thought. *And what was to come of their meeting?*

He wheeled around. Ready to escort her to her room.

"Follow me," Patrick said.

Leading the way at a brisk pace, he cast a glance back. Intrigued by the most enigmatic woman he had met since crossing paths with the Messenger.

TWENTY-EIGHT

HANNAH RAN, WEAVING AROUND CORNERS, like an enraged steed intent on destroying the creature that dared tread on its territory.

Tobias never expected such anger in the delicate princess.

Perhaps he had sparked a fire — and her years with the Prince had lain dormant inside like dry tinder. Awaiting a rogue match to set her outrage alight.

As much as he wanted to protect her, he needed her to be this fast. And so, against the kinder nature of his heart, Tobias held his tongue. He silently thanked the rage. Assuring his heart that she needed such an outlet. For he did not know what she suffered at the hands of the Prince.

Truth be told, he did not wish to know. For if he did, he would act, only to find himself at the Prince's door, outmanned and out-armed. A foolish knight throwing down his life for a lady's honour. Though if he ever discovered the Great Prince laid a hand on Gabriella, he would not rest until he slit the Prince's throat.

Tobias ran with renewed vigour. Catching Hannah and provoking her to run even faster. They leapt together up the last stairs. Determined to find the villain that dared cross into their sacred home and defy all that they honoured. If he could not confront the Great Prince just yet, Tobias would demand justice of the lowlife that took advantage of the Prince's destruction.

Hannah slowed and crouched as they approached the upper hallway. Tobias stepped before her, peering round the balustrade. The rogue had disappeared from his post and retreated. Hannah gestured to the corridor ahead. A dark passageway that likely held their wounded weasel with an arrow aimed in their direction.

In their fury, Hannah and Tobias had not moved with stealth. Speed overtook the need to be quiet. Time was of the essence. And they did not have the luxury of an elaborate plan. Tobias felt Hannah's impatience to confront the intruder. If he hoped to save her from her own anger, he would have to act. Fast.

Tobias bolted forward, sprinting down the hallway before Hannah could protest. He heard her steps quickly follow. Tobias sped his pace and dove around the corner, into the hallway. Expecting that his sudden movement would draw whatever fire might be aimed their way. He rolled tight against the wall and landed on his feet, pulling an arrow from his quiver and loading his bow. Ready to fire.

He was startled to see Syrena standing over a dead man. Tobias's arrow sticking out of his chest. But her hands around the man's neck. Tobias took note of his arrow — close to the heart. Enough to wound, but without the depth to have ended the miscreant's life. They were safe. The attacker's neck was broken. Tobias had wounded him. Syrena had finished the job.

Syrena looked up and saw the surprise in Tobias's face and she dropped her hold on the dead man. Fell back on her heels. Releasing the tension that had held her in its grasp. But she did not look apologetic.

Just as Tobias was about to call, Hannah came around the

corner. Walking toward Syrena. Hannah's eyes were locked on the man with the broken neck. She could not believe such a creature had held them hostage. He reminded Hannah of a disease-infested rat that was no longer accepted in the family's nest.

As she drew near, Hannah forced her gaze to Syrena. Her lover looked wild, overcome with the distress of taking a life. Seeing Syrena's torment, compassion filled her heart.

"Syrena," Hannah whispered, "Are you okay?"

Syrena nodded, though she was not ready to speak. She did not feel safe in this cryptic building that led her on a wild goose chase, down one hallway and up another. Then mysteriously leading her to this villain mere moments after Tobias skewered his heart.

Syrena placed a finger on her lips. She did not believe they were safe. Where there was one mercenary, there were sure to be more. Her eyes were wild. And her pulse pounded like a hunted rabbit.

We must watch for the others, Syrena cautioned. Her hands still twitching from the fight.

We will track them together, replied Hannah. Reaching gently for Syrena's hand. Soothing her so Syrena did not make unpredictable moves. They needed to act wisely when there were only three of them.

Tobias held back, keeping his sight on the hallway entrance and listening for approaching feet. He gave Hannah room to do what she did best — calm a frightened animal. Coaxing Syrena back. So they might forge a plan before moving deeper into the castle.

As Hannah moved Syrena away from the dead man, Tobias searched the rogue for any sign of allegiance. A marking on his bow or ink seared into his skin. But, as he had suspected, the man was a loner. Poaching unsuspecting passersby for gain.

"My lady," Tobias whispered.

"Yes, Tobias?" she replied.

Hannah knew their exchange aggravated Syrena, but they were safe in this protected corner. Their voices would not carry. And she did not wish to intrude on Tobias's mind unless absolutely necessary. She understood that the experience was jarring. Even more so for a man who was accustomed to hunting alone.

"When you pushed through the door, you addressed someone," he remarked. "Did you know there was a trespasser on the other side?"

Hannah blushed. She had put them in danger with her brash behaviour, thinking she had control over her feelings. And perhaps she did when they were in a place that did not haunt her heart. But since returning home, she had lost any semblance of being reasonable.

She sighed, unsure how to explain. Would he think her mad? Would he abandon them? Believing that the regent he once felt so loyal toward had lost her mind? And was unfit to rule herself — let alone a kingdom?

Hannah felt Syrena's gaze. As her lover's wits returned, Hannah could tell she understood Hannah's struggle. Though Syrena would not interfere. Hannah would have to decide whether to allow her servant to know something so personal.

For all that Tobias was sworn to protect her, Hannah also felt sworn to protect *him*. She was not assured that he could comprehend her talents. Nor should he be expected to carry such a burden. She would act as his queen. Even if she did not have the title.

As Tobias awaited her answer, Hannah drew confidence from her ancestors. Breathing in her birthright to the throne. Trusting the longstanding relationship between Tobias's people and her own.

"I thought my parents called me here," Hannah said. "In truth, I was not sure whether they were in the castle. But I allowed my feelings to get the better of my judgment. My heart was so desperate for answers that I acted without thought to the danger. And for risking us all, I humbly apologize."

Tobias dropped Hannah's gaze. And Hannah knew she had calculated well. Her expression of humility disarmed Tobias. Instead of questioning her further, he felt he had stepped out of place. No matter that Hannah's rash behaviour had endangered them. That was not for him to say. His role was to protect her at all costs.

—⁓—

Syrena was, however, far less gracious. She was not Hannah's servant. And had every right to be angry that her lover's irrational behaviour had risked their lives. Though Syrena was angrier that Hannah was lying to Tobias and withholding information from her.

How were they supposed to protect her if Hannah kept the truth from them? She protected her thoughts until she could be sure the killing rush had left her blood. The rage of confrontation. The surge of power. These were potent forces that overwhelmed the mind. Syrena felt the aggression abate but did not wish to mistake the after-effects for a motive to attack Hannah's judgment.

She could be responsible for her feelings, Syrena fumed, shooting an irritated look at Hannah. Syrena was less angry and more afraid. She did not like the secrecy that grew between them and wondered whether — even this far past the Great Forest — the Hidden Palace could reach them. If the Palace had reclaimed Hannah, they were in grave danger.

Syrena withdrew further, until she could gauge the truth. Eyeing her lover with a newfound suspicion. Pulling away and keeping her back to the wall.

—∞—

Though Hannah trusted her instinct, she was discomfited by Syrena's icy silence and the quiet concern from Tobias. Hannah should not isolate herself at this critical moment. They needed each other more than ever. Hannah needed to trust them. But the castle's voice — if that was what she heard — made her nervous.

Hannah wondered if she were losing her grasp on reality? What if she could not be trusted? Did the Prince hold sway over her home? Are the rumours of his allegiance to a wicked sorceress true? This might be her doing. What if the calling were a trap?

Shaking, Hannah stood and gained strength from her action. She was determined to take back the castle. She would not wallow in doubt. Nor could she afford for her companions to distrust her. She had come home for a reason.

And no one would stand in her way.

TWENTY-NINE

As Hannah led the way through the darkened halls, she felt Syrena's gaze burn into her back. She assumed that Tobias was equally concerned about her, but would not challenge her leadership. Syrena had, however, witnessed far more than Tobias could imagine.

Still, Hannah left her to fume. Truthfully, she wanted to spin around and confront her lover. Throw everything that tormented her into Syrena's face. Would she love her then? When she could not be sure of her sanity? What might it take for her to break and run away — leaving Hannah alone forever?

Hannah's pace increased. Ever since the Prince and the Palace possessed her, she had little faith in her own mind. Let alone the intelligence of others. And where the mind led, the heart followed. Though Hannah wished otherwise.

All three of them brewed in suspicion as they traversed the back hallways. Tense with the expectation of ambush. And agitated by the secrets each carried but would not voice.

Then Hannah gestured to stop. And held her breath.

Tobias and Syrena moved close, trusting her knowledge. Hannah was not sure how to proceed. But did not want to risk the discussion. She knew they approached a central passageway that led to the front staircase. Multiple hallways led into this atrium.

And the moment they left the corridor, they were exposed.

Hannah felt a sensation — like a light tap — inside her ears. Syrena was asking for permission to talk. Hannah's anger surfaced and she wanted to lash out.

How dare you request access to my mind? When all you want to do is examine my sanity!

But as the rage dissipated, Hannah saw that she only had herself to blame for her isolation. Syrena was offering a truce. A chance to reconnect before they strayed too far apart; making the chasm impossible to cross.

Hannah glanced at Syrena tucked close to her side, risking her life, no matter that she was unsure of her partner's lucidity. And Tobias — arrow ready, eyes sharp — prepared to battle whomever opposed his queen.

Hannah saw for the first time, that she was the one putting them in danger. Not by being in the castle, she would defend that choice. But through her cowardice. Her inability to face what might lurk in the shadows of her mind. Her unwillingness to trust. That was the real danger. Regardless of who might confront them with weapons.

Hannah turned and tucked against the wall. She needed to speak to Syrena before they leapt into the unknown that waited around this corner. Her sudden movement spooked Tobias into action and he swerved to the other side of the hallway. Syrena stepped ahead of Hannah, blocking her from harm. Her body tense and ready to fight.

If Hannah needed reassurance, she had it. How could she have doubted them? What would they think if they knew she had been so doubtful? These valiant souls ready to die without any justi-fication from her? Hannah suddenly understood why strangers followed Gabriella. Risking death to protect all that her sister embodied — courage and freedom.

Syrena? Hannah inquired.

Yes, Hannah, Syrena replied, not taking her eyes off the risk ahead.

Why did you follow me? Hannah asked. *Why put your life at risk?*

Syrena fell silent. Not sure why her lover chose this perilous moment for such an inquiry. But she sensed this was critical for Hannah. A gateway, perhaps, to a deeper revelation. Syrena trust-ed her body to signal if an attack was coming, so that she had occasion to consider the question. Syrena wondered, *Why do I follow?* Why did she trust Hannah to lead them not into a trap, but through a portal of possibility?

Aside from the recklessness of love? Syrena teased.

Yes, retorted Hannah, relieved that her lover's wit was in tact.

I follow, offered Syrena, *because I know the angels are on your side. They attend to your every wish. And believe in your ability to restore order to our world.*

She paused, so that Hannah felt her devotion.

I follow because you carry the light of community. You are as tender as a butterfly and as fierce as a mother bear. Leaping into the darkness without concern for your wellbeing. Believing that, somewhere in the heart of your homeland, lays the answer to all of the suffering we have endured. An assurance in the goodness of life — no matter what the gods demand of you.

Syrena closed her eyes, acknowledging the spirit that spoke

through her. Even as the words left her mouth, Syrena knew this gift was not for her. The grace that flooded her body was to foster courage in Hannah. A leader of tender heart and sacrificial spirit.

As she opened her eyes, Syrena sensed the tears flowing down Hannah's cheeks. And felt the gratitude in her beloved's heart. Hannah's fear had been transformed into courage.

Thank you, Hannah said. Struck, not the first time, by Syrena's power. The sacred ones spoke through Syrena with an ease that humbled Hannah. She might have come from royal blood, but Hannah knew that Syrena was a divine vessel.

Not so different from her sister, but carrying a unique magic. Hannah suspected Syrena was only beginning to discover her ability. Now that she was accompanied by kind souls. Rather than cruel opportunists who used and tormented her.

And yet, Hannah thought, that tortuous portal brought them together. The Hidden Palace alchemized something greater in Syrena and herself — by challenging them, then uniting them.

And with that realization, Hannah leapt bravely into the pit of fear. Praying that Syrena would catch her. *The castle speaks to me, Syrena,* Hannah confessed.

Syrena tensed. Then asked, *Are you sure it's the castle?*

No, Hannah replied. *There might be trickery afoot. But I do not think so. For the force opened my mind rather than taking over. I doubt the Palace is capable of such subtlety.*

Never underestimate the Palace, Syrena said. *Still, if the Palace could reach you, she would not let you live. None have escaped her clutches and lived. She must be furious and would crush the air from your chest before risking you spreading that tale.*

Hannah winced at Syrena's blunt expression, yet she knew Syrena spoke the truth.

I am sure it was not the Palace, Hannah affirmed. *What voice whispered to me, I cannot be sure. But I believe it is the heart of my castle — for it spoke in riddles. And asked me to make my own choices.*

As only the wise teachers do, grumbled Syrena. *Can you ask this infinitely astute castle if she could tell us who waits in ambush around this corner?*

I will ask, said Hannah, *but I cannot be assured of an answer.*

Of course not, remarked Syrena. *Heaven forbid we receive assistance in advance of the battle. Can you remind this eminent teacher that we are unarmed? And might be in need of an ally if she wishes you to receive another lesson?*

Despite their circumstances, Hannah smiled. She adored Syrena's humour, especially at inappropriate moments. If Tobias were not across the hall, Hannah would insist on a kiss before launching into battle. She glanced at him, considering the risk, but did not wish to throw him off his game.

Hannah closed her eyes. Confident that Tobias would believe she whispered a prayer for their safety. *Blessed castle*, Hannah said, *I am in need of your wisdom. We wish to move forward but fear an ambush. Might you give us insight, so we can take the field?*

Silence hung in the air. Each moment that passed, gave Hannah reason to doubt. Syrena reached back and took her hand. Affirming that the risk was worth the attempt.

As Hannah braced herself to take charge, she felt a chill sweep down her back.

Guide your companions to the west, came the voice. *Stay low to avoid the onslaught from the north. The infiltrators await you by the east window and the northeast wall.*

Hannah nodded. The true test lay in acting on the guidance. Hannah would only know if the voice was trustworthy by leaping over the chasm of uncertainty with a heart filled with faith. The time had come.

She tapped Syrena's shoulder and caught Tobias's eye. Then gestured to dive left and stay low, keeping the north and east walls in their sights. After that, Hannah would guide them. Presuming they landed safely and did not get shot.

Tobias gave a curt nod. Syrena squeezed her hand and let go. Touching her ankle knife to ensure it was tucked, then giving Hannah one last glance. Speaking volumes in one look — expressing fierce love and eternal devotion.

Hannah turned toward the fight. Her companions insisted that she go first. For in taking the primary leap, she would be shielded by the element of surprise. Landing in safety, while Tobias and Syrena ran forward through the onslaught of arrows and blades.

She did not argue. They were more stubborn than she, and together their opposition was insurmountable. Hannah braced herself for a leap that was not in her nature. She was neither warrior nor general. But she was a fierce mother. Protector of her friends. And devotee of her people. Determined to live another day so she might restore her home.

After a swift prayer, Hannah leapt into the grand foyer. Her jump was neither elegant nor skilled, but she threw herself with all her might. The last glimpse of daylight giving enough illumination so that she could aim for the west wall.

As Hannah landed hard on the marble floor near the staircase, her enemies reacted to the sound of flesh against stone. Arrows sailed overhead as she crouched tight against the hand-carved struts holding the rosewood banisters. Hannah ducked down and, seconds later, a knife landed in the banister above her head. Hannah cringed, feeling the force of the blade hit the wood. If she had moved slower, the dagger would have killed her.

With arrows flying and her companions in danger, Hannah would not cower. Tobias yelled to distract their assailants as Syrena sprung forward. Hannah used the melee to gain the dagger from the wood. She might not be able to throw the knife but she could do damage up close.

As Syrena fought, the flame of protection rose in Hannah's belly. Remembering her words, Hannah felt the power of the enraged mother course through her veins. More arrows flew perilously close as she watched. Within moments, Tobias and Syrena were by her side. Tobias let fly his arrows, and Hannah revelled in the pained yelps of their enemy.

Syrena watched through the struts. Trusting that Tobias slayed the visible rogues, while she sought the hidden scoundrels. Among mercenaries, some relished the battle and others waited for the easy gains. Once the arrows stopped flying, and a victor stood, the hidden villain would slit their throats before the celebration was over.

Tobias cried out. An arrow pierced his shoulder. He pulled back his final shaft, sending it whistling through the air, landing between his attacker's eyes. Then he fell to the floor, clutching his arm. He hesitated, unsure whether to yank the metal from his flesh. The tip might be poisoned. Though he did not think these men resourceful enough to find potions. He suspected they were over-confident. And did not worry themselves with subtle tactics.

Tobias prepared to wrest the weapon from his arm. When Hannah stayed his hand. She tore a strip of fabric from her cloak for a bandage. And prepared to dress Tobias's wound. Hannah assumed their safety too quickly. And Syrena sensed the attack in the wind.

In a flash, Syrena launched forward, pushing Hannah to the ground. Then used her momentum to slide across the smooth floors. While locking her eyes on her target, Syrena pulled the knife from her ankle hostler and to let loose her dagger toward the north wall.

Syrena crashed hard into the wall by the east window. As she gathered her wits for the fight, a howl erupted from behind the antique tapestry. Syrena smiled. Satisfied that her knife had found its target. The coward dropped from his hidden position.

His body landed with a *thud!* And blood pooled out across the stone.

Hannah stood. Staring at the dead man. Then turned to see an arrow lodged in the wall behind her. Had Syrena acted a moment later, Hannah would be dead.

She stared, as Syrena pulled herself from the wall. Body aching, she forged forward to ensure the villain was dead. Then retrieved her knife. And kicked him away. Her eyes still ablaze, when she caught Hannah watching.

Syrena shrugged. And Hannah smiled. Fierce love pulsed between them.

Then Hannah bent her knee to tend to Tobias. Knowing they had surmounted only the first of many trials this night.

THIRTY

ADRIAN STARED AT THE FULL MOON overhead and felt the call of Gabriella's soul.

He glanced at the sleeping Vanora. He could never be sure if she were truly asleep. Or if she pretended to rest while watching him with her magic. Either way, he could not risk responding to the call. As deeply as it pained him to forsake Gabriella in her time of need. She would understand.

For three days and three nights, Adrian and Vanora battled one another in the Great Plains. They had not moved from the place where she confronted him. There was no need to find a more suitable arena. The magic they each possessed could turn the most desolate environment into a palace and the most elegant castle to a wasteland.

This was a battle of wills. And Adrian could not say how long the war would rage. Vanora exhausted him with her guile. He wished for a battle of physical confrontation. Yet, this was her power. She had stamina and cunning. She had outwitted many adversaries and outmaneuvered many hunters.

As he sat on the edge of his sleeping mat, Adrian savoured the light of the moon. Drinking in her emotional wisdom and appreciating her gracious heart. The Moon Goddess held much in her sway. Though her reach seemed distant and her face paled compared to the Sun, she fortified the hearts of women, wolves, and trees alike.

The Moon Goddess spoke the language of mystery and awakened passion in the souls of the lost. Adrian sensed the moon had a message for him. One he must receive with care, for this was a letter from his beloved. Spoken in the language of stars and whispered to his heart.

This was an arduous test. He must hold his spirit still, lest he gave any sign of hope. One breath of delight would awaken Vanora — and extinguish his chance to receive the missive.

And so, Adrian sat in utter silence. Calming his mind. Slowing his heart. He waited. Trusting that the Moon Goddess would choose the moment with the least risk.

He felt no concern that the moon was aligned with Vanora. Nor did he believe Vanora's power was more potent at night. For though Vanora was the Shadow Mistress, Adrian knew there was no correlation between her power and the night. Shadows merely spoke a different language under the sun than under the moon.

In the day, shadows shouted with the vigour of dominance. In the night, they whispered with restrained desire. Adrian preferred the whispers. He understood the subtleties. And found the arrogant demands of daylight to be tiring. Even when they appeared in as pleasurable a guise as Vanora.

As he waited, harmonizing with the depths of sacred timing, Adrian pondered the stories he had heard of the Shadow Mistress. The one who slips into a village undetected, like a dark fog on a sunlit day, spreading rumours and unease. Pitting sister against brother. Husband against wife. And child against beast.

Careful not to glance in her direction, Adrian wondered what motivated such a creature.

Even as the question formed, he knew the answer. *Power. Vengeance. Rage.* Three of the most potent spells that took hold of a human soul. Adrian felt the urge toward compassion. And while he lauded his spirit for preferring kindness, he could not risk its softness.

Deep in the reaches of his heart, he held empathy for all Vanora had suffered. But she had travelled so far down the path of despair that to exhibit foolhardy kindness would merely give Vanora a chance to control him. And his power.

Inner wisdom gave him strength. But he could not show such valiance to Vanora. Not yet. Possibly not ever. Though he hoped a day might come that he could show her sympathy.

As Gabriella did the Great Prince? asked the Moon.

Her voice startled Adrian. And sparked such a maelstrom in his heart that he thought Vanora had awakened and bent her will on torturing him. But as Adrian felt the resonance of the voice, he knew he was in the presence of the Moon Goddess. For unlike humans, she spoke in the soft, detached tones of the stars.

Despite the trials of his day, the moon challenged him to feel compassion for the Prince. The spheres called him a hypocrite —he might show kindness for Vanora, yet be incapable when confronted with losing Gabriella's heart.

He was still unable to feel compassion for the Great Prince. No matter how long he tried, nor how much he counselled his heart to take that path. Adrian seethed like a scorned lover whenever he thought of the Prince with Gabriella.

Few visions brought him to his knees, questioned his faith, and made him willing to throw his mission to the wind. Wishing he could escape with Gabriella to a faraway land. But the thought of the Great Prince claiming Gabriella tortured Adrian more than any physical pain or mental trial.

Only his years of training kept the Shadow Mistress from sensing his weakness. And, then Adrian knew. This was why the moon called the vision to his mind. Shadows bear power only when they are not seen. He nodded, humbly grateful for the moon's wisdom. Bringing jealousy to his awareness.

Adrian suspected that Vanora held this secret. Waiting to use the pain against him. And though the wound may still draw blood, he could control his response.

You have a message for me, honoured one? asked Adrian.

Yes, my son, replied the Moon. Though, like all heavenly bodies, she did not hurry in the sharing.

Adrian resisted the compulsion to look at Vanora, now that he understood her secret weapon. His thoughts wandered dangerously in her direction. Risking tripping her defences and setting off her magical alarms. He focused on his breath. Keeping his thoughts distant. Seeking the stillness of the outer realms.

He was grateful that even one as ancient as Vanora required sleep. She was still human, and her need to sleep was the only way Adrian recovered his strength. Her onslaught retreated at night, and he gained back enough territory in his psyche to revive his power.

But Adrian feared he was losing the battle. Though he was strong, he felt his courage waning. The steady confrontation with Vanora sapped his will and challenged his resolve. Each night, he was more tempted. Each day, his resistance weakened.

Adrian despaired that soon the sorceress would breach his psychic barriers, and force him to do whatever she desired. Though he was not so foolish to believe Vanora truly desired him. She wanted Adrian as a pawn in her game. Leverage to be used against Gabriella.

Ah, my young one, said the Moon, as though Adrian had spoken to her. *That is where you are wrong.*

Wrong? Adrian asked. *What else could she possibly want?*

The moon did not reply. She waited for Adrian to puzzle out the wishes buried deep in Vanora's heart. Her silence reminded him never to misread the moon's intentions. The Night Goddess was not on his side, nor was she was on Vanora's.

The spheres were forever impartial. They spun and wove in harmony with the earth, but their distance afforded perspective. They felt no alliance to one side or the other. Adrian often wished they lent their powerful alliance to the higher path. But he was not so young or so naïve as to believe that he understood the vision of the Great Mystery.

Humans could not help but take everything personally. React individually. And wage wars in the name of private slights — real or imagined.

Adrian gazed up at the stars with envy. High in the firmament, they did not feel the arrows of cruel Princes. Or bear the onslaught of a Sorceress's vengeance. None of which had anything to do with Adrian.

Though the Moon Goddess appeared with a message, she did not offer support. She would no more give Adrian a secret from Vanora's soul than the Moon would reveal Adrian's deepest truth to the Shadow Mistress. The moon passed along a message only at the bearer's request.

Adrian sighed. And brought his eyes back to earth. The moon bore news from Gabriella. Or possibly from his homeland. Either way, he was grateful for the company. He may not know the details, but his heart felt lighter knowing he was not alone.

Adrian pondered Vanora's motives. What did she want with him if not to use him against Gabriella? If she broke his will and forced him to do the unspeakable – betray his love and devotion – Gabriella would be broken. She would be alone. And yet, he knew she would storm the Hidden Palace. Determined to make the Great Prince pay.

A chill shot down Adrian's spine as though lightning had struck. He clenched his teeth to keep from grabbing his dagger and piercing Vanora's heart.

She does not wish to possess Gabriella, he thought. She wants only to send the Messenger running to the Great Prince. Whether they kill one another or fall madly in love, they achieve the same end — mutual annihilation.

Adrian stared at the Shadow Mistress. Vanora was bent on their destruction, so she could claim the throne. Ruling the Great Lands with a harsher hand than the Prince. If she allied her influence with the Hidden Palace's cruelty, Adrian feared the world would end.

Until now, he had not imagined the fate of the Great Lands could be darker. But he saw that they had only begun to taste real suffering.

If you ride promptly, whispered the Moon, *you might escape Vanora's notice. Gabriella needs your wisdom. And you need her strength.*

Yes, thought Adrian, casting his mind forth to Casmire. He and Gabriella no longer had reason to be apart. Evil took advantage of their separation. By joining, they could magnify their power.

Casmire appeared, nuzzling the wizard's hand with affection. Adrian smiled. He felt the same urgency to be at Gabriella's side. As he prepared to swing onto Casmire's back, Adrian felt the electrical current slice through him. As though a bolt of lightning riddled through his spine. Sending Adrian to his knees. Gasping for breath.

Vanora was on her feet. And, in a flash, she landed at Adrian's side. Clasping her hand around his neck. Vanora dug her nails into his flesh.

"Let me have my way with you, wizard," Vanora hissed. "Otherwise, this will be *far* more painful."

Power surged through her hands. Devastating his senses and blinding him with blazing light. Adrian's protections disintegrated.

And he crumpled to the ground.

THIRTY-ONE

GABRIELLA FELT VANORA'S BLOW as though the sorceress had struck her, not Adrian.

She bolted upright. Sitting in her bed, she stared at the window. Perplexed. Wondering why the glass had not shattered and a storm was not whipping through her room. But her curtains sat still. And the inn remained as quiet as when she had drifted off to sleep.

"Adrian," Gabriella whispered, breaking the promise never to say his name aloud.

She listened intently but heard only the far away howl of a wolf. Not the sound that she awaited. Gabriella received no chill. No echo. Not even the tension that gripped her when Adrian silently rebuked her.

His lack of reply meant only one thing. He was in mortal danger. Or dead.

Gabriella jumped to her feet. Then, hesitated for a breath. Adrian would never want her to risk her plans to save his life. When they parted ways, he made her swear she would never seek him out. Only call to him if she needed his aid.

Adrian would take the risk to find her. Never the other way, he insisted. But Gabriella did not care. She rushed into her clothes and swung on her cloak. She pulled on her riding boots and flung her satchel over her shoulder. She stepped into the corridor, confident that she could find Adrian by following the thread of his pain.

As she glanced at the other rooms, Gabriella cursed. Katrin, she thought. Reproaching herself for forgetting the girl.

Gabriella's urgency had wiped everything from her mind.

Yet, she did not have time for complicated conversations.

She would leave a note in the kitchen, trusting that the girl would be safe at the inn. Abandoning her without saying farewell might sway Katrin's decision, but Gabriella had no choice. She uttered a prayer for Katrin to understand. And to have the sense to stay under this roof until Gabriella returned.

If she does not take offence, mused Gabriella, she may be grateful for the time to consider her position.

Gabriella moved silently through the hallway to the back stairs. She was about to run down the steps, when she froze. Grabbing the banister to keep her upright. The surge swept though her like a cyclone, as she felt the power swell for another strike. She had not encountered such force since fighting the Great Prince.

And this was fiercer. The intense rage took Gabriella's breath away.

Gabriella's fingers gripped the polished wood as her knees buckled from the brute force of the charge. She did not know why the effect rippled through her — thousands of miles away. She could only guess that the sorceress wanted Gabriella to feel the excruciating pain. Knowing that Adrian felt the impact a hundredfold.

Distance shielded Gabriella from being incapacitated, but she cringed at the thought of Adrian suffering at the hands of this beast. Gabriella understood that she was being baited. The sorceress was using her beloved against her. But she did not care. Gabriella would answer the call. Determined to stop this vicious woman.

Gabriella shook off the assault, and ran down the stairs. Years of moving stealthily through the most precarious of situations kept her from waking every soul in the inn.

She burst into the kitchen. Prepared to care for her needs, expecting all others to be asleep. She froze in the face of Gideon— the cloaked one. Though the Moon was high in the sky and the gentleman had no need to be awake at this hour, he understood her intent.

"Leaving so soon, child?" he asked, not expecting an answer. Much to her surprise, he handed her a bundle of food, wrapped in linen and well-packed to fit her satchel.

Gabriella stared at Gideon. She had not expected to see him again. And now, she was sure he was the one. Her Guide.

"I wish to stay," Gabriella replied, her heart torn. "More than anything. I want to hear all that you have to teach me." But this was not to be. At least, not tonight.

"But that is not so," Gideon returned. "For you would risk all that you are meant to learn by rushing to the side of one who can take care of himself. One who has sworn to care for you."

"That may be so," Gabriella said, "But he is struggling and she will surely kill him. I must go."

She wrote a quick note to Katrin and handed it to him. "Please care for her while I am gone."

As Gideon took the paper, he gently clasped her hand. Sending a wave of tenderness through her heart. Offering one last gift of contact. In his touch, Gabriella saw visions of cruel kings and destructive sorceresses —madness and power — flashes of magic and harsh truths. All in the service of the greater vision.

She gasped, and pulled her hand away. Struck by the mystery of this man.

Gabriella pulled the cloak over her head, turning swiftly. She must not give in to her curiosity. Or her doubt. She needed to focus for her ride would take days of hard travel. Only then would she reach Adrian in time.

"If you *must* ride to his rescue," Gideon said, "You might consider some help."

Gabriella kept moving. "I have no need," she replied. She unlatched the many locks on the back door with quick, precise movements.

"Ah, but you do," he said, placing a hand on her shoulder. He had bridged the gap between them in a flash of movement.

Gabriella turned, abruptly. "I have no time for delays, Gideon," she said. "Make no mistake, I depart tonight."

Her eyes alight with fear and fire, Gideon lifted his hand. But he did not step away. He was an imposing figure, tall and lithe, striking in his heavy cloak. Yet he did not attempt to sway her with intimidation. Instead, he spoke gently.

"You will not reach him in time using steed and saddle, child," Gideon offered. "The journey is too far. Even for you."

"I have no choice," she replied, "And with each word you delay me and increase the risk that he will die."

"You know the way is long, Gabriella," Gideon insisted. "Seven days without rest. Do you really expect Adrian to resist her assault for that long?"

"He is more powerful than both of us together," Gabriella

retorted.

"And the Shadow Mistress will knock you off your steed each time she attacks him," Gideon replied, with a certainty that Gabriella took to be prophesy. "Every fall will hurt you, but will strike Adrian deeper. For she uses your pain against him."

Gabriella choked back her frustration. In her haste to leave, she had not considered the tactics the Sorceress would use to break Adrian. The greatest of which was the impact on Gabriella.

As she calmed her reaction, Gabriella received Gideon's gift of vision. Seeing that each fall off her horse doubled the blow to Adrian's resolve. Weakening his defenses as Gabriella's peril assaulted him from within while the Sorceress attacked him.

"What am I to do?" she asked, her eyes brimming with dread. "I cannot travel that far using magic. Not without the cooperation of hundreds of people. Even then, I have not transported further than a league."

Gideon smiled. Confusing Gabriella, for she felt no hope. So heavy was her heart. But she trusted Gideon. And held her tongue.

"Do you believe there are those who wish to help you?" Gideon asked.

"Of course," she replied, brusquely.

"You say that, my child," he continued. "But do you *mean* it?"

Gabriella felt the pressure of an impending attack from Verona. She had no time for Gideon's riddles. But she also had no choice.

Bracing her back against the door, she readied herself for the onslaught. Then Gabriella closed her eyes and reached deep into her heart. Seeking the quiet place she discovered when the angels spoke. Asking her to serve, at all costs, with the heart of a Warrior and the soul of a Messenger.

She could not bridge their physical divide without the assistance of Gideon and whatever he promised. She needed a magic that was bigger than her. The only way Gabriella would save Adrian was through complete surrender.

Gabriella did not wish to continue this path without Adrian.

Not for all the promises to the angels. Or all the lives in the Great Lands. She wanted to save him for *her*. To be with him one more time.

Gabriella blushed at the selfish truth.

But her discomfort did not change her determination. She was left with one answer. Her stomach tightened and her nerves sang with fear. This declaration left her fate in the hands of others — a lack of control that terrified her.

She closed her eyes. And clenched her fists. "Yes," she whispered. Just as the attack from miles away struck, sending her reeling.

Gabriella fell unconscious into Gideon's arms.

THIRTY-TWO

VANORA FOCUSED ALL HER POWER on Adrian, pinning him to the ground. Delighted that she caught him off guard. His eagerness to depart had pulled his attention from her for only a second. But that was long enough for Vanora to feel the shift and open her eyes.

She had hardly played fair, letting the wizard believe she was asleep. All the while, she tracked his movements and snuck beneath his defences. Then with Adrian's back turned, she attacked — abandoning her subtle tactics. Much as she loved the long, slow game of bringing the powerful to their knees, she had gambled too much to let the wizard run.

The advantageous moment was when he stopped to puzzle over her motivation. Curiosity is only a breath away from compassion — the doorway into another's heart. And Vanora was more than happy to leverage that gateway. She laughed at the meek nature of those who bothered to wonder why others did what they did. The gesture reeked of weakness.

"No one denies my right to win," Vanora hissed, as she channeled a flow of energetic fire through Adrian's spine, keeping him pinned to his knees.

She felt him resist. His power was impressive. Indeed, Vanora had to block out all sounds, sights, and smells to focus on immobilizing the wizard. But the surprise of her attack had given her the advantage.

Vanora relished letting loose with her full capacity. Few humans were capable of enduring this much power rippling through their system. An untrained mortal would already be dead. But Adrian was alive and fighting.

"Not that anyone will know you struggled," she scoffed and bent forward to whisper her salty insult into Adrian's wounded psyche.

Thwack! Vanora was struck from behind, a mighty blow to her back. She screamed in pain. Tumbled to the ground, releasing Adrian from her spell. Casmire. He had reared up to bring his full weight on Vanora, striking her with his powerful hooves.

Casmire whinnied. Had he brought both hooves down on the sorceress, he could have cracked her spine in two. But he did not trust that the impact would not hurt the wizard. He had witnessed enough magic to know it was unpredictable.

Adrian struggled to his feet, barely able to see. Yet knowing this was his only opportunity. He balanced his stance, and commanded his mind to focus. Then set to pulling power directly from the earth's core. As much as he could summon in the moment that Vanora was incapacitated.

As he charged his spell, Adrian felt Vanora pulling power from the air, though she did not move from her crumpled position on the ground. She might look unconscious, but he knew she was alert and waiting. The hair on his arms stood up as the electrical charge built around them. Adrian used every sense in his body to prepare for the battle to come.

With no time to waste, Adrian did not raise his hands. He held them close and propelled the bolt of fire energy through the air, aiming for her heart. Adrian struck Vanora straight in the chest, just as she flipped over. Throwing a blast of icy air at his head.

He dove, evading the blow that would have knocked him senseless. His fire bolt landed and Vanora howled with pain. Adrian rolled to regain his footing, just as she also stood.

Vanora had lost all patience. Adrian dared to resist her advances. And now he meant to kill her. She snickered at the thought. Though her stomach clenched with the knowledge that if anyone on this earth had the power to stop her, this was the man.

And so, as much as she wanted to toy with him, exhausting him over the course of days, 'til he bled from his ears and his feet were stripped of skin. She had hoped his precious Messenger would arrive just in time to watch him die. But Vanora did not want to wait.

She would kill him. Swiftly. Decisively. Let the Messenger feel the wave of despair sweep across her world, thought Vanora. Snuffing the love from her heart. And the hope from her soul.

Adrian saw the Sorceress's naked desire to crush him. Her rage spilled over the ground. Pulsing waves of destruction emanated from her skin. Centuries of betrayals coursed through her veins. Fuelling her desire to wipe Adrian from the earth. His innocence did not matter. He had opposed her will.

And so, Adrian would die to avenge all the wrongs that had been perpetrated against her.

He felt Vanora's fury, burning with a heat that singed the grass. Lighting a glowing ring of fire around her. She appeared more like an apparition in the night than a living woman. The deeper her anger burned, the more Adrian saw her pain. The true source of her power.

Adrian did not wish to take her life. Nor did he want to teach Vanora a lesson. But to protect him and those he loved, he would have to defeat her. And that meant someone must die.

As the night waned and the first shimmers of daylight glowed over the horizon, the spellcasters circled one another. Pacing slowly in the heart of the Great Plains. Fire burned around Vanora. Droplets of water cooled into a ring of ice around Adrian. The counter-effect to the power each drew from the elements.

They stepped in unison, as though enacting an ancient dance. Searching for weakness. Recharging their energy. Each had some semblance of defence. But now that battle was declared, Adrian and Vanora did not waste effort on protection. Their intentions were clear. Be the first to kill.

The surrounding plains quivered from the impact. Adrian drew power from the earth and Vanora pulled strength from the sky. At the breaking of the dawn, the prairie grasses typically raised their faces to the sun. Delighting in the warmth and nourishment.

But this morning, the grass cowered and the horses backed away.

—⚡—

Few birds travelled this far into the Great Plains. The absence of trees provided no shelter or rest for songbirds. But the eagles came with the dawn. Anticipating easy prey as mice and gophers grabbed the bites of seed before running back to their nests.

As they flew above the battleground, not even the eagles could avoid Vanora's magic. Drawn into the magnetic pull, the eagles rolled and wrestled against her surge of strength. Narrowly escaping being thrown to the ground. They urgently called for all to fly from the heartland. The highest skies were not safe. Their cry echoed all the way to the mountains.

The rodents rejoiced escaping the eagle talons, but feared the force rocking their burrows. Waves of mice scurried from the plains, abandoning their homes in search of shelter far from this scorched patch. Preferring the beaks of hawks to suffocating in their nests.

Casmire paced far from the wizards' blows. He watched closely. This was not his fight, but that did not mean he would not guard Adrian. Vanora was formidable. And Casmire was poised for a gateway of escape, however fleeting.

The mare was long gone, galloping fast across the plains. Casmire knew she risked her life fleeing Vanora, but the horse also stood little chance of surviving this battle. Even if she lived only a few short weeks or months, he understood risking the chance to seek her homeland again.

Casmire was grateful. He did not need the distraction, nor did he trust the mare to be loyal to her kind when faced with Vanora's vengeance. If he were only responsible for his safety, he would have fled days ago. But he had sworn an oath. And he would not leave until one — or both — of the spellcasters was dead.

—ᴍ—

Midstep, Vanora clutched her hands and, as one foot landed on the earth, she channeled all of her clout into an assault. Wave after wave of icy bolts flew toward Adrian, with such force that he exerted as much effort avoiding their wake as he did evading the ice that would freeze him to the core.

He rolled and landed on his feet, firing back with a surge of flame. Lighting up the sky. Vanora grimaced as she spun away from his blows. Lodging shards of ice — large enough to slice a giant in half — into the earth by Adrian's feet.

A broad circle of earth singed around them, alternating from flame to ice.

Adrian focused all his attention on Vanora. He trusted Casmire to alert him of outside threats, though he doubted anyone would be so idiotic to approach this circle of hell. As Vanora prepared for each strike, she built a surge like a tornado gaining force. Drawing in everything around her to feed the potency of her blow. Adrian focused on the invisible field of her influence. Even still, he evaded her hit within half a breath.

Vanora loved the battle, but resented Adrian's ability to withstand her assault. The first exchanges were satisfying. Pulsing waves of power rippled through her, satiating her unending ache to punish the world.

Destruction was as nourishing to Vanora as conception felt to others. She would demolished the Great Plains with a blinding ice storm if Adrian did not counter every blow. But each miss and every near strike provoked her anger. He knew she was losing patience.

Seeing the wizard dart and dodge was entertaining, but did not satisfy. Vanora had come to win. Direct attack had become too obvious. Vanora needed a new tactic. She sent blow after destructive blow, keeping Adrian distracted while she scanned the horizon.

Vanora tried reversing direction, attacking from a fresh angle. But Adrian kept pace. He rallied back. The harder she fought, the more powerful his volley. Vanora growled. Then a realization struck her like a thunderbolt. The bastard was using her power against her!

Vanora sent a surge of ice toward Adrian, only to have the wizard spin aggressively and send the storm back at double the force. Transforming ice to fire and — for the first time — compelling Vanora to leap high into the air to avoid being scorched to ashes.

How was she to win when he matched her onslaught, and used her power against her? She should have crushed him when she had him on his knees!

And with that thought, a wave of delight rushed over her. She was going about this all wrong. Adrian expected her to attack him. To continue a furious dance. But how would he respond when her attack was sent elsewhere?

And with vicious delight, Vanora spun around. Sending icy swords flying toward Casmire.

Adrian saw her pivot too late. He had only a second to react. Though he saw multiple outcomes to her blow, only one would save Gabriella's steed.

Casmire! Adrian yelled in his mind. *Rear up! Now!*

The great stallion did not question the command. He felt the mighty wave headed his way. All his senses screamed that his life was in the balance.

Casmire threw his hooves in the air. And prayed that if the goddess deemed him worthy, he might feel the earth again.

THIRTY-THREE

GABRIELLA WOKE, GAZING INTO the kind blue eyes of Gideon. Vision after vision flooded her mind. Rattling her senses and causing her to gasp.

She scrambled to her feet, desperate to be on her way. Terrified by the time she must have lost. Her head spun, and her body swayed from the sudden upright stance. Gabriella reached out to steady herself and her hand touched a damp surface. Cold, wet rock.

Where was she? Gabriella panicked. Cold air brushed her cheek and the clammy rock beneath her palm whispered of the deepest places on earth. She was nowhere near the Great Plains. And had no notion how many hours had passed.

"Calm yourself, Gabriella," Gideon said, his voice soothing her nerves.

But as she tried to see him, waves of panic rushed over her. So complete was the darkness around them. Gabriella was sure Gideon was close by, yet she could not see his face.

What was this place? And how did she get here?

Each query sent her mind spinning in faster circles. Her body responded by veering against the hard rock. Gabriella closed her eyes to get her bearings. And felt Gideon's firm hand on her arm.

Assuring her that all was well. But her mind continued to panic. Sending her stomach into spasms and weakening her knees.

Gabriella needed to find calm. To quench the attack that still pulsed in her blood.

"Focus on my touch," Gideon instructed. "Feel the warmth of love in my hand. Allow the kindness to flood your body. Washing away the hate. Send the poison through the soles of your feet into the depths of mother earth. Trust that my affection replenishes your blood, soothes your mind, and graces your heart with everlasting strength."

Gabriella felt the peace of companionship. The tension left her stomach. Her shoulders rested against the rock. She was held by the earth. Cradled by the cave. Her surroundings were pitch black; impenetrable by sight.

But she understood in every fragment of her being that Gideon had transported her to the Sacred Caves of Leanore — a place so mysterious that the caves were spoken of as legend. Lost to another time, if they ever truly existed on this earth.

Gabriella heard of the caves through old folklore passed down by villagers. Few believed the stories and fewer still risked sharing them. Gabriella had been fascinated. Enough so, that she gathered every whisper of the story. But never found the complete tale.

When Gabriella turned the magical age of eight, her mother secretly arranged for a dying elder from the edge of the Great Forest to come to the castle. Queen Isabel trusted that Gabriella

was ready to hear what her mother believed was the most dangerous tale in all the Great Lands.

As the old woman sat on a stool in Gabriella's room, she did not care that the girl was royalty. She refused to tell the story until Gabriella shared the sacred rite with her — slicing her palm and mixing the blood of the storygreeter with the storyteller.

The Queen reluctantly agreed to the crone's demand, comforted that the ritual was as ancient as the legend. She handed Gabriella a blade and spoke silently, *Cut a tiny swath, my child. For a shallow slice will not leave a scar.*

Gabriella nodded. She took the knife with reverence, convinced this was her initiation. Gabriella did not care that the woman was decrepit nor that the blade was barely large enough to cut apples. She was sharing blood with a powerful creature.

After this, little Gabriella thought, she would be a warrior.

And she drew a line across her palm. Cringing at the pain, but not uttering a sound. The crone also cut the skin on her well-marked hand and stared fiercely into Gabriella's eyes. She cupped their palms together, not yet merging blood.

"Do you swear, Gabriella Magdalene Camphore, to uphold the secret of the caves?" Inquired the crone. "Never to share their wisdom unless called forth by the Goddess herself?"

"I swear," Gabriella replied, a chill echoing through her body. The hair on her arms standing on end.

"Do you understand," continued the crone, staring deeper into her eyes, "that to break your vow will unleash Spirit-scoffers from the darkest bowels of the Shadowlands. And wreak havoc on your family, your lands, and all those under your care?"

Gabriella hesitated. She was strong and bold, more than most children her age. And she had received many threats from guardians attempting to frighten her into obedience. But this warning, Gabriella knew, despite the dramatic words, was no deception. The old woman meant every word.

Gabriella swallowed hard and said, "I understand."

The crone clasped her hand with the strength of an imperial soldier, sealing her palm with Gabriella's. Holding the girl's gaze until she saw tears well up. Gabriella did not cry out. She returned the fierce stare and gripped back harder.

The old woman cracked a satisfied smile and released her hand. A sweeping rush of chilled air swept through the room. Startling even the Queen.

Nodding her approval, the crone took a swig of royal ale and wiped her mouth. Then began the tale of the mysterious caves of Leanore.

—m—

Gabriella pressed her hands into the sacred rock. Feeling for the pulse of ancient times. The wisdom of goddesses. The strength of angels. And the ferocity of dragons. The legend promised that those permitted to enter the caves were chosen to uphold the sacred tasks. Protection. Guidance. Vision.

She spoke into the darkness. "How long have you held the station of sacred guide, Gideon?"

Gideon smiled. He had gambled that the whispers were true. Murmurs that the young princess — child of Algor and Isabel — had been instructed in the cave's mysteries. Or, at least, that she had been initiated. The first fable was both an offering and a trial

— used to determine the listener's character.

"The wise ones came to me after my wife died," Gideon explained. "They had been watching me for years. Or so they said. I was never aware of their vigil." She heard Gideon shift. The weight of his wife's death still pressed on his heart. Though her passing had been many years ago, he still paused to regain his composure.

"When a man loses the person dearest to him," Gideon continued, "the crossing of that bridge marks his character. The wise ones were not sure how I would respond to such a devastating loss. And they were right to wonder. On many a dark day, I considered taking my life."

Gabriella's thoughts jumped to Adrian. Her heart fluttered with understanding, but also panic. She did not have time for distant memories, no matter how heartbreaking. She had to reach Adrian before he was torn from her world.

Then a thought made her gasp. Were the ancient ones testing her? Was she in the cave only because Adrian was dead? Was she being held here to protect the world from her despair?

"Why am I here?" Gabriella demanded. "Why did you divert my journey?"

"As a child, you were told secrets about the caves," Gideon said, ignoring her question. "But only as many as the elders trusted to the ears of one so young. Like a seed, they provided you with a portion of the grander fruit. They needed to see if the mystery would hold. If, one day, you might be strong enough to wield the deeper knowledge."

Despite Gideon's calm and the peace of the cave, Gabriella only felt the impending danger to Adrian. The threat was building and time slipped through her fingers. If there was one substance the gods never seemed to comprehend, that was time. She would never forgive herself if Adrian died while she mused about the secrets of the ages.

"Gideon," Gabriella said, exhaling her frustration. "I am grateful to be in the caves. I am ready for every test brought forth by the elders. But this is not the time. Adrian's life hangs in the balance. If I do not reach him soon, the sorceress will destroy him."

"Do you not think," chastised Gideon, "That Adrian, of all people, would wish for you to take this journey?"

"Yes," Gabriella replied, in a fierce tone. "But *I* am the one determined to save his life. No matter *his* wishes."

Gideon restrained a chuckle. "Indeed, wild one." He could not help but be charmed by Gabriella. She reminded him of his fiery wife. "Make no mistake, I brought you here to assist in the rescue. Not impede it."

"How could this benefit my task?" asked Gabriella. "We are further than ever from the Great Plains."

Gideon snapped his fingers. Shimmering sparks flew up through the cave; lighting the cavern like a field of fireflies. The sparks drifted delicately down to the wicks of tapered candles, nestled in each crook of rock. Until the ancient cave lit up like sunrise.

Gabriella gasped like a child. Dazzled by the beauty and magic. Iridescent rock reflected the flames. The cave appeared as though a thousand stars took up residence in the walls. Sparkling brighter than a new moon night.

Her eyes followed Gideon as he walked to the grotto's heart, filled with a shimmering lake. The candlelight danced in the water's reflection. And Gabriella swore this must be the fairy pond spoken about in fairytales. The ripples whispered sounds of enchantment — an otherworldly resonance infused with mystery. And peril.

Gabriella had encountered many a formidable challenge in her lifetime. But this one kept her fastened to the ground. She was in awe … and was troubled by the challenge. Fairies were notoriously unpredictable. If she ventured too far, she might suddenly find herself on the haunted side of the world.

Gideon turned, and stood silently at the water's edge. Gabriella felt his command. Telling her to join him. He offered a bridge to Adrian. One she must trust. But this — she quivered inside. The magic was overwhelming. Playing havoc with her senses and her mind.

These were the whispers she had only heard in stories. Tales of magical creatures that randomly changed allegiance. Beings with every reason to despise humans. The wars chased them from their sacred dells. Forcing the mystical ones to hide in caves and waterholes. Seeking refuge deep in the mountains, where humans did not tread.

Gideon waited. Gabriella saw that he was not troubled by Adrian's conflict. That was her concern. He simply offered assistance. *She* was the one who must take the leap. Against all that her body advised. And all that Adrian would counsel. But what choice did she have?

Still, she could not move her feet. Her body resisted with every ounce of its strength. Gabriella shivered. She was running out of time. She must choose.

She locked her gaze on Gideon. Accepting his support.

Gabriella focused on her guide's wisdom, tricking her feet into moving. As though all she intended was to stand beside a kind old man. She fixated on the steps required to meet him by the water. Nothing else.

As she walked — step by step — across the cave, Gabriella crossed through an invisible gateway. Treading from one world into another. Her body lit up with the proximity of magical beings. She could not see them, so she focused on Gideon. On saving Adrian.

She must not stray — for fear of losing sight of her purpose.

Gabriella heard giggles. And hisses. Whispers. And the faint sound of bells. Still, she kept her gaze on Gideon. Determined. Like an arrow sailing toward her target, she landed at Gideon's side. He smiled. And blessed her with a quick brush of his left hand.

She had passed the first challenge.

A flicker of recognition passed through Gabriella. A vague memory from childhood. That gesture. The sharp edge of Gideon's jaw. The distant sparkle of wisdom in his eyes. The ripple of a chill went down her spine. And a flash of a vision passed through her mind.

She had seen him before, she realized. In Granamore. In her castle! She had heard tales of him by another name. Gabriella understood he had always been protecting her. Watching over her. Since the day of her birth.

Gideon's gaze pierced her heart. Gabriella reached into her cloak and pulled out the blade that had protected her since she left home. She held her hand open to him, with her knife across her palm. Her eyes filled with fierce strength and tender vulnerability.

He stood quietly. Gideon nodded, acknowledging their long-standing bond. A glint of hope appeared in the depths of his eyes, as he took her blade.

Gabriella saw that ahead of her was an infinite number of tests. And she had passed one.

Gideon pointed to a shimmering silver blur at the bottom of the fairy lake. Gabriella felt the magnetic pull of its essence. The water must be immeasurably deep and, still, she felt the influence of the magical weapon.

Then she heard its call — whispering — as though it had waited many lifetimes for her. And Gabriella answered, without hesitation, plunging deep into the dusky water. Until her hand grasped the sword from her vision.

And she was sent spinning through the depths of time.

THIRTY-FOUR

HANNAH LED HER COMPANIONS toward the back of the castle. No more bandits appeared as they snuck from hall to hall. They were alone in the heart of the castle. Hannah felt a little like a ghost. Walking hallways that echoed with memories.

Unable to touch or see the people she remembered. Long departed faces smiled across hallways. Maids whispered stories and giggled over the latest boy they desired. Swapping gossip and singing as they changed linens and freshened water jugs.

Hannah smiled sadly, lost in years long gone. Nostalgic for the girl she once was —bearing a gracious heart and not a care in the world. Assured that her life would unfurl with a joyful current. Much like her blessed childhood.

Syrena stayed close. The weight of Hannah's sadness concerned her. Syrena understood the drowning wave of grief — a force that swept strong souls away to the bottom of the ocean. She watched with a hawk's gaze, tracking Hannah's movements. Ensuring that her beloved did not fall deep into the chasms of the past.

Syrena would have loved to explore this regal, if war-torn, home with Hannah. She felt the power of Hannah's ancestors. The wisdom they wished to bestow upon their kin. Instead, Syrena scanned ahead for threats. Silently reminding the ghosts that Hannah had a more imminent threat — her prideful husband and the vengeful Hidden Palace.

Hannah took Syrena's hand. And Syrena breathed a sigh of relief. Knowing her lover was still present. Syrena squeezed her Hannah's hand, acknowledging the gesture. Then let go. So they might each be prepared for attack.

Do what you need, my love, Syrena said. *I will watch the path. There must be other rogues hidden in this castle's belly, anticipating a cowardly prize. And I will be ready for them.*

Thank you, Hannah replied, already drifting back to her memories. The heartbreak threatened to bring her to her knees. She shed tears for the life she lost. And the parents she missed with her entire being.

—ɯ—

Tobias glanced occasionally at his liege, concerned for Hannah's wellbeing. But, like Syrena, he felt his duty was to ward off danger.

Tobias was proud that he escorted the future Queen through her castle. Her home was ragged, and much silver and gold had been pillaged, but he did not put stock in material displays. Nobility was founded in honourable action. And reclaiming the castle of his beloved regal family was a profound act of loyalty.

Tobias had not expected that, with each pass by a familiar room, his heart would skip a beat. Half-expecting to see Gabriella running around a corner. He smiled as he recalled Gabriella wrapping Hannah in her arms then chastising Tobias for his avoidance of her company.

Tobias shook off the wishful image. Reminding his foolish heart of his true mission — assisting Princess Hannah. He was not here to get lost in a young man's crush, Tobias reminded himself.

As though to prove his point, Tobias raised his shooting arm. Focused on the far reaches of the great foyer. Anticipating the hiding spots of imaginary mercenaries. Blocking thoughts of Gabriella with the immediate prospect of combat. He had never been so grateful for the possibility of a fight.

—ɯ—

Hannah ushered her brave companions toward the far gardens of the castle. She could not bear being inside any longer. Every nook reminded Hannah of her parents. Her heart ached at their loss. And she could not shake the foreboding sense that they had met a horrific end.

Her secret wish had been that returning home would offer some message — tucked in the walls or whispered in the corridors — something that would reveal her parents' whereabouts. She was sure there would be a trail, an essence that would lead her to them.

But with each passing step, she lost hope.

She felt no murmur of their presence. No hidden map pointing to their whereabouts. The lack of signs left Hannah feeling abandoned again. As though her parents did not care whether they lived or perished. Leaving Hannah and Gabriella to fend for themselves in a world gone mad.

Hannah wondered what they were thinking. Ransoming her to the Great Prince and sending Gabriella into the wilderness. No friends. No allies. Not a breath of where their family had gone!

The weight of her parents' decision hit her heart — as though she had been shoved in the chest. Hannah gasped for air. And Syrena turned, touching her lover's arm, and scanning the foyer for spellcasters.

"All is well," she whispered to Syrena, regaining her breath. "I was surprised by the echo of a memory."

"I do not like it," Syrena replied, suspicious. "We should leave this place. Something is amiss. We faced only one band of rogues. And the rest of the castle is abandoned?"

"I agree," Tobias said. "Why would the Prince not have mercenaries waiting?"

Hannah stood upright. Grateful to have her breath again. "Perhaps he called them home," Hannah proclaimed. "Assuming we would not be so foolish as to return."

"Do you not find that strange?" Syrena asked. "Why is your home so forsaken? When every miscreant in the land could take it for himself after your family fled."

Tobias cuffed Syrena on the arm, reprimanding her blunt approach.

"No, Tobias," Hannah admitted. "Syrena speaks the truth."

"This strange effect," Syrena insisted, "this force that draws you into the past, and knocks the breath from your chest. It reeks of magic." Syrena shot a fierce glance at Hannah. "We must leave. Now."

"We will leave when Hannah is ready," Tobias said, understanding Hannah's grief. Though he did not wish to admit his misgivings, he did not anticipate a pleasant resolution to the long-standing secret of the regents' disappearance.

"There is one last place I would like to visit," Hannah said. "But we must traverse the far gardens to find it."

She led the way through the winding corridors. Hurrying now that she did not anticipate messages from her parents. Hannah rushed to escape the pressing feeling of tragedy that hovered around every corner.

Hannah dashed past dining rooms and studies and closets where she and Gabriella had hidden from one another. The memories that once called her home now chased her from the castle. She sought solace in the only place she hoped might not be haunted by the absence of all she once held dear.

Syrena and Tobias struggled to keep pace with Hannah's quickening feet. She was tormented by something they could not see, running toward a set of broad wooden doors. They could only assume the doors led to her beloved garden.

Hannah wrestled with the heavy bolt that secured the doors. Forcing free the barrier that held the doors shut for years. Then pushing open the portal onto the guarded expanse that perched behind the castle.

The rush of fresh air burst upon Hannah, freeing her from the claustrophobic pressure of crushed hopes. She gazed out on the gardens that once held many a game of hide and seek between two beloved sisters.

Though the flowers had wilted and the vines had grown wild, the structure of the garden held true. Strong trees stood firm in their long rooted homes. Apple, cherry, and plum nestled closer to the castle, amid the cultured plants and flowers. The wild presence of fir, pine, and cedar held the barriers. Waiting, Hannah sensed, not for her return. But for the homecoming of their beloved child

— Gabriella.

As Hannah breathed the liberating air of the wild space, she understood for the first time why Gabriella had spent each day in the far reaches of the woods. She sought refuge and silent understanding. Freedom and acceptance without the suffocating pressures of the court.

Hannah had loved everything that Gabriella had fled. But now, with all that she adored in ruins, Hannah wanted only to nestle among the trees. To feel their reassuring embrace. And forget the secret yearnings that had lured her home.

She descended the steps, heart rushing at the thought of greeting the trees. Sensing the homecoming she had wished to find in the castle. But was more than willing to accept in the dark woods. As Hannah moved off the stone of the castle steps, a sharp chill rushed up her spine. And she knew she had made a horrible mistake.

The trap they all suspected awaited in the castle, had been set outside. In the place she least expected. Hannah was too distracted by the torment of memory to feel the warning of prescience.

And when her foot landed on the garden soil, Hannah fell to the ground. Ensnared in a deep slumber.

Unable to awake until the spell's creator returned to set her free.

THIRTY-FIVE

THE BOLT OF LIGHTNING SEARED so close to Casmire's belly, he feared he might burst into flames. Before she could fire another shot, he bolted. Flying far and fast, away from the battlefield. Casmire was furious for having to leave the wizard with that tormentress.

But he knew he was being used. His presence put the wizard in deeper danger. Vanora had figured out what neither Adrian nor Casmire could see. The wizard's weakness was those he loved. He might bear the loss of strangers and friends, but he would never break his vow to protect Gabriella's steed.

And so, Casmire galloped faster than he had ever sprinted in his life. Head down, senses heightened. He flew across the Great Plains. Headed toward a small speck of shelter far in the distance. The foothills to the Ceres Mountain range.

Even as he pummelled the earth beneath his hooves, he felt Vanora's blows. Shards of ice blasted past his head. Narrowly missing his ears as Casmire swerved sharply. Trusting his instincts to avoid the vicious attacks of a predator.

He had survived many onslaughts from winter-starved wolves and patient mountain lions. Though, on those occasions, he had Gabriella's intuition to protect him. This time, he was alone.

He glanced back to see Vanora watching him. He was not yet out of her reach.

Casmire dug deep into his muscles, surging forward. He must not give in to doubt. For that would mean he had failed Gabriella. He would be fast enough. He must outrun the sorceress' magic. Faith. In his valour. In Gabriella's mission.

At this moment, it was all he and the wizard had left —

—⁓—

Vanora applauded the steed for acting against his desire to defend the wizard. She had heard tales of this valiant horse and had counted on his idiotic loyalty to come to the wizard's aid. Instead, he ran for the hills.

She laughed at the quaint thought that a *horse* could out-maneuver *her!* Then savoured the delicious vision of Gabriella's ear-splitting grief over her demolished steed — twisted and unrecognizable on the Great Plains. She would be bereft that the wizard failed her. And Gabriella would never trust anyone — least of all the Divine — to be on her side. Ever again.

Yes, thought Vanora, building the surge of electricity to incinerate Casmire. This would be most satisfying. Let the wizard try to outpace her blow.

Adrian felt the surge of power as Vanora set her sights on Casmire once more. He knew he should let the steed fend for himself. Casmire had wisdom far and beyond what Adrian understood. But Adrian would never forgive himself if this was the blow that not only killed Casmire, but decimated Gabriella.

As Vanora prepared to fire, Adrian took the action he knew

to be as unwise as throwing his body into a surging volcano. He ran straight for Vanora. Then, with ample momentum, he leapt. His body flew through the air, with Vanora sensing the ill-advised attack too late.

Adrian crashed into her, just as she fired her fatal blast. Knocking Vanora to the ground.

Releasing their collective power into a spinning fusion of pulses. The cyclone whirled between the two sorcerers. Adrian could not fight the consequence of his action. He could only ride the waves of surging power, praying that he stayed conscious.

As he felt the surge of darkness swell inside his mind, Adrian heard the sharp whinny of Casmire. Unsure whether the cry meant the steed had survived or had been struck.

Then Adrian's world went dark.

—m—

Vanora struggled to consciousness, untangling her body from the wizard.

Much as she had toyed with taking his sexual will for her own purpose, she despised him for violating her with physical violence. She pushed away his limp body, desperate to have him off her.

As she crawled backwards, gaining distance, Vanora slowly came back to her senses. She was no longer the weak, vulnerable little girl who had been attacked in the night. By men she did not recognize.

She had been possessed with finding them. But they were ghosts. Secret warriors who massacred her sisters, kidnapped her parents, and violated Vanora. Even worse, they left her behind —

alive and scarred by haunting memories.

Vanora shook off the lingering past, and came back to her body sprawled in the burnt grasses of the Great Plains. She began to laugh. A cruel, mad laugh.

She found her feet. Her shaking legs drew strength from the earth. Until she was sure she could stand on her own. She had regained consciousness before the wizard, celebrating the cruelty of fate. He would pay for his foolish courage.

Vanora banished her vulnerable fear. And called back her anger. Feeling her figure blaze with the fire of destruction. She was ready to end this battle. She would tear the wizard limb from limb for touching her.

She stepped toward the wizard's crumpled body. She would be quite the laughing stock if she fell for her own charade. But she quickly sensed his heartbeat was fading. His mind was too dark. And his soul was preparing to depart.

She sighed, deeply satisfied. This one was ripe for killing.

As Vanora stood over Adrian's body, she relished her victory. She briefly considered suspending his slow, exquisite death. But she would only find such a delay entertaining if the Messenger was here to torment.

"Well, here we are," whispered Vanora, crouching down, hissing at Adrian, "in the middle of a scorched plain, after hours of battle, and still…"

She tipped up Adrian's chin, revealing the fullness of her repulsion. Staring at the man she knew many found attractive. But was now broken and unconscious. In moments, the birds would be free to pick the meat from his bones.

She dropped his chin, letting his head crack against the ground.

Then rose to her feet. Sneering. "Still, she did not come. I am beginning to believe this precious Messenger does not exist," scoffed Vanora. "Or if she does, she is dead."

She held her palms to the earth, calling up metals from deep within its core. Molten lava surged toward her hands, as Vanora soothed the angry liquid into a long column of steel. Blowing an icy breath along the pillar to cool the metal.

Vanora unleashed a maniacal laugh, scorning the gods for choosing such a weak opponent.

Then she thrust the metal bar toward Adrian. Plunging it deep into the soil behind his back. She cast her head back, screeching into the sky. Sending chills reverberating across the Great Plains.

Vanora snapped her fingers — magically wrenching Adrian's unconscious body up against the pole. Knocking his head for good measure. She ripped apart his shirt, and raked her nails across his chest. Ensuring that whoever found him would recognize her mark. And bound his half-naked, bleeding body upright.

Not wasting another moment, Vanora threw her hands up to the sky. Calling power from the sky. Dark clouds gathered overhead. Bolts of lightning surged above her. Even as the darkness blocked out the sun, the lightning lit up the Plains.

Vanora smiled as the power surged around her. Pulsating toward the wizard. Still, he did not wake. She laughed at this pathetic man who her attendants insisted would not yield to her assault. She would eviscerate them for their incompetence.

She cupped her hands, building the powerful surge in the clouds. As Vanora waited for the lightning to build to its highest possible force, she grinned at the thought that she would wipe the wizard from the earth in one blow. Simultaneously causing the

Messenger a pain unlike any she had experienced in all her years.

The death of her homeland. The loss of her parents. The abduction of her sister. The decimation of her people. This pain, this agony, was going to make every moment of the past years feel like a celebration.

Vanora pulled the electrical current down in her palms. Then whipped her hands toward the ground. Like a conductor calling in the last chord of a mad symphony.

Commanding the sky gods to crush the wizard for good.

THIRTY-SIX

GABRIELLA WAS UNPREPARED for the impact of travelling through time.

She rippled like a wave, pulsing through the air. As though she no longer existed. As though, by swimming to the bottom of that magical pond, she had given permission to be transformed into spirit and sent careening through the sky. In a manner of travel that wracked her mind, yet fed her soul.

As she whistled through the passageway like music escaping an instrument, Gabriella held on to one thought. And one thought only. Adrian, alive in her arms.

Even as she moved faster than a beam of sunlight, she saw the inherent challenges. Gabriella held to her single intention. But she could not help seeing glimpses of other times. Other choices. Unfolding all around her.

Her parents whispering in their chambers. Deciding the fates of their children. Sinking to their knees to cast prayers on the ears of the Divine. The crumpled body of her sister. Unmoving in her home garden. A sanctuary that made Gabriella's heart ache.

She had no idea how she saw these things. Or if the images were real. Had these events happened? Or was she seeing moments that never came to fruition?

Gabriella could not dwell on the imagery for fear of going mad. The only choice she had, as she soared on the wings of time, was to focus on where she needed to be. The Great Plains. Next to Adrian while he still lived. She dedicated all her ability on seeing her beloved.

The light spun faster. Her stomach flipped. And her travel picked up speed.

She prayed that she possessed the magic needed to break free from this plane to return to her world. Gabriella closed her eyes tight. Holding strong against the forces that pressed on her. She had not anticipated that the journey would be disorienting. Gabriella had heard tales of magical forces but when others whispered of mystic portals, they made the experience sound like stepping from one world into another without missing a breath.

This was profoundly different from those recountings. Gabriella felt suspended between two realms. Hurtling at the speed of an arrow. As though she was being tested and tried. Pulled and prodded. Torn asunder.

At the very moment Gabriella was unsure she would last another moment, a force shoved her forward. Breaking her free from the hurtling tunnel of light. Sending her into a wide-open, cloud-filled sky. Gabriella felt like she had been dropped from an eagle's talons.

She opened her eyes in time to see a grassy plain hurtling toward her. As she plummeted closer, she saw an immobile body. The familiar shape. Her dearest companion. Casmire.

Unmoving in the middle of the plains. Gabriella opened her mouth to scream. No sound escaped. Instead, the force of her flight knocked the air from her chest.

As the ground rushed toward her at lightning speed, she instinctively tucked her head to prevent her neck from snapping. The force of her landing brought her over twice before she found her feet — dizzy and disoriented — but ready to fight.

As Gabriella found her balance, she felt ire surge from the core of her being. Fury from the depths of the Netherworld, called forth by the need for revenge. Gabriella had not felt such a commanding hatred in years. Demanding reckoning. Justice. Death.

Compelling her hands to destroy the woman who killed her beloved Casmire. She had trained for years to deny such bitter fuel. This kind of wretched bile. But now, dizzy and fatigued, she did not stem her fury. Her utter loathing for one who had abused her power.

Gabriella reached back and felt the fairy sword tucked between her shoulders. How the sword had not flown free and sliced her in two, she would never know. Nor did she care.

Her heart was consumed with the vision before her eyes. Vanora's back. Adrian bound to a metal post at the epicenter of the Great Plains. And an immense thunderstorm gathering overhead. She did not need to imagine what Vanora intended to do with all that power.

When Vanora threw her arms up to the sky, Gabriella had but a moment to act. She pulled the fairy sword from her back and ran with all the power in her legs. Casting forth a spell as Vanora pulled down the forces of the sky.

Gabriella murmured incantations that felt as though they came from the soul of the earth. Calling the elemental forces. Pulling in the power that Vanora believed was for her sole use. Diverting every ounce of lightning toward Gabriella's sword.

As the Messenger descended on Vanora, the sorceress uttered

a cry of surprise. But it was too late. Gabriella swung the fairy sword with a strength she had never experienced. It was a blow intended to annihilate Vanora. And release her soul to the sky. Never to torment this realm again.

But Vanora's instinct was strong. She clasped the sword. Wrapping her hand around the fairy metal, grasping at the conduit of magic. Such magic! Soft yet deadly. Gentle yet wildly strong. Vanora's eyes were wide with awe.

All the lightning in the sky gathered, and shot down the sword. Pinning the magical sheath to the earth. With Gabriella's hand on the hilt. And Vanora's hand on the blade.

Sweeping the two women to the dirt with the intensity of a hurricane.

The punishing sound of bodies hitting the ground woke Adrian with a start. He gasped as air was forced from his lungs. Then peered into the storm, unable to believe what unfolded before his eyes.

A sword that pulsed with the power of generations. The fairy sword that called to a chosen leader. A sceptre forged to mark the warrior who would challenge the darkest evil, and restore strength to a decimated people.

Adrian snapped free from the fire-torched bindings that had held him prisoner. And called back the power of the storm. He trusted the Goddess to give him the strength to see the end of this fight. Even as he pulled power into his hands, he felt Gabriella's heart reach out.

You cannot do this alone, my love, Gabriella said. *We must do it together. If we fight this battle without each other, we will surely die. Let us vanquish Vanora as one, so we may live.*

Adrian did not question Gabriella. He felt the ancient voice of Gaia speak through her. The time had come. *I am ready,* he replied.

Vanora sneered at Gabriella. Furious, yet emboldened. She might be bruised, but she was exhilarated. Prepared to decimate the Messenger that brought hope to the Great Lands. This child was no match for her experience.

Vanora held her hands close, gathering a fireball that would incinerate a lesser sorceress. She smiled, as the ball grew to a size that would set a house on fire, let alone a feeble girl.

As she hurled the fireball at Gabriella, the Messenger dove, pulling the sword from the ground. She leapt to avoid Vanora's fireball and it exploded against a tree, reducing it to ash. Forcing the sorceress to build her weapon once again.

Then Gabriella spun as Adrian threw his hands to pull power from the sky. A chain of lightning poured from the heavens into the fairy metal — and Gabriella twisted, and with one thrust drove the sword into Vanora's heart. The sorceress gasped and fell to her knees. Dropping her small fireball, setting the grass around her alight.

Vanora tried to yank the blade from her chest. But her hands slipped through the light. As though the weapon did not exist. She was powerless to stop the life seeping from her body.

As she fell to the ground, fire ignited all around — surging into a bonfire worthy of the darkest night of the year. Sparks flew high to the heavens. Releasing Vanora's soul to the birthing grounds.

Gabriella swayed from the force of the magic. As the power left her, she crumpled. Adrian surged forward, catching Gabriella in his arms. And together, they fell to their knees on the ruins of the Great Plain.

THIRTY-SEVEN

THE HIDDEN PALACE FELT the tremor in the earth.

A surge of magic that she had not felt since her own birth. The force was so strong, the Palace clung to the earth beneath her stones, for fear her walls might tumble. And her mortar might melt.

High in the Palace corridors, the Great Prince felt the quake. Stronger than the physical power, however, was the release in his soul. Whatever caused the surge, and the Prince knew it was connected to Gabriella, it had set him free.

His mind was clear. His heart was sure. And he would not waste this moment.

The Prince flew like the ravens of the night. Soaring faster than his servants. His feet barely touched the floor, so quickly did he leave the halls of the Palace. Surging out into the cold air. He did not stop to think. Nor did he waste time wondering whether eyes would mark his movements.

The Great Prince was focused on one thought. Finding his beloved.

Leaping onto the back of his fastest stallion, the Prince departed before the Palace could sense his rebellion. He had one window. And through it, he would soar.

The stallion's hooves pummelled the dirt. Running like the Lord of the Underworld was on their heels. Feeling the urgency of his rider. Grateful to be galloping far from the evil edifice that held them prisoner. Disappearing far into the wild woods.

—⚋—

The Palace rumbled. Her walls held firm. She felt into the firmament to sense whether the ripples in power threatened her. Fortuitously, she was nestled deep into the bedrock of a far-flung mountain. Guarding her from such intense magic.

But she understood what this tremble foretold. The sorceress had proven incapable of killing the Messenger.

Just like the others. All of her strutting and bluster amounted to nothing, growled the Palace. Wishing, not for the first time, that she had hand to smash windows — and skulls. Instead, she was reduced to pulling the puppet strings of feeble-hearted men like the Great Prince.

The Palace grew tired of waiting for someone capable of crushing the impudent girl. Though the Prince chopped the head from every person who helped the Messenger, still they followed her.

She would not take this any longer! Her walls trembled with rage. Servants fell to their knees. Soldiers gripped their weapons. Wondering whether the day of reckoning had finally arrived.

Enough with these games, the Hidden Palace whispered.

The Messenger must return. If no one else is capable, then I will destroy her. Once and for all. I will call her to my walls with temptation. Dangle the one she cannot help but rescue.

The Palace saw a vision of Hannah asleep in the garden of her ancestral estate. Her companions bowed over her. Distraught by her slumber. Unable to wake the spellbound princess. The Palace grinned. Savouring the pain of humans. Her good humour restored.

Once I have the Messenger in my possession, thought the Hidden Palace, *I will end this game. And all of its players — save one.*

The Palace breathed deep and —

The Prince. Where was he? She sought him out in her turrets, her halls, her rooms. But all that she received was echoing barrenness. She refrained from howling her displeasure. She could not afford to shake her mortar, so close on the heels of such powerful magic.

Still, she wondered what he planned. Where he thought he could run that she would not find him. The Palace deliberated. And allowed herself the luxury of time to decide.

Whether, after her day of reckoning, *any* life would be spared.

GRATITUDE
My great, big, heartfelt thanks to:

My oh-so-lovely reader & editor, Kathryn Cottam. Your passion and guidance are inspiring.

The dazzlingly talented Roberta Cottam for her elegant cover design. I would be lost without you.

My gracious and lovely map illustrator, Vanessa Mayville. You are abundantly gifted.

The generous Won Ng for her proofreading skills. Your precision is amazing.

A second round of big thanks to Roberta Cottam for her brilliance in layout.

Sweet hugs to my friends & family for your abundant encouragement on this ever-winding path.

Gracious thanks to my readers for your generosity and support.

Special love to my insightful husband, Kevin Corkum, for being my dedicated partner on this journey.

And ever-flowing thanks to the Divine for trusting me with this tale.

ABOUT THE AUTHOR

Kate lives deep in the charmed realm of British Columbia, gathering inspiration in the woods. Her Celtic heritage inspires the poetic style found in both the *Great Lands* series and her second series, *Fated*. Kate spends time in the United Kingdom and the United States, where she researches, writes, and weaves a little magic. In 2017, she can be found on podcasts and YouTube, as well as speaking at creative and transformative events.

Follow her blog and connect with her at www.kmtremills.com.

A GLIMPSE INTO

HELEN STEPPED OFF THE ELEVATOR. She wasn't sure what drew her here. She had followed an instinct. Luring her up sixty-one floors to the top of this glass sky rise.

She stood for a moment in the entryway.

Gazing around, she absorbed that no man's land between elevator and business. Imagining how many people passed through this space. Matching what they wore to the finest details of the wallpaper, the door frames, the frosted glass. She smiled. Knowing these were the tiny specifics most people blurred past in their day.

For Helen, each detail was a clue. A fascinating mystery to be solved. She knew that someone had chosen each item, no matter how banal, to give an impression. To set a mood. Every thing selected to intimidate or welcome, depending on the business at the end of this passage.

Helen knew she stood on a bridge between worlds.

On her last birthday, Helen had created a game to follow any pull her instinct presented with enough force. No matter where it took her or how much talking she needed to do. She promised to follow.

Usually it involved picking an unsuspecting business or event, seeing how far she could get and how much she could find out. She gathered as many clues as she could before she opened their door, then kept the game going as long as possible. Other people went to movies. Helen invented her own little plots.

She knew Manhattan had millions of people, but it could be a lonely place at the best of times. Never mind expensive. So she created a fun source of entertainment to get to know the city, while meeting people she would never run into in her normal life. Not that Helen was remotely normal.

She had been on her way to a housewarming party with no intention of detouring into an Upper West Side skyscraper. Helen strode extra fast when she was forcing herself to a destination. She didn't like parties much, especially ones where she had to bring a home-oriented gift, but she reluctantly admitted they were a place to meet friends. Or potential job prospects.

She would have gone straight past the building had she not spotted the Logan & Associates logo. The moment she saw it, she felt a spine-tingling chill, and stopped in her tracks. The chill was her sign that there was something special about the place. Something mysterious.

Helen couldn't explain it. But she suddenly had to know who Logan was and why he needed associates.

She found herself pulled into the lobby by a curiosity so strong she would have sworn someone was tugging her blouse. The building was remarkably quiet. She looked around but did not see a soul in the lobby. Even the security guard was strangely missing from his desk.

Helen didn't question her luck. She headed straight for the elevators, quickly checking the building's directory for Logan & Associates before disappearing through the elevator doors.

Now that she stood in front of their logo, emblazoned on the wall, Helen wondered what could have possibly enticed her up sixty-one floors.

Their conservative emblem announced their importance like a law firm yet with too much flair to be such a practical enterprise. Sparkling silver, the logo's material implied expensive services and the size laid claim to the entire floor. Yet the name was so banal, she would almost assume they didn't want anyone making the trip.

What kind of company offers high-end services to a limited clientele, Helen wondered as she moved her gaze from the logo to re-examine the entryway. She suddenly picked up on the missing washroom. And the lack of art on the walls.

They aren't looking for exclusive clients, Helen thought, *they don't want clients at all. Or, at least,* she corrected herself, *they don't want anyone who isn't invited.*

Helen smiled. Jackpot! And the chill shot up her spine. Just like when she saw their name. If she needed any confirmation, she had it. There was something mysterious about this place. Which made her game all the more exciting.

As she turned her gaze to the office behind the glazed glass, she wondered how to play this. The best approach was to let the receptionist take the lead. Helen preferred to be in charge, but when the dance was this unscripted, she knew to follow where other people loved to show the way.

Luckily, she had dressed for the party. Most days, she would never wear pants that required an iron, let alone a blouse discreet enough to be worn to a job interview. She glanced down at her flirty blouse, and shifted the shoulders back to adjust the plunge down her chest. Well, almost discreet enough.

Helen shook off her doubts and pushed open the glass door. She wasn't surprised to see the waiting area empty. But she had expected a receptionist. Not seeing anyone at the front desk, she moved lightly yet confidently into the quiet space.

As she moved past the simple, modern furnishings and the non-descript glass table, she was no closer to figuring out what this place was. Luckily, she spotted a pile of magazines in the far corner of the waiting area.

Helen was a pro at figuring out a business within five minutes of seeing their reading material. She walked straight past the front desk, around the edge of the waiting area, and reached toward the stack tucked in the corner. As though no one expected them to be read at all.

"May I help you?" a voice asked in an unhelpful tone.

Helen practically jumped out of her skin. She whipped

around to see the receptionist leaning out from behind an absurdly large computer monitor, looking far from amused. Helen wondered whether this woman was really a receptionist or a guard dog with her finger poised on an alarm button.

Helen smiled effortlessly and stepped toward her opponent. She didn't actually care what the woman's real job was. Helen reveled in the challenge. Hostile receptionists were like a rite of passage. If she hadn't piped up, Helen would have been disappointed to move past so easily.

"Why, yes," Helen began, approaching the front desk.

Helen's eyes swept over the clean, sharp lines of the white barrier between her and the reception area. The chest-height obstruction said much more than anyone else might imagine. Discretion. Restraint. Secrets.

Where others noticed simple elegance, she saw protection and suspicion. Logan & Associates didn't want anyone sneaking up on their receptionist and catching a peek at her work. Helen smiled innocently and leaned in to create an air of intimacy with the cool guardian of the front desk.

"I have an appointment with Mr. Logan," Helen said, glancing over the barrier at the immaculate desktop. Not a sheet of paper in sight.

The receptionist gazed back without flinching. Then asked, "Which one?"

"Senior," Helen responded quickly.

She had no idea where that answer came from. Helen cursed her fast tongue.

Why did she say Senior? She should have opted for Junior. Helen always had better luck with younger men. Between her playful tone and complete lack of interest in their opinion, they couldn't help but be drawn to her.

"Your name," the receptionist demanded.

"Helen," she replied. "Helen Troy."

"Take a seat, Miss Troy."

As she perched on a white leather chair, Helen was nervous, but excited. She had secured an invitation inside this secret place. Not only was she going deeper into the labyrinth but she was officially rescued from her party.

Who knows, she laughed to herself, *she might even get a job out the deal.*

While she waited, she picked up one of the neatly stacked magazines. Intrigued to find an interior design magazine on the top. She glanced around surreptitiously as she flipped the pages.

No way this is a design firm, she thought. *Not a stitch of art. No minimalist yet pretentious furniture. No discreet yet oh so obviously placed awards for clients to notice.* She gazed down at the magazine. *Unless this is meant to distract me from whatever horrible problem I have by gazing at harmless, pretty pictures.*

Helen looked up, trying to catch a glimpse of the inside workings of Logan & Associates. No one walked by. No one showed up for appointments. No one called. She was alone with the sullen receptionist.

She began to wonder if anyone worked in this place. The more she wondered, the more the quiet grew unsettling.

Helen's mood shifted. She no longer felt excited. She felt vulnerable. She was alone in a strange office with one exit. If anything went wrong … she glanced up at the door. Thinking about how quickly she could get to the stairwell.

Wait. Had she seen a stairwell? Or just the elevator? She wondered. *Skyscrapers had to have a fire exit. It must be code. But she couldn't recall seeing the door. Or the bright red Exit sign that lit the way in case of fire.*

Helen admonished herself. She was getting worked up over nothing. She must have missed it. Her instinct had never steered her wrong. That intuitive pull had landed her all kinds of amazing jobs, apartments, and even the occasional fun affair.

But she couldn't shake the feeling that this place was strange. Like whatever they did here was definitely *not* a game. And that feeling clashed with her reason for doing anything.

By her twenty-seventh birthday, Helen decided she'd had enough drama to last several lifetimes. That night, after many drinks, she swore on an invisible stack of bibles that she was never taking anything seriously again. Not love. Not money. Not even life itself.

As far as she could tell, life was some elaborate game played by the gods. Where dice got tossed and you had no say in the numbers that showed up. Helen had lost that toss too many times in twenty-seven years.

She was playful by nature. But she decided it was time to up the stakes — so her game was born. If life was a crapshoot, she was going to have as much fun as possible. Helen wanted to play life full-tilt, following her intuition. Life was for living. Not for getting attached. And definitely not for staying in one place too long.

Nope. Helen was about as far as you could get from every other twenty-seven year old on the shores of Manhattan. Most twenty-somethings with enough chutzpah to get to this island,

and afford the rent, were filled with more ambition than one human being had the right to carry. The very thought of it made her nauseous.

They were determined. Helen gave them that. Determined to climb any and every wall presented. To what aim, she had no idea. Their pathological need to prove themselves seemed just as random, and infinitely less fun, than her decision to let her intuition take her wherever it damn well pleased.

When she committed to her game, Helen was so excited she made the mistake of telling people at parties. She loved the idea of letting life lead the way! Pure adventure. Letting go of the reins. She was sure people would be inspired or at least intrigued.

Not so. The response she typically got was horror, confusion, or a blank stare. Not one ounce of curiosity. Not one person wanting to tag along and give it a try. She had expected more of people in New York. Especially the artists.

Somehow, her lack of ambition did not make her intriguing. Helen discovered that it made her suspicious. Like she made the whole thing up just to trick them and steal their gold when they weren't looking. Though she had ancestors who might have done that, she was still insulted.

Helen felt a twinge. Someone was staring at her. She turned to see a young associate waiting. Eyes flitting from Helen to the floor then back to Helen. She cradled a pad of paper in her arms like a shield and had a nervous energy that made Helen think of a startled fawn.

The jumpy associate did not ease her fears. Helen figured the young woman was naturally twitchy. But for some reason, Helen had a feeling she made the little fawn extra nervous. And the longer she waited, the more uneasy the associate grew. Helen had to decide. Either she was in or she was out.

They stared at one another for a very long moment.

When Helen thought the young woman was poised to bolt, she stood up and smiled. Then gave a quick nod.

The associate sprang forward down the hall without as much as a glance back. Either she had no interest in an introduction or she figured she would never see Helen again. Helen wanted to ask questions, to gather as much information as she could before getting launched into the interview.

But the fawn kept a far enough distance to discourage conversation. Helen shrugged off the awkwardness of being led without a word and used the time to look over the unusually silent surroundings.

She walked past stretches of secluded cubicles. Not so unusual, though Helen found herself a bit surprised to see people. She half expected the place to be as deserted as the lobby. Despite the number of diligent employees at their desks, not a peep was made. Only the hushed rhythm of keys tapping and papers shifting.

When she tried to make eye contact, not a single head glanced up. Every face stayed glued to the task at hand. Her presence was of no interest. Or they had too much work to worry about the new recruit.

Giving up on human contact, Helen caught sight of the tall windows above the cubicles, displaying the sun falling over the skyline. No matter which way she turned, her view was filled with light gleaming off elegant skyscrapers and landmarks. From this height, the city took her breath away.

But then, she had fallen in love with New York at first sight.

A fact that might have worried her … for a few reasons. First, she had promised never to fall in love. And second, she was no romantic. As nostalgic as she sometimes felt for eras like the 1930s with their sensual approach to life, she knew romance was a fantasy. Even with a city, love affairs brought trouble. Setting you up for overblown expectations and crushed dreams. She preferred to follow the whims of her heart. Not someone else's.

Lucky for her, New York never stood still. If a place could be more restless than Helen, it was Manhattan. The city was always shifting, always changing. She had picked the perfect relationship. Like being with a new lover every night.

The associate stopped abruptly. Catching Helen off guard. She stopped as the young woman stepped aside, to the right of a heavy-looking wooden door. Helen waited. Thinking the fawn might lead the way.

But the young woman just stared. Blinking at Helen, like she should know what to do. Helen smiled and stepped toward the door. Glancing at her guide for any clue she had guessed wrong. Nothing.

So Helen reached her hand out to grasp the doorknob. Turning slowly. Wondering, for a brief second, whether she really wanted to go through with this.

The latch clicked. And the associate bolted. Springing away in the flash of an eye. Leaving Helen alone.

Fair enough, she thought. *Into the deep end we go.*

And she pushed the door open.